Gathering Goodness

Faith, Family, Friends & Horses

Linda Amick Algire

Fawn Song Books

York, South Carolina

Cover Artwork & Design Kayleen MacDonald
Book Layout © 2017 Book Design Templates
Copyediting by Espoir Editing

Gathering Goodness/ Linda Amick Algire—1st ed.

ISBN 978-1-7337884-2-7 (Hard Cover Edition)
ISBN 978-1-7337884-0-3 (Paperback Edition)
ISBN 978-1-7337884-1-0 (Kindle eBook)

Library of Congress Control Number: 2019903086

Printed in the United States of America

For Doug—My Encourager

Now to him who is able to do far more abundantly than all that we ask or think, according to the power at work within us, to him be glory in the church and in Christ Jesus throughout all generations, forever and ever. Amen.
Ephesians 3:20–21 (ESV)

Rejoice in hope, be patient in tribulation, be constant in prayer.
Hebrews 12:12 (ESV)

Also by Linda Amick Algire

Thank You God for Everything—Especially Horses

My Horse Flicka, Short Story, Horse Tales for the Soul, Vol. 2

# Chapter One

Appleridge, Ohio

Patches of blue poked through the green foliage of large old-growth trees providing a perfect horseback riding day for best friends, Jennie McKenzie and Belinda Peterson. This would be their last ride together for the summer. The best friends were packed and ready to move into new beginnings as college freshmen.

"Let's go, Julep!" Eighteen–year–old Jennie leaned forward and wrapped her long jean-covered legs around her bay mare.

Julep leaped forward from an imaginary starting gate. Laughing, Jennie released one rein and quickly brushed Julep's long mane out of her face.

Caught off guard, Belinda quickly squeezed her mare Sugar. "No fair! Come on, Sugar, let's go!"

Jennie and Belinda both loved speed—so did their mares. The wide trail was the perfect stretch to let it rip. Both horses pinned their ears as they galloped. Sugar stretched her chestnut neck forward and nipped Julep's rump. Julep responded with a little buck—hey, stop it!

At the top of a small rise, both girls sat deep in the saddle—slowing to a trot, then a walk—before entering a grassy meadow. The horses pranced and tossed their heads, eager for another race.

"Wow...what a...perfect day...for our last ride." Jennie looked over at her friend as she took little catch-up breaths.

The horses had barely broken a sweat.

Stroking Sugar's neck, Belinda frowned. "It's just our last ride before college. You know my sister will let you ride Julep anytime you're home."

"Yeah, but it won't be the same. Tomorrow I'll say goodbye to horses, hang up my boots, and move on to the next chapter of my life." Jennie turned in the saddle. "And Julep will be Megan's horse."

Belinda shook her head. "I can't imagine you saying goodbye to horses. You'll come back to Appleridge—right?"

"I'll try, but money will be tight, so it won't be often. Besides, I'll be making a new life in the city." Jennie thought of herself as an in–with–the–new and out–with–the–old sort of girl. Appleridge would soon be the old and Chicago the new.

"I'm not wandering too far from the old homestead, and, girl-friend, you better get your little self back home as much as possible." Belinda made an attempt to be humorous, but her voice only pretended humor. She didn't want to be one of Jennie's out–with–the–old friends.

Jennie didn't answer. Instead, she reassuringly stroked her mare's neck. Julep's head was up, eyes alert, looking for a rabbit to jump out of the shadows and eat her alive. Late afternoon shadows are scary.

The sun, barely visible over the tops of the tall trees, started its dip toward evening. Belinda pointed to a small trail leading into the woods. "I think that's the quickest trail to the trailer parking.

Jennie nodded.

The narrow trail wound around trees and several moss-covered boulders. The only sound was an occasional snap of a twig, the rustle of leaves, or a hoof hitting a rock.

Belinda's thoughts swirled like angry bees. *Geeze, give me a break. She's just leaving for college, not the moon. What about me? Is she going to forget about me, too?*

Oblivious to Belinda's swirling bees, Jennie relaxed in the saddle and smiled. *I can't believe in a few days I'll move into an apartment and start a new life in Chicago. I wonder when Belinda starts school.*

"Hey, when do you leave for school?" Jennie's question disrupted her friend's silent tirade.

"I move into my dorm this weekend. Too bad you aren't going with me because you know we'd be perfect roommates."

"And you know Chicago has always been my plan." Jennie liked having plans.

"Oh, I forgot the Big Plan. What's so special about Chicago, anyway? Did you pray about it?"

Jennie heard the challenge in Belinda's voice. "Pray about what?"

"Did you pray about going to Chicago?"

"Well, no, I guess not. What does that have to do with anything? Did you pray about going to Ohio State?"

"Actually, yes. I prayed about it, and my Ohio State scholarship was an answered prayer."

"How do you know the scholarship was an answer to your prayer? That's sort of crazy." Jennie thought this talk about prayer seemed silly.

"Because it answered all my doubts and it felt right."

"Well, moving to Chicago feels right to me. Besides, I don't think God really cares where I go to school."

Defending her decision, especially to Belinda, annoyed Jennie and her voice made that clear.

"Ok, maybe school in Chicago is the right plan, but, gosh, why are you so eager to forget everything here?"

Looking straight ahead, Jennie shrugged. "Hey, let's trot."

They trotted single file, following the curvy trail through mature hardwoods for a half mile before slowing to walk. Belinda and Sugar carefully navigated a washed-out section of the trail. Jennie and Julep followed.

Forcing a smile, Belinda twisted in the saddle to look at her friend. She didn't want to spoil their ride, and according to her best friend, at least for now, their last ride. A change of subject was needed—and quickly.

"I saw Jeremy James at the grocery store."

Jennie smiled. "I haven't seen Jeremy in ages. How is he?" *Ok, this is better. Maybe all that trotting bounced Belinda into a better mood.*

"Oh, he seems fine—I'd say more than fine." Belinda fanned her face with her hands. "He asked about you. I told him you're going to Columbia College way out there in Chicagoland. He'll be near me in Columbus. He's going to Capital."

"He asked about me? I'm surprised." *I'm not really surprised.* "I feel bad for teasing him about his name." *I loved teasing him about his name.* And her face said she wasn't one bit sorry.

"Yeah, you loved calling him 'Jeremy James the boy with two first names,' and I think he liked the attention."

"Well, his mom didn't like us very much." Jennie always tried to stay away from Mrs. James at 4-H events.

"That's for sure, especially when we beat her boy; Julep and Sugar held their own in the show ring."

"And still could." Jennie reached over to stroke Julep's warm neck. "Hey, let's get going. We don't want to get stuck out here all night." She wasn't kidding. They needed to pull out before the sun hit the horizon and the park gates were locked for the night.

SUGAR LOADED into the trailer easily and Belinda walked around to check on Jennie. "Hey, are you selling your trailer?"

"Saying goodbye to horses means we won't need a horse trailer any more. But first I'm pulling it home to give the inside a good scrubbing. It's helping me move to Chicago."

"I'll tell Dad. He sees a lot of the 4-H families and I bet a few are looking for a nice used trailer." Belinda paused. "I guess I'll see you at Cedar Tree tomorrow. Megan is totally excited."

They hugged awkwardly. Jennie stepped back. "You know I'm happy for Megan and Julep, right?"

"Sure. I know you are." *I don't think you look very happy.* "Hey, I'm sorry for being snarky. I just hate saying goodbye, you know?"

"Yeah, I know." Jennie took a deep breath and climbed into her truck. She would be glad to finish all her goodbyes in Appleridge and begin her hellos in Chicago.

GRABBING the end of her long-sleeved T-shirt, Jennie wiped her face. Releasing the sleeve, she searched her pocket, but found nothing but a tattered tissue too small to blow her nose. She needed more than the torn tissue. This was turning into a two-ply paper towel day. Digging into the center glove compartment of the truck, she found a couple of leftover fast food napkins underneath a tire gauge and burned-out flashlight.

She wiped her face with the napkin. Taking a deep breath, she walked to the barn. This was Julep's last day at Cedar Tree Farm—her home after Grandpa sold his farm. Today, Julep would move to the Peterson farm for a new life with Megan

Peterson—her soon–to–be new girl. Everything was going according to plan—except for these silly tears.

Why am I being so silly? Megan will give Julep the perfect home and I'm excited about college. I'm fine. It's only natural to feel a little sad, because goodbyes are sad.

A chorus of nickers welcomed her steps, topped off with a high pitched whinny from Julep.

She pulled a couple of peppermints out of her pocket. Julep heard the crinkle of the peppermint wrapper and stood at attention, ears forward, waiting for the sweet treat.

"I'm going to miss you, girl." Entering the stall, she kissed Julep on the forehead before burying her face in the long thick mane.

"Hey, Jennie, are you ok? What's happened?" Sherry, the barn help, stood outside Julep's stall.

Taking a deep breath, she wiped her face again before looking at Sherry. Julep turned her head and nuzzled Jennie's arm as if to say, *I'll be ok.*

"Julep's leaving today," she managed to squeak.

"Oh, girl, I know. But she'll be fine. Megan's a great kid and her family will take good care of her." Sherry liked the Peterson family. Dr. Peterson was the Cedar Tree Farm vet.

"I know, but I'm going to miss her."

"Hey, we'll all miss her—and you, too."

Sherry liked Jennie, but didn't know her well. It was time to change the subject. "Hey, I've always wanted to know, who trained Julep?"

"We bought Julep when she was four and I was only nine, and even though that's what's called *green on green*, she ended up teaching me more than I taught her."

"And now she'll have another young girl to teach. She wouldn't like standing around waiting for you to finish school, and she's a perfect choice to replace Megan's old pony. That little guy deserves his retirement."

"Yeah, you're right."

"Well, girl, I need to get busy. If you need anything just holler." Sherry pushed her wheelbarrow down the aisle.

Jennie opened the tack trunk sitting in front of Julep's stall and pulled out a well-used grooming brush. She flicked away a bit of dust on Julep's back wishing she could easily flick away the strange ache in her chest. In spite of her carefully orchestrated plan, saying goodbye hurt. Taking a deep breath, she followed the sound of Sherry singing as she cleaned stalls.

"Hey, if you have a couple of minutes, I could use some help loading my tack trunk into the back of the truck."

"Sure thing. This is a good time if you're ready." Sherry leaned her stall fork against the wall, wiped her hands on her jeans, and followed Jennie down the aisle.

"I love this trunk. I always thought it was too darn nice to sit in a barn."

"Thanks. Dad made it. Mom says he worked on it for months. I guess I'll use it as a coffee table or maybe a blanket chest from now on."

I'll take it to Chicago, along with Julep's brushes inside, capturing her sweet smell for as long as possible.

Jennie shook her head wondering where that thought came from just now.

It sure doesn't fit with my say-goodbye-to-horses plan.

"Geeze, it's heavy." Sherry grunted as she lifted her end.

"Sorry. Dad made it to last forever."

7

Horse girls have muscles from lifting saddles and bales of hay, but the tack trunk was a challenge. Slowly, they carried it down the barn aisle and outside to the truck. Eyeing the distance from the ground to the tailgate, they set it down, repositioned their hands, and grunted through one final lift.

"I sure hope you have someone to help you unload this thing." Sherry didn't wait for an answer. "Is that it? Maybe I shouldn't ask." Laughing this time she paused for an answer.

"That's it. At least that's the only two-person job. Thanks, and, hey, don't worry about Julep's stall. I'll clean it after she leaves."

"Ok, thanks, I appreciate the help." Sherry hummed as she returned to her work.

Jennie took a deep breath.

Cleaning Julep's stall one last time is a fitting end to this chapter of my life, and then I'll go home and start the next.

Buckets, blankets, and a bridle were stacked outside near the barn door for Megan to keep. Jennie carried her saddle to the truck and placed it on the passenger seat. She wasn't ready to sell it, yet. She shut the truck door just as the Petersons' silver truck and horse trailer crunched gravel as it rolled to a stop.

Thirteen-year-old Megan jumped out, her huge grin revealing new silver braces. "Look at Julep's new halter!"

"Wow, look at this!" Jennie pointed to the brass plate on the halter engraved—Mint Julep.

Megan bounced as she walked. "I promise to take real good care of her."

"I know you will, sweetie." Jennie reached for the new halter and took it into the barn. She asked Julep to lower her head and gently placed the halter over her ears and adjusted the buckles for a perfect fit. Squeezing her eyes shut for a moment, she led the horse out of the stall and down the wide aisle toward Belinda who waited by the barn door.

Jennie's hand fingered the little Canon Power Shot camera tucked in the pocket of her jean shorts. "Hey, how about taking one last pic?"

"Sure, but you'll see Julep at our farm. She isn't going anywhere else." Belinda noticed her friend's red puffy eyes.

Ok, those eyes tell the real story—my best friend WILL miss horses, especially her Julep.

"I hate seeing you so sad."

"I'm ok. It's all good." Jennie made a brave attempt to smile, posing with Julep's face right next to her own, as Belinda clicked away.

Good shots.

She handed the lead rope to Megan and Julep walked up the ramp and into the Petersons' horse trailer without hesitation.

"Good girl." Jennie took several steps forward, not ready to break the connection. Not ready to say goodbye.

Dr. Adrian Peterson moved efficiently, loading buckets and blankets. Load the horse up and go was his remedy to avoid what promised to be an emotional situation.

Jennie fastened the security bar behind Julep's rump and lifted the trailer ramp as Dr. Peterson and Megan climbed into the front seat of the truck.

Belinda waited with Jennie. "Do well in school, girlfriend. I'll see you during the holidays, and call when you can, ok? Keep in touch, and don't you go and get yourself another best friend." She could usually make her friend smile. Not today.

"Thanks. And don't you go and get yourself another best friend. I heard those kids at Ohio State can be real friend stealers." Her attempt at humor also fell flat.

They hugged—a long hug. Ready or not, they were moving into the adult world.

Jennie reached into the horse trailer and laid her hand on Julep's bay rump. Her hand remained there until the truck pulled away, taking Julep—and a little piece of her heart—with them.

# Chapter Two

Chicago, Illinois

Four Years Later

*T*ugging on both backpack straps, Jennie jogged up iron stairs to catch the 8:05 southbound train. Moving quickly, dodging several commuters checking their phones, and squeezing between two men with briefcases, she reached the less-crowded end of the platform. It was a learned skill—avoiding the crush and getting a good seat on the train.

Her thoughts moved as quickly as her feet. Graduation was in less than three weeks—and then what? She wasn't sure. Her mom said to pray about it. How in the world do you pray about something like careers and where to live? As if God cares.

She usually prayed before meals. She even prayed at night, sometimes, when she wasn't too tired. But did God hear her prayers?

Ok, I'm sure God hears my prayers, but does my little life really matter when he has a whole world to worry about?

She hit the pause button on her personal debate as the train swished into the station. The doors slid open, and she rushed into an empty car. Slipping out of her backpack, she chose a seat in the middle of the many empty seats and sat down.

Two young men, dressed in business attire, followed. One chose a seat directly behind her seat and the other sat across the aisle. No other commuters boarded the car before the doors swooshed closed.

This is strange. It's always standing room only this time of day.

Jennie braced as the train pulled away from the platform.

"Hey, girl, are you still in school? I bet you're not in high school because you look a little old for that. You look just right to be my girl." The man sitting across the aisle laughed as he continued, "Yup, you look just ripe for some loving."

Staring straight ahead, her body froze as a million scenarios raced through her head.

"Girl, we're talking to you." This time the voice came from behind Jennie and only inches away from her head.

They didn't like being ignored. The one sitting behind Jennie reached over the seat. Sensing his movement, she stood up quickly, shaking off his hand, and walked quickly to the front of the car.

Ok, calm down. I'll just get off at the next busy stop and follow the crowd. When did they leave their seats? I can't remember how far it is to the next stop. Oh God!

"Where're you going? Don't you like us? We like you. Yup, we really do."

She grasped her backpack tightly—in front of her chest, like a shield.

This isn't funny. Why are they laughing?

The mocking continued as the punks moved slowly up the aisle—stalking their prey.

She glanced at the half-glass door leading into the next car, took a deep breath, and lunged for the handle just as the creeps leaped forward to block her escape.

"God, please help me!"

The men froze. The train screeched to a stop. The doors flew open. She rushed out and ducked into a crowd of commuters pressing forward to board the train. Moving with the crowd, she found herself back on the train in a different car.

The doors slid closed, leaving the two creeps outside on the train platform with scowling faces. Jennie grasped the handrail and the train jerked forward.

Thank you, Father, thank you, thank you!

Everything appeared normal except for the rapid beating of her heart. Her fellow travelers remained tucked away in their own little morning-commute world. No one noticed a slim girl with tears in her eyes.

God, did you hear me? Is this what people call a miracle?

Wheels screeched as the train braked to enter the station near Columbia College. The doors opened, and she followed the crowd exiting the train and navigated the steps to State Street.

Thank you, God, thank you for helping me. And thank you for giving me this peace I feel right now. How is this possible? How can I go from being so very afraid, to this incredible peace?

This certainly was a very strange start to her day. Her emotions were flying as fast as the train—fear to joy in what seemed like only minutes.

God, I feel you with me, please stay by my side.

Sometimes Jennie felt lonely in the middle of the crowded city. Sure, she had acquaintances—classmates, Mr. & Mrs. Samuelson at the deli where she worked, and the couple who lived in the downstairs apartment. She loved her two roommates, both dancers. Kyiko and Kate were her best friends in the city.

To survive four years of school, Jennie worked hard and lived simply. She liked the word "simply." It was a better word than "cheaply." Simply meant she was creative and thrifty versus just barely surviving.

God, it's me again. I need some more help. I need a job. I'm scraping the bottom of the barrel. Graduation is in less than three weeks and I don't have a plan. You may have a plan for me, and I think it's probably better than anything I can dream up.

She grew up attending church, but she never talked to God like he was a good friend. Her prayers never felt like a conversation—at least not until today.

Wow! I can talk to God like a friend and he'll answer.

The sun peeked between the tall buildings, as Jennie walked and prayed. Its unseasonable warmth on this late April morning was welcome in a city still recovering from a harsh winter. She smiled.

I was so scared on the train, and I'm worried about graduation. I don't have a clue what I'm going to be doing in a month, but I'm happy—really happy! I've been content, but I haven't been really happy for a long time. God, this is so strange. Sorry, I didn't mean you are strange. It's just strange to feel so bad and minutes later feel so good. Thank you for this miracle.

Pausing at the corner street vendor, she stepped up to the counter to buy a blueberry muffin and small carton of orange juice. Change dropped into her front pocket as both arms threaded their way through backpack straps in a well-rehearsed dance. Hands now free, she picked up her commuter breakfast and searched the street for the Mounted Police Officer, Jerry, and his partner, Rocky, a dark bay stocky horse with a white star on his forehead. She loved getting close enough to smell his deep horsey smell. No sniffs today. Jerry and Rocky weren't on their usual beat.

Taking a detour to her academic advisor's office, Jennie impatiently rocked her body side to side as she waited for the receptionist to look up from her fascinating computer screen—

which happened to be flashing some sort of game—before speaking.

"Hi, I'm Jennie McKenzie. Mrs. Smyth left a message asking me to stop in today."

"Yeah, she left this envelope and said you should call her if you have any questions."

Jennie reached for the envelope with her name handwritten on the front. "Ok, thanks."

The receptionist offered a dismissal nod before swiveling her chair to face her computer monitor.

In the hallway, her back against the wall, Jennie opened the envelope.

Wow, I got the interview!

Jennie's stomach summersaulted.

Whoa, I feel a little sick. Ok, maybe a lot sick. Hey, self, this is good news. If I get the job, I'll stay in Chicago and actually begin a career at a large newspaper.

Her stomach wasn't listening.

Listen, stomach, we don't have time to mess around. This may be an answer to my prayer. God, do you always answer prayers so quickly?

Both her heartrate and her mental conversation increased as she jogged up two flights of stairs and entered the classroom slightly out of breath. She didn't take her usual seat up front. Today, she wasn't her normal self.

What is he saying? No new assignments? We should spend the next two weeks polishing our résumés and editing portfolio pieces? My college life is ending. As if I need another reminder.

SCANNING the street again, Jennie didn't see Patrolman Jerry and Rocky.

Maybe they're on vacation.

Disappointed, Jennie climbed the stairs to the train platform, and this time, she entered the train with a group of tourists. No one noticed Jennie but she noticed everyone.

JENNIE'S SHOULDERS softened as she lifted her face to the warm afternoon sun filtering through large maples, and listened to the shouts of small children playing at school. What a great day to be outside.

Her thoughts drifted back to her own childhood—roaming with the neighborhood bunch and biking as a pack to the park, disappearing from sight until they were called in for supper.

It probably isn't safe for children to have as much freedom in the city. It probably isn't safe in Appleridge, Ohio anymore, either. Things are different now.

Kicking off her shoes in the empty apartment, she dropped her backpack and sunk to her knees in front of the kitchen cabinet.

Where are you, pickle jar? Today's a perfect day for brewing some sun tea.

Jennie found the huge jar she'd washed and carried home from the deli a few weeks ago. She also found a bag of trail mix. A high-calorie snack, for sure.

I'll dance the calories away in my modern dance class, followed by rehearsal with my always-bursting-with-energy roommate, Kyiko. That's my story and I'm sticking with it.

She laughed at her silly self as she stretched her legs, one at a time, careful to chew her food before bending forward with a sweep of her right arm, like a dancer at the barre.

Am I good enough to dance in the senior showcase? Well, Kyiko must think so.

She loved dance. Too bad she discovered dance a little too late to make it her career. Her roommates were both reaching for careers as dancers. Kyiko's future as a performer and chore-ographer looked promising, and Kate studied dance therapy as she worked in a center for abused children, using dance to help them become comfortable with their battered bodies.

Jennie filled the former pickle jar, now ice tea jar, with water, added four family-size tea bags, and carried it to the wide win-dow ledge in her bedroom.

With the window pushed up as far as it would go, she tight-ened the screen. She didn't want to find her three-year-old black cat, Beauty, balanced outside on the window ledge two flights closer to heaven.

Beauty wound herself around Jennie's legs begging for their proper petting ritual.

"Hey, Beauty. I missed you."

Jennie walked to the kitchen in search of lunch and a chance to jot down a few thoughts in her journal. She popped open a can of Diet Coke and added a peanut butter and strawberry jelly sandwich to her fight against starvation. Twenty minutes later, the page remained blank and her plate was empty.

Father, I need a bit of help. Did I get the job interview because it's your plan? Somehow, it doesn't feel as good as I thought it would. Thank you for loving me enough to even care about my life, and, oh yeah, for being patient with me when I can't quite figure out what it is you want me to know. I've been called stubborn, but I'm not trying to be stubborn, I'm really not. I'm very confused. Help, please help. Amen.

Jennie wrote one word in her notebook—thankfulness.

Her pen flew as she wrote a quick list of all the things she was thankful for—the words poured onto the page—her health,

family, her cat, surviving college without student loans, staying safe in the city, her roommates, dancing in the recital, her job at the deli, this warm spring day, sun tea, tights with no holes, sniffing police horses. She didn't want to stop, and she didn't realize until later, the list didn't include the Tribune interview.

When she finally stopped writing, she noticed the time and leaped out of the chair.

"Oh no! I'm going to be late for class!"

And dance protocol meant no entry to class after the music began.

She frantically tugged on black tights cut to expose bare feet, a black leotard, comfy gray sweats, a large black T-shirt, and wobbled on one leg and then the other to add white socks and running shoes.

Geeze, why don't I just sit down like a normal person to put on my shoes and socks instead of pretending I'm the balancing queen?

With two feet planted firmly on the floor, she stuffed a hand towel, banana, wheat crackers, and a thermos of water into her backpack.

The window!

Beauty sat next to the tea jar, watching a few brave sparrows as they fluttered and teased a black cat, with tail swishing in a slow rhythm like a clock pendulum.

She didn't trust the old screen. After moving the jar to a patch of sun on the floor, Jennie struggled to push the sticky window down, leaving a couple of inches open for fresh air, but not enough space for a certain feline to escape.

Jennie raced out of the apartment for another mass transit journey—this time to the dance center.

How many steps do I jog and how many stairs do I climb every day? Actually, maybe a few more wouldn't hurt. My costume for the showcase will show every extra ounce and I just ate enough to feed an entire dance company.

The costume hanging in her closet was a skin-tight bronze–colored unitard.

She wrinkled her nose. A few barbecue grills were at work with winter rust scraped off or covered with foil.

I guess the first warm day of spring has sprung all the old grills from their winter hiding places. A grilled cheeseburger sure would taste great right now. Why am I so starved? Probably because I need to watch what I eat and I think about food all the time.

Bursting into the Dance Center lobby, she didn't stop to socialize. In the main dance space, she dropped her bag against the wall, kicked off her shoes, and removed her sweats before carefully stepping over stretching dancers to her usual spot—up front on the left side.

Her favorite musician waited beside his drums and keyboard. She nodded and smiled.

Oh boy! It'll be a fun class with Isaac's drum rhythms and original tunes.

For the next hour Jennie's world contained only dance.

KYIKO and Kate, one on each side, rushed to Jennie as she walked out of class.

"Well, hello to you two, too." Opening her water bottle, she gulped half of it.

"We only have the room booked for two hours." Kyiko rushed ahead.

"And she'll work us to death in two hours!" Kate stuck with Jennie but they didn't dawdle.

Kyiko's choreography was challenging. They danced until their leotards changed to a darker color—soaked with sweat.

THE SUN pulled a disappearing act, taking away the afternoon warmth.

"Wait a minute." Jennie dug into her back pack for a sweatshirt—a forgotten sweatshirt.

"I think it's good." Kyiko dropped her gigantic dance bag to the sidewalk with a thud, and searched through a jumble of sweats, tights, and leotards to find Jennie a sweatshirt.

"What do you guys think?" Kyiko already knew the answer. She was proud of her work.

"I love my part, and thank you, thank you, thank you for only giving me one turn—even if it's a double." Jennie didn't find turns easy. She loved leaps.

"I love our pieces!" Kate didn't want to be left out of the conversation. Besides, she did love Kyiko's choreography. It was fun and challenging. "You have a real talent."

Kyiko grinned at her friends as she picked up her bag.

A GAME of rock-paper-scissors determined the shower line-up. Jennie lost two rounds and graciously accepted the last shower spot. She picked up her phone. She needed to talk to her old friend, Belinda. Maybe she would share what happened on the train. Belinda wouldn't think she was crazy.

Belinda's phone rang five times before she heard the perky message.

"Hey, it's me, but not really me. You'll need to leave a message." It was good to hear Belinda's voice.

"That's funny, it's me. It's me, too. Nothing big—I just felt like talking to you. I bet you're busy graduating. Later, gator."

FINALLY! Jennie positioned her body under the massaging shower head, turning slightly, allowing the spray to sooth-tired muscles. Closing her eyes she soaked up the warmth—for a few minutes.

"Oh, no!"

Two and a half showers were finished and so was the hot water.

The small bathroom was steamy warm from the previous two showers, and a brisk rub with the towel before tugging on clean sweats, a sweatshirt, and warm socks helped her warm up.

"You guys took all the hot water!"

Kate and Kyiko sat on the floor, picking their favorites from a pile of DVDs for a dance movie marathon.

"I'm so sorry." Kate's silly grin wasn't exactly a picture of sorry.

"One of these days I'm going to be first and then laugh at you when you end up freezing." Jennie also wore a silly grin.

"Come on—watch with us." Kyiko, still running on adrenaline, planned to stay up all night. "We're going to watch, *Fame*. I like that old movie."

"I'm going to bed. Some of us need to work in the morning."

"Yeah, well, what can I say?" Kate didn't try to change Jennie's mind. "'Night, Jennie, sleep tight."

Beauty slept curled up on a Jennie's "missing" sweatshirt, and didn't offer to move when her human climbed into bed. Shivering, she pulled the quilt up to her chin. Why was it so cold? Tossing back the quilt, she got up, and pushed the window down to the sill. It would probably be a good idea to refrigerate the now nicely brewed tea, too. She carried the heavy jar to the kitchen.

"Yay, you changed your mind and just in time." Kyiko held the remote in her hand ready to press Play.

"No, I just remembered the tea. Help yourself."

"Thanks, I'm good." Kate raised her can of Coke. Kyiko's can of Sprite sat with her on the floor.

"Well, goodnight one more time."

Kate responded. "And sleep tight this time."

Keeping socks on cold feet, Jennie snuggled under her quilt.

"'Night, Beauty, I love you."

In her dreams, Beauty galloped across a huge pasture, mane and tail flying.

JENNIE REACHED for the snooze button, hoping to score a few more minutes in bed. Beauty had other ideas—sitting on her chest and kneading the covers with her front feet.

"Come on, Beauty, you have food, you have water, and you have a litter box. Let me sleep."

Reluctantly, Jennie climbed out of the warm bed and into a cold room.

What happened to spring?

Dressed in khaki pants and a navy polo shirt with the deli logo, she brushed and braided her long hair into one braid down her back, brushed her teeth, and added mascara and lip gloss. Her coat and backpack waited on their hook behind her bedroom door—just where she left them. Her roommates liked to tease her about being a bit of a neat freak.

No breakfast needed. One of the benefits of working in the deli meant it was easy to grab a freshly baked muffin or bagel.

The sun, just peeking up over the horizon, promised a nice day. Thinking about the incident on the train, Jennie quickly glanced up and down the street.

I'm fine, really, I'm fine. Criminals do whatever bad things they do all night and then crash somewhere before the first rays of morning. That's my theory, anyway.

Mrs. Samuelson opened the deli's back door moments after Jennie knocked.

"Come in and have some hot tea. You look a bit chilled."

After helping her backpack and jacket find an empty hook in the back room, Jennie gratefully accepted the offer of a warm blueberry muffin and hot tea.

"Yummy. Thanks, Mrs. S."

Mr. and Mrs. Samuelson treated Jennie like the family they didn't have. But as much as she loved them both, working in the deli wasn't a reason to stay in the city.

I will find a good job in Chicago or go home to Ohio. I'll either stay or I'll leave. That's a little bit better than simply repeating, 'What am I going to do, what am I going to do,' like a Chicken Little.

She always found comfort in silly humor.

There wasn't time to continue her funny musings. Saturday morning customers, with hungry eyes, lined up for breakfast sandwiches, muffins, and bagels with different flavors of cream cheese. And since most wanted their bagels toasted, the deli soon smelled delicious.

Jennie and Mrs. Samuelson worked the counter as Mr. Samuelson toasted bagels and manned the grill frying eggs. Warm weather, events at Navy Pier, and the Cubs playing a home game at Wrigley Field enticed a large crowd—eager to start their day with a deli treat.

CUSTOMERS KEPT them busy and the hours passed like minutes. Deli doors closed at three, Jennie completed cleaning

duties quickly, walked out the door at 3:23, and burst into the apartment by 3:46.

"Hey, you ok?" Kate peeked around her bedroom door, half dressed.

"Sorry, I jogged home and I guess the momentum pushed me through the door."

"You're funny." Kyiko ran to the bathroom to stake her claim. "Are you going out with us tonight?"

"No, I'm just going to stay here. I'm tired as a dog. I'm still pooped from your rehearsal yesterday." Jennie liked to tease Kyiko using English slang she usually couldn't catch.

Kyiko looked at her. "I don't understand why you are talking about dog poop."

Kate jumped into the conversation. "Dog-tired and pooped both mean really tired."

"Jennie, I guess you are dog-pooped." It was Kyiko's turn to tease.

"Yeah, I guess I am."

Kate couldn't resist adding, "And don't forget bone-tired. That goes with dog and poop, too."

"And you call me the funny one." Jennie laughed as she found a glass and filled it with ice for this year's first pour of sun tea. Leaning on the kitchen counter, she checked her phone. No calls, no messages.

She was tired, but also restless. Maybe a short bike ride to the lake and back would help her relax.

I better hurry. As Dad likes to say, daylight is burning.

She traded khaki pants for bike shorts, and decided not to change from her polo shirt since it was already deli dirty. This time, thinking ahead to the evening cool-down, she tied a sweatshirt around her waist. As she rolled her bike from her bedroom to the front door, Beauty followed and meowed.

"What's the matter, sweetie?" Jennie leaned the bike against the wall and lowered herself to the floor. Her phone rang as Beauty gracefully hopped into her lap for a few minutes of adoration.

"Hi, Mom, you just caught me."

"We haven't heard from you for a while."

"Sorry. I'm trying to figure out what happens next."

"Well, that's a problem. You're running out of time, Miss soon-to-be college graduate."

"I'm tempted to stay in school. I'm sure I can find an interesting grad program to hide in somewhere." She was only kidding, although the thought had crossed her mind. Maybe she wasn't ready to meet the world as a professional.

Her mom was silent, as if she was considering the possibility of graduate school for Jennie.

"I never know if you're serious or being funny. Not that further education is funny, but since you referred to it as a place to hide, I have to think maybe you're joking."

"I did think about it, but I can't afford more school right now. I wasn't joking about hiding, though."

"Honey, come on home until you figure out a few things. Maybe your perfect job isn't in Chicago or Ohio. Maybe it's somewhere else—although I hope it's not too far from Ohio."

She hadn't considered that idea. Maybe she was supposed to live somewhere besides Chicago or Appleridge.

"We can borrow or rent a trailer to move you home, if needed, but to be honest, honey, your dad hopes it's not needed. Pulling the trailer through the streets of Chicago last time just

about drove him to drink. Maybe we could squeeze everything into the back of his truck?"

"Ok, got it. I'll come up with a plan. I found out Friday I have an interview for that Tribune job, but I'm going to turn it down. What's wrong with me?" Jennie didn't expect an answer.

"Nothing's wrong, sweetie. If you're not jumping up and down with excitement maybe that's your answer."

"Yeah, that's sort of what I thought." Jennie was silent for a few moments. "Mom, I'll figure out something." She snickered. "I certainly don't want to drive my poor dad to drink anything but his usual root beer."

"It's good to hear you laugh, sweetie." Ellen McKenzie took a breath. "I also called to tell you about a couple of other things. First, Megan has been accepted into a horsemanship program and will spend the entire summer with a horse trainer in South Carolina. This trainer doesn't think Julep is good enough to be in his program. I think he said he would find Julep a home and Megan a better horse."

Jennie stiffened. "What! That's crazy!"

"I agree, it sounds suspicious to me, but I promised Megan I would give you a heads up."

"Mom, tell her absolutely not. We have an agreement. They can't sell Julep, or give her away, without first offering her to me. It was a verbal understanding but I trusted the Petersons."

"They know, but you'll need to either take Julep back or give them another plan."

"This decision is easy. One way or another, Julep is coming back to me."

"Well, sweetie, if that's your decision, I think you just made a lot of other decisions, and ones that need a bit more thought. Pray on it. I'll tell the Petersons you'll make the decision for

Julep. I don't think Megan will sell her or give her away, but it sounds like she will eventually need to find a new home."

"Please tell them I'll call." Jennie was upset but didn't say anything more.

"I will, but I have more, and it concerns the family that bought your grandpa's farm. Mr. Jerome has been offered a great job in another state, and they're asking for the land contract to be dissolved and for your grandpa to take the property back. They've also asked for half of their downpayment returned. Of course, he could take them to court for breaking the contract, and keep everything, but you know your grandpa, he isn't going to take anyone to court. He feels Mr. Jerome merely wants the best for his family."

"What is Grandpa going to do? I thought he used the money to help pay for his senior apartment." Jennie temporarily forgot her own worries.

"He thinks he'll be fine for a while. He still has all the downpayment money tucked away in the bank. Dad just hates the thought of trying to sell the property again, but your uncle and I will help." Ellen McKenzie paused. "I'm not going to keep you. I know your phone minutes are limited. I just wanted to touch base. Love you."

"Love you, too, Mom—bye."

No longer interested in a bike ride, Jennie rolled her bike to the bedroom and rooted in her tack trunk for her Julep box of mementos instead. The trunk still held Julep's brushes, but they no longer shared her scent. In spite of the brave speech to her mom, without a good job, Jennie wasn't sure she could take Julep.

I'll find a way to keep Julep. Poor Grandpa, now he has to sell the farm all over again?

Suddenly sleepy, Jennie picked up one of Julep's brushes, curled up in a ball, and pulled the quilt made by her grandma up around her neck. Beauty curled up beside her stomach and they both fell asleep.

Chapter Three

*J*ulep cantered across the pasture. Jennie dropped the reins and stretched her arms overhead, touching something...*Ouch! What?* Beauty swatted Jennie's hand.

I'm not on Julep and I'm not at Grandpa's farm.

Her head heavy from a restless night, Jennie did a slow roll to a sitting position. She remembered her last day on the farm. She cantered Julep through the pastures, just like in her dream. She missed Grandpa's farm, but mostly, she missed Julep. In spite of all her brave talk before moving to Chicago, Jennie missed horses.

Strange how life can go according to plan and, yet, still not feel right.

Jennie grabbed the bathroom for a quick shower before walking to Lake View Lutheran church. It was a bit of a hike, but the weather was pleasant—on the chilly side but sunny. She attended church most Sunday mornings, while her roommates slept. She invited them once, but they both said they didn't do church. That was fine. She didn't want to be one of those pushy Christians.

It wasn't a dress-up sort of church. She pulled on her nice pair of jeans and her favorite soft sweater was just the ticket.

Hey, that's another one for Kyiko. I'll have to find a way to use the expression—just the ticket.

As she walked, she prayed.

Thanks, Father, for all the things on my thankfulness list. And, please be with Megan as she travels to South Carolina, and, hopefully, without Julep. And help Grandpa as he figures out what to do with the farm. And maybe help me find a job because I really want to keep Julep. And, God, am I supposed to be a pushy Christian?

Jennie walked happily.

FOLLOWING the worship service, Jennie opened her arms to catch two little girls running in her direction.

"Jennie, Jennie!" Four-year-old Anya and six-year-old Elisa greeted her with Sunday school papers scrunched in their small fists.

"We're going to McDonalds and they have a super big playground." Elisa held out her arms showing how huge. "Mommy said you can come."

Anya giggled as her sister talked. The girls adored Jennie— their sometimes babysitter when Scott and Tracy pleaded for a date night.

"Are you ok with Mickey D's?" Tracy asked as she walked up to Jennie, and also motioned for Scott to grab Anya before she snatched another donut from the coffee bar in the church foyer.

"Yeah, that's good." It wasn't Jennie's favorite place, but it fit her carefully managed budget, and perfect for two energetic youngsters.

JENNIE and Tracy carried lunch trays to an empty table near the playground. The girls took a few quick bites of their Happy Meals before scampering to the play area, closely followed by Scott, munching on his cheeseburger. He gladly took Anya and Elisa duty giving Tracy and Jennie an opportunity to talk.

"So, catch me up. We haven't seen you for a while and you're about to graduate. What happens next?"

"I'm not sure."

"Wait, I don't think I've ever heard Jennie McKenzie say 'I'm not sure.' Didn't you get that interview?"

"I did and I turned it down. I think I'll go home to Ohio."

"What changed your mind?" Tracy rubbed a little ketchup off her hand with a napkin.

"I had a strange experience on the L."

Jennie shared what she now thought of as her *it's a God thing* experience.

"So you're going home because you're afraid?" Tracy asked.

"No, I'm not afraid, but I called out to God for help, and then, somehow, I can't explain it, but somehow everything stopped, and, well, it was sort of like a miracle. It was like he heard me ask for help."

Jennie was shy about sharing her story, but Tracy was a good listener, and she understood God stuff.

"I mean, it was all so strange. It was strange the car was empty during rush hour. And then, the guys where dressed like professional businessmen but they acted like street punks. It just didn't fit. And after I called out for help, it was like God snapped his fingers and fixed everything."

"I think you definitely experienced a God thing." Tracy reached out to touch Jennie's hand.

"I know, and now I talk to God all the time. We have great conversations."

"You didn't talk to God before?" Tracy squeezed Jennie's hand softly before letting go. French fries were calling.

"Oh yeah, I pray in church, and we always prayed before meals at home, but now I talk to him like he's my best friend."

"Maybe it's because he IS your best friend." Tracy smiled as she chewed before adding, "I think he must be talking to you a lot right now."

"Yeah, and I think he's leading me back home to Ohio." Jennie told Tracy about Julep and her grandpa's farm.

"So, your grandpa sold his farm on a land contract the first time?" She waited for Jennie to answer, and after Jennie nodded, she continued, "and maybe he would sell it on a land contract again?"

Jennie knew Tracy was leading the conversation somewhere, and then she had a thought, and then a bunch of thoughts.

"So maybe he would sell it to me on a land contract with terms I could afford, and then Julep could come home." Jennie sat back in her chair. "Wow."

Tracy echoed Jennie. "Yeah, wow."

Both sat quietly for a few seconds and then Tracy asked, "May I pray over you?"

Jennie nodded yes, although she was ready to bolt out of the chair and get started on a NEW plan.

Father, we thank you for your friendship and for our friendship with Jennie. Thank you, also, for watching over her as she commutes all over this city. Please guide her decisions for a new life after college. Give her peace and wisdom. And if it be your will, Father, bring Julep home to Jennie. We know you want us to be happy and Jennie is happy with horses. In your holy name, Amen.

Scott noticed a break in the conversation and brought Anya and Elisa grudgingly back to the table to finish their lunch, promising more play time later.

"Thanks so much for inviting me to lunch." Jennie walked around the table to give the girls a little tickle. "You two, behave."

She declined Scott's offer to drive her home and promised to keep in touch. Jennie looked for the nearest L stop. She wasn't afraid.

A mounted patrolman sat quietly on his dark horse and Jennie crossed the street to get a closer look. It wasn't Jerry so she didn't speak, but she edged as close as possible and took a huge breath, capturing the wonderful smells of horse and saddle leather.

I really miss horses, and I sure won't find one on the streets of Chicago. Well, at least not one to call my own.

Jennie felt another piece of the puzzle slide into place—Julep would fill the horse-shaped hole in her heart.

Please God.

Chapter Four

*C*omputer turned on, comfortable in socks but no shoes, a glass of ice tea sitting far from the keyboard, Jennie began to write a series of letters written from a horse's perspective. She called them *Dear Equestrian*.

Hours later, her stomach cried for attention in the now-dark apartment. Three things were absolutely clear in Jennie's mind—she lived to write, she loved to dance, and she had a soul for horses. She would go home.

Wow, one big decision down and it felt great. It was time to check in with the Master Planner.

Father, thank you and that's all I have to say right now. Just thank you.

Her parents didn't answer their phone, but they'd get the message. "Hey, Mom, Dad, I'm coming home."

Her roommates walked through the door and she jumped up to share her news.

Kyiko squeezed Jennie in a hug. "I'll miss you, my funny friend. But, remember, I want to ride horses!"

"I want to ride horses, too!" Kate chimed in as she gave Jennie a hug.

"Hey guys, I don't have horses, yet. But you're welcome to come to Appleridge for a visit anytime."

MRS. SAMUELSON wrapped her arms around Jennie and cried.

"You can work here as long as you need. Don't worry about giving a notice."

"Thanks, Mrs. S. Do you and Mr. S want to come watch me dance? I'm in the senior dance showcase at school. Mom and Dad can't come because they'll be here next week for graduation and can't get away for both weekends."

"Oh, that would be wonderful. We'll be your parents for a night." Mrs. S thought the invitation deserved another long hug.

ELLEN and Ed McKenzie made reservations for the nights before and after graduation at the Sheraton on Interstate 80—less expensive than staying downtown, and less intimidating. Jennie knew her parents didn't care for city driving and crowds. She was determined to fit everything in her dad's truck—he would be ecstatic.

FRESH résumés were on their way to Ohio newspapers and businesses, and she prepared a proposal to buy her grandpa's farm. Now it was time to make two very important phone calls.

Mrs. Peterson answered in two rings. "Yes, we'll keep Julep until you can get home. Belinda's going to be thrilled."

"Thanks, Mrs. Peterson, I'll make arrangements for Julep as soon as possible."

Of course, Jennie didn't know what she would do if Grandpa couldn't accept her proposal to buy the farm, but she would find somewhere and somehow to give Julep a home.

Glancing at her notebook, Jennie practiced her proposal. Sharp as a tack, Charlie Gantzler was more than capable of having a good conversation. That is, if she could catch him at home long enough to have a conversation. He didn't let much grass grow under his feet.

Each morning, her Grandpa strolled to the Bake & Shake—a small bakery that sold old-fashioned milk shakes, baked goods, and simple lunch sandwiches—to meet a group of local gentlemen, of his vintage, for some good coffee, and often very interesting conversation. Some days they tried to solve all the problems of the world, but they usually told a few jokes and indulged in a little local gossip. Most people called them the B & S group but sometimes the tag was shortened to the BS group—and it wasn't always used in a complimentary way. The group broke up long before the lunch crowd, and, especially, before the after-school crowd of young milkshake aficionados.

Jennie glanced at her watch. Grandpa and company should have solved all the problems of the world at the Bake & Shake by now.

Grandpa answered on the first ring.

"Hello, Jennie girl." She heard him chuckle. Obviously he thought he was clever knowing it was Jennie.

"Hey, Grandpa, how did you know it was me? Did you get caller ID?"

"Yes, it was added to my service a while ago, but I didn't know until I bought a new phone."

Jennie jumped right into the conversation she'd practiced. "I talked to Mom and she told me about Mr. Jerome's new job and I have a proposal for you." Jennie's voice quavered a little. "I'm moving back to Appleridge and I was wondering if you would consider selling the farm to me, with contract terms I can afford? Of course, the terms would change as I could afford more."

There was a long silence and Jennie felt a stab of disappointment.

"Well, there, I'm surprised. I didn't think you were planning to come back but I'm real glad. I didn't like the thought of my Jennie girl staying in that city all alone."

"I know. I'm surprised, too. I don't have a job but I'll find something, and I'm thinking about boarding a few horses at the farm. The college is only fifteen miles away. Maybe I can rent both a stall and a room for a student who wants to bring her horse to college."

"Mr. Jerome took real good care of the house, but he didn't have horses, and he didn't keep up the pastures." Grandpa paused with a sigh. "But I like the idea of keeping the old place in the family. Your uncle and mom didn't want the place. Your great-grandpa bought the land, built the house and barn, and you would make four generations at the home place. I like that, I really do."

"So, Grandpa, do you think it's a possibility? You could have Mr. Casey write a formal agreement."

"Do you think you could pay at least the utilities, insurance, and taxes? I can get by for a little while not making any money, but I can't keep up those expenses, and my old bank account is going to take a huge hit when I return half the downpayment."

"I think so, but do you have an estimate of what those things cost? I made up a budget but I guessed at those numbers."

Jennie was trying to contain her excitement. She didn't want to make a promise she wasn't absolutely sure she could keep. It wouldn't be fair, and, in fact, harmful to Grandpa, if she couldn't handle the expenses.

"Well, then, if you could cover those things, I think we have a deal."

"I'm going to call Mom and tell her what we've discussed. I want to move to the farm, but if I can't, I'll find something else and a place for Julep."

"Ah, yes, I heard about Megan and the internship but sure didn't understand why Julep isn't good enough for that horse trainer."

"My thoughts exactly, but I'm excited about being with Julep again. I never dreamed that would happen."

"I'm happy for you, too, Jennie girl. I'll look forward to having you home." Grandpa hung up the phone.

"Ok, love you, bye," Jennie said to herself. Grandpa never said goodbye. When he was finished talking, he simply hung up. She didn't let that thought linger long, because she was too busy jumping up and down and shouting, "Yes! Yes! Yes!"

Beauty raised her head from her nap and meowed. *Can't you see I'm napping?*

Jennie called a few friends in Appleridge to see if they had any job leads and found out the library had a part-time opening in the circulation department. What writer didn't love being around books? She found the job application online and sent it off. She was aiming for a job in journalism but willing to accept any opportunity to make some money. She would soon have a dependent to support.

Listening to the rumbling noises erupting from her stomach, Jennie made her favorite lunch of a tuna salad sandwich with pickles, no mayonnaise, on light bread. She was someone who always worked on maintaining a healthy weight, and being ever mindful of her performance attire, she was now counting every calorie.

With her stomach happy again, she called home. Her mom was surprised to hear Jennie's plan, but once she realized Jennie was not only serious, but had also done her homework, she offered encouragement.

"Your dad and I can help clean up the pastures and do some small repairs, and I think your idea to board a couple of horses and maybe get a roommate to help with expenses is good, too, especially if you find someone who is nice to have around most of the time."

That was the thing about her mom. Jennie could always count on her to be an encourager. She could have said, "Be careful, you may not get a good roommate, or the place will need quite a few repairs," but instead, she worded her comment in a way that caused Jennie to be mindful of a few things but still encouraged. No lecture, no judgement. Encouragers are special people and she thought her mom was very special.

JENNIE WORKED a few extra days in the deli to help Tina, the student taking her place, learn the job. Although she was a little timid with the customers, Tina seemed to enjoy the work. It was a nice job working for nice people, and working for nice people didn't happen very often in life.

Belinda finally returned her call for a catch-up conversation, and to share her bit of news.

"Hey, I'm so sorry it took me so long to call, but I knew we would stay on the phone for hours and I was busy graduating."

"Well, congratulations, you beat me. I have another week before I wear my cap and gown. What happens next?"

"Well, that's sort of funny. Especially, after you ended your message with "later, gator." I'll be home for the summer and then I head to vet school at the University of Florida in the fall."

"I'm so impressed. You'll be a real gator, and I'll be a farm owner."

"Mom told me and I'm happy for you. Hey, I'll be working this summer, and you will, too, but I'll help get the farm ready. Maybe we can ride. I didn't get another horse after losing my Sugar but Sam still has his Quarter Horse, Sadie, and I know he would trust me to take her out on a few rides."

"Wow, I would love to ride. Are you and Sam still a couple?"

"Sam is a good friend, and I love being with him, but we're not a couple. I need to finish school, and if we're meant to be together, it will be. Did you hear he went to farrier school?"

"Great, another item checked off my list. I was going to ask for a farrier suggestion for Julep and any other horses I may board."

"Sam's good; of course, I may be slightly biased."

She could actually hear Belinda smile.

"I also want to talk to you about this internship thing that Megan is taking. I wasn't quite as enamored with this guy, JJ. I'm glad you didn't agree to give him Julep. We need to talk more about this in private—and soon."

"We'll definitely talk. Hey, does this mean that someday you'll be my vet?

"Right now, yes, I think. I would like to do mostly equine, and maybe some small animals. I'm not interested in hogs and cattle. My dad would like me to take over his practice but things have changed and vets tend to specialize more."

Belinda seemed happy and that was nice. She was also concerned about Megan's internship and Jennie found that interesting. They would definitely need to talk more.

PERFORMANCE butterflies took flight. Jennie loved to dance, but dancing for an audience was way out of her comfort zone.

Maybe I won't see the audience because of the bright stage lights and I can pretend it's just another rehearsal. Yeah, right!

Carrying her breakfast of peanut butter toast into her room, she made an attempt to work on her *Dear Equestrian* letters. She couldn't focus—her mind was definitely on dance and not on horses.

Maybe a short bike ride to the lakefront will calm my nerves. It's a nice day to sit on the stone steps, watch the water, and do a little thinking.

As she watched the water, her emotions ran the gamut—nervousness, fear, happiness, excitement. After she moved, there wouldn't be time or money for dance classes.

Riding a horse sometimes feels like dancing. When I dance, I try to feel the music, like I always tried to feel for Julep when I rode. I wonder if dancers make natural riders. I guess I'll find out when Kate and Kyiko visit me in Ohio.

Peddling back to the apartment, the deli beckoned. She was hungry but she didn't want a big sandwich bulge in her stomach.

Maybe a small bite won't hurt. It sure is easy to understand why so many dancers struggle with body image and eating disorders.

"THE TICKETS are waiting for you at the box office. They're under my name."

The joy on Mrs. Samuelson's face made Jennie happy she offered the comp tickets to the couple.

"I'm so excited! Mr. Samuelson and I haven't had a night out for a long time. We may even go out for pizza!"

"Somehow I didn't know you liked pizza, Mrs. S, but I'm sure it will be a treat because it's different than what you usually eat here."

"Yes, I think that's the attraction. Well, that, and I won't be the cook."

Jennie gave Mrs. S a hug and pedaled home—her home for a few more days, anyway.

Chapter Five

The house lights flickered as a signal to send the audience back to their seats. Intermission was over. Kyiko was next. She was showcasing three pieces of choreography—a solo, a duet with Kate, and the dance for the roommate trio. Jennie finished stretching on the hallway floor and claimed a spot at the ballet barre backstage.

Kyiko moved across the dark stage and found the white glow tape marking her spot. Several seconds later, the lights came up and the music began. She performed her solo piece to live music, written and performed by a good friend at the school.

Kyiko danced beautifully. Her choreography was original and fluid. Jennie forgot to stretch and watched, one leg resting on the barre, mesmerized by the performance. The audience's enthusiastic applause brought her back to real time.

Next was Kate and Kyiko's duet piece. Jennie removed her leg from the barre and gave up any pretense of using it to stretch. Instead, she positioned herself in the wings to watch, stretching in place to keep her muscles warm. The choreography was comical, athletic and challenging, with strange lifts, turns, and leaps to music crazy and fast. The audience showed their appreciation with stomping feet and whistles.

The house lights came up and a member of the faculty walked on stage to invite the audience to a small reception following the evening performances. Kate and Kyiko waited backstage, hands on their knees, taking deep breaths. The announcement gave them just enough time to recover, but not enough time for

Jennie to give congratulatory hugs. She silently found her mark on stage.

Lights up, the music began, and Jennie lost herself in the magic of dance—forgetting about several hundred people watching. She would remember this night forever.

THE DANCERS walked to the front of the stage, holding hands, with Kyiko in the middle. As the audience clapped and cheered, the trio lifted their clasped hands and bowed. Jennie and Kate took a step back as they bowed again leaving Kyiko alone in front. During the third bow, Mr. Harper, Kate's dad, carried three bouquets of spring flowers to the stage and presented them to the dancers. And the audience approved.

The evening wasn't over, yet. All the performers gathered for a short final bow or curtsy known as a reverence to honor the musicians and audience. And tonight's reverence was especially beautiful.

KYIKO was beaming. With no time to shower, a fresh dab of deodorant was the remedy. They quickly changed into street clothes and rushed to the lobby to celebrate.

"Oh, Jennie, it was beautiful." Mrs. S looked younger in her new dress. Her husband, Otto, stood quietly by her side—smiling shyly. Minutes later, they left, holding hands for their pizza date. How cute.

Kate's parents walked up. "Ladies, we have reservations for a celebratory dinner tomorrow evening. Tonight, we thought you three dance sensations would just want to go home, eat a few snacks, and relax." They sure didn't know Kyiko very well, she loved food but relax wasn't in her vocabulary.

PLAYING rock-paper-scissors for the shower line, Jennie found herself last, again, but she was quick and avoided the big freeze. Kate and Jennie didn't bother drying their long hair, and Kyiko finger combed her pixie-short hair. It was time to eat and celebrate, laugh, eat some more, and rehash their performance. The subs and salty chips hit the spot. Calories be gone for tonight. Finally, with stomachs full and adrenaline gone, all three went to bed exhausted. Tonight's performance was the movie playing in their dreams.

TINA was working the early breakfast shift and Jennie didn't need to be at the deli until 10:30, but that didn't stop her alarm clock named Beauty.

"Geeze, Beauty, go away."

Breakfast was leftover subs and chips—the breakfast of champions.

Jennie scanned her closet for something to wear to their celebratory dinner. Her favorite mid-length navy blue sleeveless dress, along with a cream cropped cardigan was perfect. It would be fine dining tonight with no costume or calories hanging over her head. What a treat!

THE LARGE deli crowd wore blue baseball caps and shirts. It was an afternoon home game for the Cubs. Too bad the Cubs were playing away next weekend. Jennie was sure her dad would love to catch a game at Wrigley Field.

"I didn't realize you were so talented. You dance beautifully." Mrs. Samuelson looked at Jennie admiringly.

"Kyiko is the real talent. Her choreography shows off everything I do well. But thanks, and thank you so much for coming."

"It was our pleasure." Mr. Samuelson's comment surprised Jennie. Otto didn't usually join their conversation, probably because she and Mrs. S never gave him much of an opportunity.

"Well, I better go. The Harpers are taking us out to dinner tonight. Hey, did you enjoy your pizza last night?"

"We did. We ordered it loaded." That made two comments from Mr. Samuelson. Go, Otto!

THE APARTMENT was empty. Yay! This time she was first in the shower with plenty of hot water to wash away deli smells. She didn't bother to wash her hair again. Tonight she would wear it up in a messy bun. Suddenly sleepy, she pulled on her sweats and snuggled up with Beauty for a little before-dinner nap.

WHY WAS the apartment so quiet? Jennie sat up but remained wrapped in the quilt for a few more minutes with Beauty snuggled by her side.

Kate rushed into the apartment and called dibs on the bathroom.

Jennie called out, "I showered when I got home. Take your time."

"I'm not worried about you. I need to get in before Kyiko. She takes forever getting ready." Kate ran past in her bathrobe.

Dressed and enjoying a glass of ice tea, Kate and Jennie grinned when Kyiko arrived at the speed of sound.

"The bathroom is all yours." Jennie laughed at her roommate.

"But you better hurry if you don't want to miss dinner!" Kate added.

"Silly friends, you wouldn't dare leave me." And they wouldn't.

STUFFED with delicious calories, Jennie followed Kyiko into the apartment.

"That was so good. I'm glad I don't need to wear my unitard tonight. It would look like I swallowed a bowling ball."

"I love Kate's parents. I don't think she really wanted to spend the night with them at their hotel, but I'm glad she did it. It made them so happy." Kyiko scurried to beat Jennie to the bathroom.

"No fair!" I just need a minute and then you can take all the time you need." She pushed Kyiko aside, rushed in, and locked the door before her roommate could answer. It helped that she was six inches taller and a few pounds heavier than petite-but-quick Kyiko.

After a good hour in the bathroom, Kyiko left with her date. Jennie changed into comfy sweats and snuggled on the couch for another list-making session. She made lists of things to happen before moving home, and things she wanted to do at the farm. Ok, maybe another list of expenses, and what she could do to earn money.

The job interviews lined up for her first week in Appleridge were encouraging, but none were terribly exciting. She had an interview for an entry-level job at the Appleridge library and could possibly get that job easily. That is, if they didn't think she was overqualified.

How can anyone be overqualified? If you understand the job description, know the salary, and still want to apply for the job, why should it matter? A few extra qualifications are just a bonus for the employer.

JENNIE HIKED to the early service at Lake View. She enjoyed the worship but didn't see Scott and Tracy. No lunch out with friends today.

She walked slowly home, thinking her week of gluttony may have ended.

No classes, no dance rehearsals, and only two more days at the deli. Ok, good, now what? She needed a few more *Dear Equestrian* letters for her portfolio. The monthly Ohio Equine Gazette seemed interested in the letters, and she had an appointment to show them to the editor.

Dear Equestrian,

I know you think I need to be protected from bugs, but I like to roll in the mud and dirt to make a barrier from those nasty flies. Of course, I do appreciate that smelly stuff that comes out of the bottle. The stuff you use when we go out riding, because I don't like the buzzing around my ears. That bottle stuff—I think you call it fly spray—it seems to keep those nasty green-headed flies away. I hate the green-headed flies, don't you?

Have you noticed the bottle makes a weird noise? It sounds like an animal in pain. Scary! I will get used to it eventually. Keep trying, but don't get mad when it surprises me. Maybe you could show me the bottle first before you start spraying?

When I'm tired and sweaty after a long ride, I like being sprayed with water from that thing that looks like a snake. But please make sure you give me a warning before you hit me with the water, because that's what it feels like—like I'm being struck. And also, use warm water; I don't like it too hot or freezing cold. And don't spray it directly in my face. I like it when you wipe my face gently with a wet cloth, and let me rub my face up and down on a nice dry towel. That feels so good!

After my bath it's nice to go and roll in the sand or dirt. I know that doesn't make you happy, Dear Equestrian, but it feels wonderful to me, and the rolling helps my muscles and joints after our work together. Dirt is also a good bug barrier like we talked about before. And it gives you the opportunity to groom me before our next ride. I know you like that, don't you?

Thank you for taking care of me, Dear Equestrian, but always remember I also know how to take care of myself.

Wishing you lots of rubs and scratches,
Your Favorite Horse

Dear Equestrian,

I think we need to talk about horse trailers. Ok, I know you want to go places and do things with me, and I want to go, too. But there's a problem. You scare me. You make me get inside this scary box and then you slam the door shut before I have a chance to be comfortable inside. Why? Why can't you take a few minutes and wait for me to relax? When you slam the door, you make me feel trapped and I'm afraid.

Please walk with me to the trailer, that very scary box, and pause. Maybe we could both take a few extra minutes and a deep breath, while I try to find a way to be brave. Ask me to walk inside but be ready to accept only a few steps. Step-by-step is the way I learn, and learning sometimes takes more than a few minutes. Can we practice? That would help, Dear Equestrian.

Some days I am brave, but then I get scared and change my mind. Please allow me to back off the trailer a few times. Give me just a little bit of time to get brave again. Walking in and out helps me to understand, and also helps me to feel it is my choice and I'm not being trapped. That is a safe feeling.

And when I load confidently and you shut the door, please remember you have precious cargo. At least I hope I'm your precious cargo. It's hard to balance and ride standing in a horse trailer, so take those corners slowly and stop gradually. Help me to stay balanced. When I don't lose my balance, I'm more confident and don't mind the ride.

Please, please, please don't forget to open all the vents and windows. I need air. Air helps me to feel better about being in a tight space and not feel scared.

In all things, I need to trust you to keep me safe. I will earn your trust and you will earn mine. Then we can have our great adventures together.

Wishing us safe travels,
Your Favorite Horse

JENNIE CONTINUED to write into the evening. She heard Kate and Kyiko return home and still she wrote. In a few more days she would be home, she would find a job, she would have a horse again, and she would write. Her life would be perfect.

Chapter Six

ennie sat on the apartment steps, ready to dash to the street and claim the empty parking spot for her parents, Ellen and Edward McKenzie.

There they are!

Mom and Dad looked tired. It was probably the last hour of driving in the city that took its toll. Still, when they spotted their daughter sitting on the steps, they smiled.

Ed McKenzie eased into the empty parking spot and both climbed stiffly out of the truck, stretched, and hugged Jennie.

"It's so good to see you, honey." Ellen felt the need to explain their later-than-planned arrival. "We made a quick stop to check in at the hotel before coming here."

"Did you stop for lunch?"

"No, but we had a few snacks." Jennie's mom held open the tote bag she grabbed from the backseat of the truck.

"Snacks helped but I could use a little lunch, my treat."

"No need to treat, Dad, I brought some things home from the deli, but I'll take you up on the offer for dinner out tonight." Jennie led them up the steps and into the apartment.

"Dad, I rented a van to move my stuff, but then cancelled because I think it'll all fit easily in the truck. Some things, like my computer, can ride with me in the backseat. I sold my futon and computer desk to the student taking my room. She also wanted the dresser but that stays anyway because it belongs to the apartment."

"Well, that's good, and you're welcome to take your old bed-room furniture with you to the farm."

"Thanks. I heard they opened an Ikea in Columbus. Maybe I'll get a few things for the house there—maybe a bigger desk. I want something simple but with a large workspace and plenty of drawers.

"I bet you have something already picked out, dear." Her mom followed the conversation but focused on her food. "These salads are delicious." Ellen chewed thoughtfully. "Especially this tuna salad."

"It's Mrs. Samuelson's special recipe." Jennie made a thick sandwich. She couldn't figure out why she was so starved all the time.

"Are these chips from the deli?" Jennie's dad was somewhat of a potato chip connoisseur.

"Yeah, they make their own chips."

"Maybe you could make them at home?" Ed was hopeful.

"I'll try, but I don't think it's worth buying a deep fryer."

"No, I don't think a deep fryer is something you'll find in your mom's kitchen anytime soon."

"Now Ed, fried foods are ok for a special treat." That was all Jennie's mom needed to say.

ED McKENZIE eyeballed his daughter's things. "The weather report looks good, and I've brought straps and a tarp just in case we need them." He looked at Beauty. "I hope she doesn't meow for eight hours or she may end up riding in one of those storage tubs in the truck bed."

"Dad, don't you dare! She'll take a cat nap—eventually." At least Jennie hoped so. "I don't have a lot to move. I had to be thrifty so I didn't buy anything I didn't absolutely need."

Ellen got up to give her daughter a hug. "We're so proud of you. You wanted to graduate without debt and I know it wasn't easy. I see one small splurge, if you can call her a splurge." Ellen sat back down and patted her lap, offering Beauty a seat.

"Having her furry body tucked under my chin at night was my therapy. We helped each other." Jennie rubbed Beauty's head, remembering the tiny frightened kitten she found at the deli back door.

"Jennie, are you going to spend the night with us at the hotel?" Ed McKenzie had a look of someone ready to get up and moving.

"Yeah, I thought that would be fun."

"How about moving everything to the hotel tonight? It will mean a bit more loading and unloading, but it will save us from doing it tomorrow. I'll call the hotel to confirm we can leave a few things and Beauty in the room during graduation."

Ellen chimed in, "That's a great idea, Ed, and tomorrow we'll just enjoy the graduation."

"That's my plan." He looked at Jennie.

"Ok, but Beauty can stay here during graduation. I'm afraid she'll get out when they clean the room."

Ed called the hotel, and, yes, they would allow Beauty to stay in the room at night for a small pet fee. He got up ready to get everything loaded. Jennie secretly laughed, knowing her dad was eager to get back to the south suburbs and away from the city. He would be happy to eat dinner at a well-known chain restaurant instead of sampling something new, and possibly different, in Chicago. She hoped he would enjoy eating at The Berghoff following graduation. The restaurant was an old Chicago tradition full of good German food and history.

It didn't take the three of them long to load the tack trunk, bike, and Jennie's storage containers, while Jennie's mom stood

by the truck as guard. Her smart dad brought a hand cart for the heavy tack trunk. He was a good packer and mover. They taped down the lids to all the tubs so they wouldn't blow off and get lost during the drive. With blue May skies overhead, they didn't bother to add the tarp. Jennie climbed into the back seat with her computer, printer, and Beauty in the cat carrier for their trip south on the Dan Ryan Expressway, accompanied by frequent meows. Oh boy! That didn't bode well for their trip to Ohio.

Beauty explored the hotel room with interest and then jumped on a bed for a nap with her blanket and favorite toy—an old make-up brush she stole from Jennie several months ago.

Tired but also hungry, Ellen looked in the hotel directory and located an Outback restaurant. Jennie's dad liked Outback and he was picking up the tab. Besides, it was one of her favorites, too.

"THAT WAS a nice breakfast." Jennie sat back and smiled at her parents.

"It's a better-than-usual free hotel breakfast." Jennie's mom always enjoyed anything she didn't cook. Paper plates and napkins went in the trash, and after refilling their coffee cups, they went to the atrium to relax and talk about the farm.

"I drove out there about a week ago. I ran into Mr. Jerome at the grocery store and he invited me to come on out. They're moving the first week of June and having a yard sale next week to get rid of a few things. He said for you to come out before the sale and buy anything you may want."

"How bad is it, Dad?" Jennie leaned forward.

"Good, all things considered. The pastures need some work, but since he had them mowed several times a year, it hasn't become a forest. The barn is used for storage but it didn't look like he tore out the stalls or any other walls. The fence lines need to be cleared but they're in decent shape. They have two large dogs that roam the pastures. That's probably why the fences look good. All your grandma's flower beds are gone but I don't think you like to garden, anyway."

"No, as beautiful as Grandma's flower beds always were, I don't think I'll have time to keep up a garden, so that's fine with me. What about the house?"

"I saw the kitchen and it's nice. Mrs. Jerome has good taste. She's sad to leave the farm."

"Your dad and I have been cleaning out the basement and garage. Before taking anything to the donation center, we saved everything for you to pick through first. Well, except for a few things your sisters stole for themselves."

"Sallie and Connie already have their own homes. What did they need?" Jennie hated to hear herself whine.

"I think Sallie took a few cookbooks and Connie wanted that old kitchen table for her craft room. By the way, they're eager to help you fix up the farm so don't be mad."

Her mom seemed to have an *ie* sort of thing when she named the girls Sallie, Connie, and Jennie. She couldn't count how many times she was teased about her name when the boys in her elementary school learned that a female donkey is called a jenny. She tried to explain she was an *ie* Jennie and not a *y* Jenny, but the grade-school boys still thought her name was funny.

"Oh, I'm not mad, Mom, it will be great to see them, and my nephews. It's hard to believe my sisters have toddlers."

Ellen glanced at her watch. "We need to get ready. It's your big day."

THE THREE McKenzies climbed into the truck for their last trip into the city. Beauty was in her carrier, meowing during the entire white-knuckle trip.

Ed McKenzie didn't have much to say as he navigated the heavy traffic, but he noticed the commuter train running on the tracks between expressway lanes.

"That's the ticket. That's what I would do." Ed motioned to the train.

"I can't imagine making this commute on a daily basis—not even on a train." Ellen McKenzie ran a sewing business from home. Her commute was short and easy.

"I've used public transportation for four years and its good most of the time." Jennie didn't share her recent experience with the two professional-looking thugs. Maybe someday she would tell them about how God answered her prayer in a big way, but she wasn't ready to do it today.

Beauty just continued to meow.

KYIKO and Kate raced down the apartment steps to greet Jennie's parents. Kate was dressed and ready to leave, and amazingly, Kyiko was, too.

Beauty stalked out of the cat carrier in a huff, and strutted to her former bedroom for one last nap on the futon, now stripped of its sheets and quilts.

The dancers gracefully folded their legs and climbed into the backseat of the truck— graduation gowns and all—three thin dancers but still a tight squeeze. They met the Harpers at the venue and two sets of parents found four good seats in a row. The lights dimmed as both mothers searched their purses for tissues. They wanted their tissues in hand and ready.

"Jennie Hope McKenzie," the announcer read. Jennie walked across the stage to receive her diploma, her mom wiped a few tears, and her dad simply smiled. Jennie Hope because she was the last hope for a boy to carry on her family's name. Her dad's older brother, Roger, was killed in Viet Nam and he was the only sibling. Of course, Roger was also a free spirit and the family often joked that a child could be out there somewhere. They all agreed a child would be a welcome surprise.

Following the ceremony, hugs, smiles, and plenty of pictures with friends captured memories. The girls didn't want to leave but eventually hunger won.

STUFFED with great food, the parents and roommates returned to the apartment for the dreaded final goodbye. An uncooperative Beauty was gently shoved into her carrier and then it started—hugs, tears, more hugs, more tears. Jennie glanced back at the apartment one more time, waved at Kate, Kyiko, and the Harpers, climbed in, and fastened her seat belt. Let the next chapter of her life begin.

Chapter Seven

ennie placed a little scoop of scrambled eggs in a paper bowl and wrapped it with a napkin. Beauty would enjoy a special treat.

"I'm not sure why they call breakfast a *free* breakfast. The cost of the hotel room easily covers a plate of fake eggs and a couple of pieces of pre-cooked bacon."

"Now Ed, it's very convenient to have breakfast here at the hotel." Ellen thought maybe free breakfast meant they were free to eat and get on the road without the need to search for a breakfast place. She liked to look at the glass as being half-full most of the time.

"Well, I guess you're right; it isn't a bad start to the day."

Jennie helped her dad load the truck. He covered the back with a tarp and strapped the load down tight. Traffic was heavy on Interstate 80, but thinned out once they crossed into Indiana and found Interstate 64 south. They picked up Route 30 for the rest of the trip to Appleridge, passing several huge wind farms near the Ohio border. This was flat, open country with farms and field crops, and apparently, a good supply of wind. The landscape felt open and huge, especially after the crowded streets and buildings of Chicago.

Jennie rolled down her window. "Ah, I smell sweet country air. Well, it was. I think we're passing a dairy farm now and the air isn't quite as sweet. I love the smell of horse manure but I don't like the smell of cow manure very much."

She was strange that way. A lot of horse lovers were a bit strange that way.

Ellen spotted a sign advertising a local Dairy Queen. "I bet that would be a good stop for a quick sandwich and ice cream cone."

They weren't disappointed. Jennie ordered her ice cream in a cup, instead of a cone, because she wanted her soft serve ice cream topped with syrupy strawberries.

A SIGN announced Appleridge, Pop. 6,976. Jennie sat up and leaned between the front bucket seats.

"Hey, Dad, would you drive around the square so I can look at everything?"

"Missed old Appleridge, did you?" Her dad made a turn.

She heard the tires hit the old brick streets and saw the library and town hall in the middle of what locals called The Green. There were a few people sitting on benches under the covered walkway connected the two public buildings.

"That's new." Jennie pointed to a large gazebo sitting between and slightly in front of the two buildings.

Ellen positioned her body to look at Jennie. "The Appleridge Apple Festival Committee donated the funds and the high school building construction class took it on as a project. It's pretty. They did nice work."

The town boasted several small stores, a grocery store, quite a few churches, and a local restaurant called, simply, The Café. Jennie always thought the name was funny because it reminded her of a cartoon where the restaurant sign simply read, Eats.

And there was the Bake & Shake, Grandpa's office. Jennie didn't tell her parents she called the Bake & Shake Grandpa's office.

"Could you drive to the park so I can see the lake, too?"

"Sure." Her dad didn't mind. He enjoyed taking the tour.

They drove through the park with baseball and soccer fields and a picnic shelter then parked at the edge of the small lake. A trail of steps leading to a small ridge beckoned, but they didn't get out of the truck. Jennie looked up and saw what remained of an apple orchard. Johnny Appleseed was certainly busy when he passed through this part of Ohio. Volunteers cared for the orchard and apples were free for the picking.

"Thanks, Dad." She thought Appleridge looked different. Not bad, but different. Of course, she was also different after four years in Chicago.

PULLING a suitcase on wheels to the house, Jennie noticed flowers already planted, risking a late May frost.

"Mom, what a brave soul to plant flowers before Memorial Day, but they look great!"

"Thanks sweetie, I like the way they turned out with all pinks and purples this year."

Jennie's mom was often found drooling over pictures in garden catalogues during the cold winter months.

"Oh my, I'm stiff." Jennie stretched.

"You're too young for that, young lady." Her mom kidded as they climbed the steps to Jennie's old room.

"Mom, I don't want to stick around too long. I know you and Dad like being empty nesters." Jennie was teasing but she also thought she was correct.

"It's ok, you're fine. You can stay as long as you need. But be warned, we usually have one of the grandsons on the weekend." She smiled as she sat down on the bed and petted Beauty who returned from exploring the house and was now searching for a new nap place.

"Wait until you see how they've grown. They're a handful so you are officially recruited to help when your sisters want a break."

"Ok, I'll work out and get in good shape so I can chase the little guys. I can't wait to see them."

JENNIE UNPACKED, found hangers for some of her clothes, kept some in the storage tubs, and set up her computer and printer on the folding camping table she found in the garage. She carried her notebook downstairs to sit on a kitchen bar stool and work on her lists. Ellen was busy setting out a few snacks.

"I think we'll get visitors once your sisters know we're home. I thought we would just have a few easy snacks tonight."

"That sounds good."

Jennie added a few things to her notebook. She didn't have a car and would need to find something cheap. She would like a truck. Would she need to take out a small loan? No, she hated that idea. She hadn't made it through school debt-free to start getting loan happy now. She needed a job—any job, and preferably one within walking distance.

Jennie's dad walked into the kitchen with a huge grin on his face. "Mom, are you ready?"

"Why, yes, I am." Ellen also wore a silly huge grin.

"Your mom and I drove the truck to Chicago because we promised to help you move your things, but, recently, we bought something a little more comfortable for the trips we plan on taking now that I'm retired, and we want to show it off."

They walked outside to look at the new Buick Enclave sitting outside the garage. Her dad, as a GM retiree, could get a decent discount on the purchase, but it was still more vehicle than he ever owned.

"Wow, Dad, it's nice! I bet you missed driving it on the trip to Chicago."

"You bet. We almost told you to rent that van. We're a bit spoiled now."

"I'm surprised you kept the truck."

"Ah, you're quick. We kept the truck because we're giving it to you as your graduation present. I wish it was a brand-new truck, but we had it fully serviced, new tires, and it still looks and runs great."

Jennie jumped up and down. "Thank you, thank you, thank you! It's perfect!"

Wow, she didn't expect that item to be checked off her list so fast! What a great present. What a generous present. She was thrilled.

Chapter Eight

Appleridge, Ohio

Clothes littered the bed the morning of Jennie's library interview. Running out of time, she settled on pressed khakis, a fairly new white linen shirt, and her navy cropped jacket, with a scarf added as a nod to current fashion.

Peanut butter toast and a banana sat forgotten on a plate as she updated her notebook and crossed off *buy a truck*. With a fresh résumé printed, she walked outside into a beautiful Ohio spring day and climbed into her new—at least new to her—Silverado.

THE INTERVIEW went well, with, of course, the expected question addressing her qualifications. They couldn't come out and say she was too qualified for the job but that was the root of the question. She answered as truthfully as possible—she was a new writer, who wanted to supplement her income in an environment she would enjoy, and where she was extremely skilled. Yes, she was flexible and could work extra hours. Yes, she was available immediately. Yes, the salary was acceptable. And, the valid and perhaps selling point, her technology skills were excellent. She did her best.

JENNIE FOLLOWED her urge to visit Grandpa and ask him on a lunch date. Well, that is if he was home, of course. He was home.

Jennie hugged her grandpa tight. "I missed you, Gramps."

"I missed you, my Jennie girl. Let's head to the Bake & Shake. I noticed they have chili dogs on special today." Grandpa never let much grass grow under his feet.

Jennie took her dog without chili but loaded it with ketchup, mustard, onions, and relish. The hot dogs were especially good in freshly baked buns. The Bake & Shake didn't have a full kitchen or a grill but they practiced creative cooking with a few burners, an oven, and slow cooker. They were best known for their baked goods and, of course, ice cream and milk shakes.

Catching up on Grandpa's activities took a while. He was a busy senior.

"Jennie girl, how about a little trip out to the farm? Mrs. Jerome said we could come on out any time to look around."

"I would love that."

The farm sat a few miles out of town in a neighborhood of small farms. The larger spreads were further out in the country. Jennie rolled down her window as they drove and enjoyed the sweet smell of the country.

Simply known as the old Gantzler place, the farm never had a real name, until one day, out of the blue, Grandpa gave it a name—Fawn Song Farm. Jennie didn't think her grandpa was known for his musical ability, but he told stories about his mother, who could make grown men weep with her singing voice.

Jennie also remembered pictures of a favorite mare named Fawn in her grandma's photo album. It was easy to figure out how he came up with the farm name. Her 4-H friends used to hold contests to see who could say the name three times as fast as possible without getting tongue tied—Fawn Song Farm, Fawn Song Farm, Fawn Song Farm. Whew!

"Grandpa, do you care if I keep calling the place Fawn Song Farm? I'm going to create a logo for my boarding business."

"That would make me happy." His voice quivered.

He was a sentimental man and she knew her question brought out a bit of emotion. She wanted to thank him for helping her buy the farm, but couldn't find the words without getting a bit weepy herself. He would understand.

They pulled into the drive and parked beside an older SUV and waved at two small children, a boy and a girl, swinging on their playset. The children stopped swinging and watched as the strangers walked to their back door. Grandpa knocked and, after a minute, Mrs. Jerome answered. She glanced over to the children on the playset as she opened the door.

"Mrs. Jerome, we don't want to bother you, but I wanted to introduce you to my granddaughter, Jennie, and ask if we may take a little walk out to the barn and into the pastures. Jennie will be living here after you leave."

Jennie smiled and stepped forward to greet Mrs. Jerome.

"Why, of course you may, Mr. Gantzler. I'm glad you stopped by. Thank you so much for what you've done for our family. Most people would keep all the money and then sue us for breaking the contract just to get more."

Grandpa took her hand. "I wish you and your family many years of happiness in your new home. I know you didn't make this decision easily."

"I love this place, but this is a great opportunity for my husband, and the increase in pay makes it easier for me to stay home with these kiddos." She reached down to touch the heads of the children who had left their play to come see the visitors.

"The dogs are in the back pasture. They'll lick you to death, but please don't let them out."

"Thank you, we'll only be a few minutes, and we won't open the gate. I don't want to be licked to death." Jennie laughed at her grandpa's comment.

"You go on ahead. I'm right in the middle of putting together a casserole for dinner and our cat, Sassy, would be on the counter stealing a taste of our supper if I left it unattended."

The kids giggled because they knew their mom was right.

"Oh, I have a cat so I totally understand." Jennie laughed because she often caught Beauty on the kitchen counter.

"Thank you, ma'am," Grandpa stepped back, "and I hope to see you again before you leave.

GRANDPA and Jennie looked about as they slowly walked out to the barn. The place was exactly as her dad described. The pastures were mowed and didn't look too bad. The fence was the same fence. It was getting old, but looked to be in decent repair. The barn was being used as a storage building. It was hard to see into the stalls, but with a little cleaning the barn would be a horse barn again. Jennie's biggest investment would be a lot of hard work.

"I would like to make some improvements, eventually, but it looks like a good cleaning and a bit of organization is all that's needed to get it horse ready, Gramps."

"I thought they were good people. I'm making out fairly well in the deal. It's like I rented it for a few years and it's still a good asset."

"How about going out to the Petersons' for a visit and to check on Julep?"

"I would love that, Grandpa. I can't wait to see her again. Do you think they'll mind?" She was being silly. The Petersons considered her family.

"I should think not. You were a regular fixture at their place. I'm surprised you haven't been out there already. You girls used to be joined at the hip."

"Belinda's been away for a few days, and I didn't want to go out until she was home. I feel a little strange—like I don't deserve to get Julep back."

"That's nonsense. The Petersons helped you and now you're helping them, and all of you will continue to love on Julep." Grandpa fastened his seat belt and adjusted his baseball cap.

The Petersons' farm was about two miles away as the crow flies. Jennie turned into the long drive and saw the barn first.

"They always keep their place so nice. Strange, I don't see Julep in the pasture."

She drove slowly as the Petersons' two dogs sniffed the moving tires of the truck.

"Good dogs; here, boys." Jennie called to them as she climbed out of the truck.

Before Grandpa climbed out, Belinda was running from the house. Hugs and smiles followed but something seemed off. Belinda stepped away as Jennie asked about Julep.

"I'm so sorry. Dad and Megan left for South Carolina yesterday and they took Julep. My dad doesn't like to be told what to do and he doesn't like to be corralled into buying a horse."

"I didn't want her given to the school and your mom promised I could have her back." Jennie's voice quivered.

"Don't blame Mom. You know how stubborn Dad can be when he thinks he's right. He won't give her to the school. I don't know what the trainer will think, but it wouldn't be a good idea for him to argue with Dad."

"I know you're disappointed, but it'll be fine." Grandpa was now standing beside the two girls. "When and if Megan gets a

new horse, Julep will come home. And you'll be better prepared when that happens." He looked at the house.

"Now, let's go inside and see Susan. I'm sure she's been worried about how you'll feel." Grandpa led the way.

"Thanks, Mr. Gantzler. Mom has been worried. She tried to talk Dad into leaving Julep here but he wouldn't listen. I'm not sure why Megan wants a new horse because Julep is perfect. But then, I can't figure out why she wants to spend the summer in South Carolina with this trainer who thinks he is *all that*." Suddenly both girls looked at each other and snapped twice with attitude as they repeated *all that* and laughed. Something they used to do in high school together. Belinda hoped getting Jennie to laugh would break the tension. And it did.

Jennie didn't blame Mrs. Peterson. She remembered how stubborn Dr. Peterson could be because she knew him well. Grandpa was right. She was disappointed because she wouldn't see Julep until the end of the summer, but she also had a lot on her plate before she took on a dependent. Even a dependent she loved as much as she loved Julep.

Several homemade gingersnap cookies and a glass of ice tea later, Jennie looked around the Petersons' comfy kitchen. She remembered eating many meals with Megan, Belinda, and Susan Peterson in this room, although not too many with Dr. Peterson. He missed a lot of meals in his profession.

Grandpa stood up and placed his ball cap on his head. A sure signal it was time to leave.

"Hey, Jennie, let's meet at the Bake & Shake tomorrow for ice cream. We have a lot of catching up to do."

Jennie gave Mrs. Peterson a hug and answered Belinda, "Sounds good."

As they drove down the farm lane, Grandpa cleared his throat.

"You will need to consider the possibility that Megan will decide to keep Julep. I'm sure they won't give her to the school, but she is a great horse and may work out well in the program."

"Oh, Grandpa, I hope not. I know she's Megan's horse, I accepted that idea four years ago, but when they said I could have her back, that's all I've thought about. It feels like I'm losing her again."

"It will be a loss but it could happen." Grandpa looked away. "When you looked for a good home, Megan was your first choice. Trust that you made a good choice."

Grandpa loved her enough to talk honestly, instead of fussing about the situation. He was a good man. He believed harsh words in anger never solved the real issue, so he didn't use them, and he wasn't going to add fuel to the fire of Jennie's disappointment, either.

She dropped Grandpa off at his apartment and drove home. Her mom was in the kitchen and she shared the news about Julep.

"I'm so sorry, but I trust Dr. Peterson and Megan will do the right thing. I only wish they wouldn't have suggested the possibility of you getting her back before they were absolutely sure."

"Yeah, me, too, I was so excited." Jennie sat down on a kitchen bar stool and leaned her elbows on the counter.

"I took a message from the library. Here's the number. I'm surprised they didn't call your cell phone."

"I think they did. I have a missed call. Gee, I never seem to hear my phone. Good thing I listed the home number along with my cell."

She was a little nervous about the library calling back so soon. What could it mean?

It meant she had the job! And could she start next week? Of course, she said, "Yes!"

Chapter Nine

he library dress code required khaki pants and a white short-sleeved polo shirt with the library logo. On cold days, a navy sweater was added. Jennie had somehow chosen a similar outfit for the interview. How perfect. It was comfortable attire, plus she already had all those khaki pants from working in the deli. At least a few were still in good shape. Maybe she could wear khaki shorts in the summer—probably not.

She breezed through a ton of paperwork and a quick lesson on the library computer system. The job wasn't too difficult and most of the library patrons were friendly. Jennie recognized quite a few faces, and all seemed surprised to see her behind the circulation desk. She smiled and nodded as she checked books in and out. After several hours helping library patrons, she took her turn shelving books. She liked the solitude of putting the books in order on the cart and rolling it out to the book stacks.

She liked her schedule. Three days a week she opened the library in the morning, and two days a week she closed the library in the evening. She worked every other Saturday, and when she worked Saturday, she had Friday as her day off. The library was closed Sundays, although there was some talk about opening on Sunday afternoons. She hoped that wouldn't happen, but some libraries in larger towns were experimenting with the idea.

Today, her serious self told her she needed to go home and write following her shift. Her fun self didn't feel like writing, or

doing any sort of work. It was going to take a bit of discipline to stay on task, especially after moving to the farm next week.

THE JEROME FAMILY moved out, and Grandpa stopped by the library to present her with a set of keys. She couldn't wait to drive out to the farm after work.

Maybe I'll stop at home and pick up Mom first. No, she's working on a large sewing project. I won't bother her.

Ellen McKenzie was a skilled seamstress. When the girls were at home, a corner of the basement was her sewing room, but now, with several spare bedrooms, her workroom was upstairs. When the girls were in school, she attended all their school events, but she expected them to inform her in advance, so she could schedule the time off work.

Ellen had more work than she could handle. Friends encouraged her to hire a few people and rent a storefront. Ellen resisted—she wanted to earn a living, but didn't need to make a killing.

Jennie never understood. Didn't everyone want to make a lot of money?

The biggest advantage to having a mom who sewed extremely well was a closet of beautiful clothes. Jennie still wore the same things she wore when in high school—classic and versatile.

She turned her truck into the farm gravel drive and stopped to take a mental picture of her new home.

Gone were the Jerome kids' toys and swing set, the Jerome cars, and their porch furniture.

This is my home. This is my new life. I can't wait to find boarders. The farm needs horses.

The few things Jennie purchased at the yard sale were stored in the basement. The house would look a little empty for a while, but she didn't like clutter, anyway.

The new key turned easily and she stepped inside. She imagined the house filled with the things she would someday purchase—as soon as her budget gave permission.

Good memories filled rooms. They weren't quite so empty after all.

She pulled her ever-present notebook out of her bag to add a few items to her growing lists. She still loved making lists on paper. It was satisfying to check off each item—one item at a time.

The walls were a neutral cream throughout and wouldn't need to be painted. The carpet had been ripped up and the wide board floors refinished.

This is nice. Maybe I can find some nice inexpensive rugs.

The old floors still had blemishes that couldn't be sanded smooth—they had character.

I sure wish they would have refinished the woodwork instead of painting it white, though. Oh, well, it's nicely done. Oh, they painted the bricks around the fireplace, too, but it's, actually, nicer than before.

Grandpa replaced the windows about thirty years ago. They weren't the most energy-efficient models but they were in fairly good condition. The roof was about twenty years old. Hopefully, she would have a little bit of breathing room before replacing windows or a roof.

The movers doing their job left a little mess.

I'll come back tomorrow with a few cleaning supplies. Oh yeah, and lamps and timers.

The lights going on and off at random times would give the house an occupied look.

Turning the page she started a barn list.

Let's see, I'll keep two stalls for myself—one for Julep, she silently prayed, and one for maybe a young horse. Two or three boarders will be good. And, I'll turn the last stall into a feed room and small hay storage area. I wonder how much it will cost to concrete the floor. Maybe I can also pour concrete outside to make a wash area for the horses.

Finding the right boarders would take some time. Jennie wanted boarders who loved their horses and who would respect her time and home.

Tomorrow, I'll change into jeans and come armed with buckets, brooms, rakes, and tools.

She started another list: tools needed.

Chapter Ten

ear Equestrian,

We find the things that are important to you humans quite strange. For example, why do you worry about shelter when we would prefer to be outside in the rain? We enjoy having a shelter in the wind and cold, but a spring rain is fine, and being given a choice is very nice.

It is also nice to have a private place to eat our meals. We don't like it when we get chased away from the last few tasty bites. But as soon as we finish our feed buckets, please let us go back outside.

Here is a hint, Dear Equestrian—put out more piles of hay than there are horses in the herd. That way, there is always an extra hay pile to find when we get told to move by a more determined herd mate.

Since we're talking about food, let's talk about water. There seems to be a fad of putting goldfish in water troughs. No, we don't like goldfish in our water troughs. Would you like a fish in your water glass? We understand goldfish do eat the slime on the sides of the tank, but, unfortunately, they poop a lot more than they eat. Yuck. If you wouldn't drink it, why would we? We like a clean tank of water, so please take an extra few minutes to dump, wash, and refill the tank when it's dirty.

And one more thing—let's talk about grooming. We like grooming because all that scratching feels good. You must like it, too, because you seem to do it a lot. We also think it feels good to roll in the mud and sand. Sometimes you seem mad when we get dirty, and we don't understand.

We don't mean to complain because we know you're trying your best. Horses and humans certainly have different thoughts, don't we?

Wishing you lots of carrots and clean water troughs,
Your Favorite Horse

JENNIE TURNED off her computer and stretched. Her life seemed like a juggling act most of the time. She fell into bed exhausted most nights, but she was happy.

Jennie's only disappointment was being told Julep would remain in South Carolina for the entire summer and possibly longer. She didn't want to be angry at Dr. Peterson, because he also recommended her farm to her new boarder, Marcy Streeter. He wouldn't send anyone he didn't personally vet first—ha, no pun intended.

Marcy and her two ponies named Riley and Stuffin would arrive next week. The stalls were ready, pastures mowed, hay and supplies stored. Marcy loved her two outgrown ponies, meaning they formerly belonged to children who had grown too big to ride a small pony, but they were a perfect size for driving. She drove them as a pair at carriage events.

Marcy promised to teach me more about driving ponies and horses. I can't wait!

Cassy Morton picked Jennie's farm as the perfect fit for her warmblood horse named Treasure. They would arrive in early July for a few summer classes. Cassy was starting her freshman year at the local college.

I've got time for a walk around the property before my afternoon shift at the library.

As Jennie eyeballed the now-mowed former gardens, she saw a large, flat area for a future practice arena and had a silly thought.

I suppose a daffodil or tulip will pop up occasionally but fresh-cut flowers are always nice.

Jennie's farm didn't have all the amenities of a large equestrian center—things like an arena, an indoor wash bay, or even a bathroom in the barn. Marcy and Cassy both picked Jennie's farm because they wanted a safe place, reliable care, nice pastures, and good-quality hay. Jennie could easily provide all those things. Well, maybe not easily—keeping a farm was a lot of work.

At least so far, she had plenty of help. Her dad and handy brothers-in-law enjoyed using power tools, and, fortunately, they also had an extensive collection of tools to use.

The property had good bones. The house sat in front, with the original old barn behind and to the side, and the newer horse barn behind both the house and the old barn.

I'm sure glad Mr. Jerome didn't pull down the old barn. Dad and company did a nice job fixing it up. I'll keep my truck in front and equipment in back.

Cassy's horse was being hauled to Ohio by a professional company with a semi. Jennie eyed the drive. The part leading to the barn needed more stone. Jennie made another note: load of gravel and price?

Marcy drove her own truck and trailer.

Marcy can keep her trailer near the barn. I sure wish I could get that load of gravel before she arrives.

A fence across the front of the property with a gate would be a good idea—she starred it on her list. She had an entire notebook full of ideas. Of course, she wasn't silly enough to believe everything on her list would magically appear.

Jennie walked to the house and sat on the back porch steps for a quick prayer.

Dear Father, thank you for all the good things happening in my life. You are so good. I know I need to work hard, and I will. Please take care of Julep. Whatever happens, please keep her safe. Amen.

She couldn't remember where but somewhere she read, "Thankfulness leads to joy, turns selfishness into serving, and ego into humility." She vowed to always thank God first before she asked for anything.

Money is my big issue, Father. I guess it's a pretty big issue for most people who have big dreams, but I'm going to turn the money issue over to you, too. Amen.

And with that thought, she went inside the house and dressed for work.

Chapter Eleven

ear Equestrian,
Let's talk about fear. Sometimes we don't show our fear because we try to be brave, but we are often fearful. You see, Dear Equestrian, fear is our link to survival. Our only defense is to run, and we have a heightened awareness of things that we may need to flee, in order to survive.

Over the centuries, you may think this instinct to sense danger and run would lessen, but it hasn't. It's still very strong. Please help us to become brave. You can't force us to be brave. It doesn't work that way. Force never helps. What helps is patience—lots of patience.

We have long memories and we will remember everything we experience, both the good and the bad. Please teach good lessons, and if you teach well, every ride won't require a lesson.

That will be a great day for us both.

Wishing us long rides and safety,
Your Favorite Horse

PONY DAY! Marcy, Riley, and Stuffin are on their way. Finally, horses to smell in the morning without sneaking a sniff on the street. My clock is now on horse-time!

Jennie cranked up her well-used but still-running riding lawn mower. She had a bit of time to mow on this beautiful summer day before Marcy and the ponies arrived. Old jean shorts and a stained T-shirt were her mowing attire. She added work boots to

complete her ensemble. She didn't think boots and shorts strange at all.

With only the front yard mowed, Belinda pulled into the drive with the same old truck she drove in high school—the Red Roan. The once red truck with its scratches, dings, and years in the sun had a blotched look, like a red roan horse with a mix of red and light colors. Jennie laughed.

"Hey, why are you laughing? Not at my Red Roan girl, are you?" Belinda teased through the rolled-down window.

"No, I'm laughing because we both have our high school wheels, named ever so fondly. Mom and Dad gave me Blue Boy as my graduation present."

"Well, at least Blue Boy is in decent shape. But, yes, it's funny." Belinda climbed out and gave Jennie a long hug.

"Here we are at your very own abode. I never thought you would be a farm owner in Ohio, but it fits, it really fits."

"Listen to you, Miss I'm-going-to-vet-school. But yes, it fits, and vet school fits you, although you were always determined not to listen to your father."

"Yeah, but once I admitted I really wanted to be a vet, I forgot it was also what Dad wanted. But I'm not, and I repeat not, going to take over his practice. I may go into research, or I may specialize in equine, but I'm not going to run a practice in town."

Jennie and Belinda continued to talk as they walked to the barn—the mowing and trimming forgotten.

"Megan called and said the internship was going well. It isn't as much fun as she thought it would be, and she isn't getting a lot of horsemanship time, but she thinks things will change when she isn't the newbie. Right now she is more of a worker bee."

"How's Julep?"

"Julep is doing well, but this trainer is pressuring Megan to buy another horse—probably one he just happens to have for sale. Dad says, no, nada, not yet. She wants to stay down in South Carolina for her senior year of high school. I'm not so sure that's going to fly with Mom and Dad. Supposedly, she and a few others will be homeschooled while they travel to competitions and events."

"I can't imagine your parents letting her stay and miss her senior year at Appleridge High. Well, not unless she already has what she needs for college. Will they insist that she attend college?" Jennie stopped walking to look at Belinda.

"I think they'll definitely insist on college, but I also think she could skip most of her senior year and still get into a decent school. She doesn't think about anything other than horses and art projects. I suggested the University of Findlay. They have a good equine program."

"Yeah, it's a good school and not too far away."

"All I know is they aren't thrilled about her following this up-and-coming trainer around the country as free labor."

"Hey, what's this guy's name, anyway? We can't keep calling him this up-and-coming trainer."

"His real name is Johnny Johnson but he likes to be called JJ. I think he should be called Mr. Full-of-Himself because he has a huge ego. I've heard he's been written up in several magazines as an amazing horseman, mostly Western disciplines. I saw him at last year's Quarter Horse Congress and I didn't see the attraction, but he has quite a huge following. He's entertaining, and I guess he tells people what they want to hear. Megan is a huge fan of his methods—a real groupie."

Belinda looked around the barn. "Wow, you did a great job fixing up the old place. I love the new feed room, and you even poured cement for a wash rack outside."

"Dad and the brothers-in-law did most of the work, but I helped. My sisters married great guys who love to work on improvement projects. Who knew?"

"Well, I'm sure they knew, because I've always admired both Sallie and Connie. They have great taste.

"Hey, do you want to go to the Bake & Shake for a sandwich and shake?" Belinda was starving. She was always hungry, ate anything and everything she wanted, and somehow stayed thin.

"Marcy and her ponies are coming in today, but I'm not expecting them to arrive until after lunch, so, yeah, let's eat, but maybe no shake for me. I'm your weight-challenged friend, remember." Jennie was teasing because with all her jobs and the farm work, she was still at her dance performance weight.

JENNIE KICKED off her dirty shorts and replaced them with a clean pair, changed into a polo shirt, a little wrinkled but ok, dampened a wash cloth, and quickly washed the dirt from her face, neck, arms, and legs. Her hair was in a messy pony tail, but wasn't messy hair in style? A swipe or two of deodorant and she was back outside in ten minutes. They climbed into the Red Roan for the short drive into town—talking non-stop. Belinda rattled off Sam's cell number for Jennie to share with Marcy and Cassy.

"I saw Sam at the feed store last week but forgot to ask for his number. He seemed to be in a hurry." Jennie pushed her blowing hair from her face.

"Sam's usually booked solid most days because he's a good farrier." Belinda couldn't hide the pride in her comment. "He's intrigued about hoof function and likes to show me client photos, and, of course, as a soon-to-be vet student, I'm interested."

"How interested are you?"

"Stop it. Vet school first, then we'll see."

Belinda parked the car on a side street and they talked all the way to the bakery. The place was swarming with little kids wearing grass-stained baseball uniforms, some eating ice cream, and some standing in line, not so patiently, waiting for their cones. Jennie snagged a small empty table.

"Well, look here. Could it be two of my favorite 4–H friends?"

Both Belinda and Jennie turned in their seats and stared into very familiar face. Suddenly, Jennie wished she had taken a little bit more time cleaning up.

"Well, well, if it isn't Jeremy James, the boy with two first names. Are you still stinging from being beaten by two girls and their ponies?" Belinda kept a straight face as she teased.

Jennie was usually the one to tease Jeremy about his name, but after hearing her friend do it today, it didn't seem very nice.

Belinda wasn't finished. "Did your mama ever forgive us or you?" That part wasn't funny as Jeremy's mom demanded he win, and he paid dearly when he didn't.

Jennie motioned for Jeremy to grab a seat.

"You ladies are still very funny. And, yes, you are correct, Mom wasn't happy I didn't earn enough points for the state show last year. Of course, I tried to explain I was double teamed by the double twins. She got over it—eventually. Like maybe last week." Jeremy smiled as he talked. He clearly didn't hold a grudge.

Jennie finally found her voice. "What are you doing in Appleridge?"

They slid their chairs to make room for Jeremy to pull up his chair.

Jeremy motioned to the ball players happily licking cones. "I'm on nephew duty today, and his team is celebrating their first victory. How about you, home from school? Moving on or staying in Appleridge?"

Jennie motioned for Belinda to go first. "I'm here for the summer, graduated from Ohio State in May, and heading to the University of Florida for vet school, and, yes, hopefully returning to Appleridge, eventually."

"Wow, that's exciting. I can definitely see you as a vet. Your dad is a great vet."

Jeremy saw Belinda stiffen. "Of course, I'm sure you will find your own greatness because you aren't a bit like your dad."

"It took me a while to admit I wanted to apply to vet school, but the desire is there, so I'll follow my heart, and let Dad think he won."

"I guess in a way we both suffer with pushy parents, your dad and my mom. But hey, we turned out great." Jeremy squeezed Belinda's arm and turned to Jennie.

"Jennie?"

"Well, I graduated from college and now I'm back here."

Both Jeremy and Belinda looked over at Jennie, waiting for her to continue.

Jennie quickly asked, "What about you?"

"Graduated from Capitol in May, and I'm heading to seminary in August." He paused for their reaction and wasn't disappointed; it came quickly.

"You're going to be a pastor? I never would have guessed, but very cool." Belinda was always honest. Jennie remained quiet but smiled.

"I didn't expect it, either, but after Dad died, there were a few things that caused me to look at my life differently. I looked around, and things that I thought were important were no longer important, and other things became more important. Mom thinks there is status, of sorts, in her son being clergy, so it works.

"Well, I need to roll; it looks like the ice cream is gone and the messing around has begun. I don't remember being quite so active when I was nine. I thought I was a perfect angel."

Both Jennie and Belinda couldn't resist laughing.

"Hey, here's my number. If you want to get together before the end of summer, give me a call." And with that Jeremy went to save the Bake & Shake from nine-year-old boys.

When Jeremy left the Bake & Shake Jennie felt bad. "He's right. We didn't want him to win and we were mean."

"Yeah, we didn't like his pushy horse show mom, so we didn't want to like him, either. Especially when he joined the other club because his mom said our club had too many backyard-bred horses."

"I know, but those backyard horses named Julep and Sugar whipped his butt. Sorry, that wasn't nice then and it's not nice now." Jennie hung her head in fake shame, but she had a grin on her face she couldn't hide.

"But true. I always felt sorry for Jeremy. I think he wanted to stay in our club. Even though we teased him, we were friends, and we always had fun hanging out with him. His mom didn't give him a choice." Belinda paused, "Hey, why didn't you say more? You have a lot of exciting things happening in your life right now. What gives?"

"I don't know. I guess I wanted to listen to you guys." Jennie was trying to appear nonchalant, although her heart did a few

gymnastics while they talked to Jeremy. Or rather, Belinda talked and Jennie sat and smiled.

Her friend didn't prod her for a better explanation. Jennie was surprised, but relieved. She wanted to share her news, but her mind wouldn't send words to her mouth. She thought about the expression, tongue tied. If it meant you couldn't form words, that's exactly what happened.

"Hey, let's share a milkshake after we finish our dogs." Belinda glanced at her watch.

Jennie nodded. "That's a good compromise for your -challenged friend who wants a shake, too."

They sipped the thick shake cautiously. Neither wanted a brain freeze.

"I'll just drop you off. I know you'll be busy when your boarder arrives with her ponies, and I promised Mom I would stop at the store. Are you going to church tomorrow?"

"I'm going to the early service. I like the worship band instead of the organ."

"Mom and Dad won't budge from the traditional service. They think the worship band is too loud, but if I can get out of going with them, I'll sit with you." Belinda was making an effort to be a dutiful daughter before she left for school.

As Belinda and the Red Roan disappeared, Jennie contemplated changing back into her mowing clothes to finish the lawn. She glanced at her phone, the phone she never seemed to hear, and saw a text. Marcy was still about three hours from Appleridge and things were going well. Great! There was just enough time to hop back on the mower and finish, with plenty of time to clean up—hopefully, a little better this time.

Jennie couldn't wait to meet the ponies. Marcy's warm personality, along with her horse knowledge, or in this case, pony knowledge drew Jennie in immediately. Anyone who drove a team of ponies across open fields and through hazards and obstacles must be crazy fun. Jennie couldn't wait to find out.

Chapter Twelve

arcy climbed stiffly out of her truck. "Whew, so glad I'm finally here. What a long drive." She walked over to Jennie and gave her a hug.

Well, that answered Jennie's question. Hugging is ok. Jennie was from a family of huggers, but some people didn't like to be hugged.

"I'm glad you're here. I'm excited to meet Riley and Stuffin. Their stalls are ready, but I'm sure you'll want them out in the pasture after being in the trailer all day."

"Pasture would be perfect, for now. We may need to talk about a paddock with no grass at some point. They're what I call *easy keepers*."

"I thought about that, and I have a paddock area attached to the barn that may work, or we can add some temporary fencing and create a special place."

"Great! Thanks. My furniture arrives on Monday, and I start my new job on Friday. I won't have much time to exercise Riley and Stuffin for a while, and that'll mean they'll pack on the pounds."

Marcy opened the front trailer doors, unhooked the lead ropes, and threw them over the ponies' backs. She walked around, opened the back doors, and took down the ramp.

"If you want to take one, I'll take the other. I usually handle both at the same time, but this is new territory and the trip was long, so we'll see."

Jennie reached for the rope as Marcy backed a pretty bay pony down the ramp.

"This is Riley and the gray is Stuffin."

"Wow, they're gorgeous, but I expected them to match."

"It's nice when a pair or four in hand are color matches. It's a good look. But my ponies are perfectly matched in their movement. Once the judge sees how well they synchronize, the color never seems to matter."

"I'm learning already. I love it." Jennie led Riley over to the pasture gate.

"Do you want to walk them around the pasture to show them the fence lines before we turn them loose?"

"No, I'm not worried. Even if they want to run and kick up a bit, they have plenty of room and the fence is easy to see."

Jennie liked how the ponies stood patiently for their halters to be removed. Marcy stepped back and pointed to the pasture as a signal they were free to leave and the ponies trotted away from the gate. Both plopped down on the ground for a good stretching roll, got up, trotted a little, but stopped when they found the grass too enticing.

"Well, so much for new pasture excitement." Marcy was already walking away, eager to unpack her trailer. Jennie stood quietly, enjoying the view—two ponies in her pasture.

"Wait, I want to show you something new." Jennie led Marcy to the tack room and opened one of the special closets her dad built.

"What a nice surprise! I love them!"

"Dad made one with racks for your harness. You may want to keep your carriage in your trailer for now. Several feral cats are hanging around the barn, and I'm afraid they'll attack the seat upholstery. Dad said he may be able to build something to keep

it safe from dirt and cats, but we didn't know how big to build it."

"Thanks, but don't worry. Keeping it in the trailer works fine for me." Marcy was definitely a hugger.

They checked on the ponies and found both at the water tub.

"Well, that answers my question. They didn't drink on the trip, and I considered keeping them in stalls for the night so I could check their water buckets in the morning."

"We can leave them in their stalls tonight if you want." Jennie was new at this boarding business and eager to please.

"No, I saw them drink. It's a nice night so let's leave them out. I'm pooped. I'll leave after I show you what they get for breakfast, and the rest of their stuff can stay in the trailer until I have time to organize my super-nice tack closet."

"Two closets."

"What?"

"You get one for each pony."

"Wow! I probably won't need both, but I'll see what happens when I unpack the trailer. I'm not looking forward to all the unpacking and organizing when my furniture arrives, but organizing the tack closets will be fun. Maybe I'll start tomorrow." Marcy had dimples. "Show me where to park the trailer. I'm ready for a shower and a good book in bed."

Marcy backed her trailer into the spot Jennie chose, and unhitched like a pro. She joined Jennie by the pasture gate for one more look at Riley and Stuffin contentedly munching grass.

"I'll be out tomorrow to check on the munchkins."

"Ok. I'll be at the 9:30 service at My Savior Lutheran, if you want to sit with me." Jennie was usually shy about issuing an invitation to church, but she felt a little tug in her heart to step out of her comfort zone with Marcy.

"Thanks, but I've been a little mad at God lately." She wasn't offended by the invitation.

"I understand. Just know you're welcome. It isn't a traditional service and we dress casual."

"I may take you up on the offer—sometime. I won't drag this body out of bed tomorrow, but this move is starting to change my perspective about life." And with that comment, Marcy was in her truck and down the drive.

Jennie wondered where she was staying since her furniture wouldn't arrive until Monday. Maybe she should have asked. No, even if she and Marcy became good friends, they needed to give each other space.

Jennie stood for a few more minutes watching the ponies. She would come back out and check them before going to bed. It felt good to have horses on the farm. And it felt good to have a new friend.

Chapter Thirteen

*L*ong rolling thunder startled Jennie and her eyes popped open.

Oh no, a storm, the ponies!

Yesterday's jeans and T–shirt were conveniently on the bedroom floor. Bare feet slid into boots at the back door. After a race through the rain, Jennie found Riley and Stuffin huddled under the barn overhang. She led the ponies into dry stalls and tossed each pony a flake of hay.

She believed horses could usually handle what nature threw their way. The dry barn and flakes of hay were more for her benefit. She would sleep better with the ponies safely tucked inside the barn.

Jennie's fingers tapped her phone. *Ponies in stalls with hay.*

Marcy was exhausted from the drive, but just in case the thunder woke her, the text would help her go back to sleep.

IN WHAT seemed like minutes, instead of hours, Jennie's phone played Misty Mountain from the Hobbit movie. She attempted to shut off the music, but knocked the phone to the floor instead. She tossed the covers aside. Riley and Stuffin waited for their breakfast. This time she jumped into a clean pair of jean shorts and T–shirt, and also grabbed socks.

Both ponies nickered.

"Hey guys, you ready for breakfast?"

Oh, I love barn mornings with low nickers and the smell of hay.

"Maybe I should stop calling you guys. Sorry, Stuffin, I know you're a mare."

The ponies licked their buckets clean, then put their noses over the stall doors, eager to get outside and back to munching grass. They had eaten every stem of their thunderstorm treat of hay.

"Enjoy it while you can, Munchkins. I have a feeling you'll soon be on a limited-grass diet."

Riley and Stuffin were eating machines.

SHOWERED, dressed, and in the kitchen with partly dried hair, Jennie fixed her favorite quick breakfast of a granola bar and peanut butter. Spying her notebook, she reviewed her lists. She smiled at all the check marks, and there were quite a few.

Her little home was quiet this morning. She chased away a stab of loneliness.

Father, I don't talk to you enough. Thank you for everything you have provided these past few months, as I jumped into this new life. Thank you for the help and resources that just seem to happen, but I know nothing happens that isn't your plan. And, Father, something has been bothering me since I saw Jeremy. Please forgive me for everything I said and did that was cruel and uncaring when we were younger. I told myself it was only teasing, but now I think it was hurtful. Give me the strength to apologize to Jeremy the next time we meet. And, I would like a next time very much. Amen.

Wow, prayer certainly was revealing.

JENNIE SANG and swayed to the uplifting worship music. Marcy didn't meet her for church but Belinda did. She would invite Marcy again but wouldn't push. She planted the seed, but it was up to the Holy Spirit to help it grow. Jennie wasn't sure if

she was responsible for the fertilizer or not. Maybe just being a good friend is the fertilizer.

"HEY, IT'S EARLY but how about lunch?" Food was never too far from Belinda's radar.

"It's barely 10:45, girlfriend. But I'm in if we can at least wait until eleven. We'll still beat the Baptists to the buffet, as my grandpa likes to say."

"Very funny, but also very true," Belinda agreed. "If you don't get to a restaurant by 11:30, the lines are long with all denominations of hungry church goers. So where should we go?"

"Let's see, there aren't a lot of choices in Appleridge on Sunday. Maybe I could stop at the grocery and pick up a few things for salads, and you could get dessert. We'll meet at the farm to eat. I haven't been to the Dairy Fresh since I've been home and I'm craving their soft serve ice cream in a cup with strawberries. Do you want a sundae? Hey, and maybe get some of their special fried mushrooms. I think they open up at eleven, don't they?"

"And you call me bad! It sounds like my kind of lunch. I'm off. See you soon." Belinda turned and walked to the Red Roan.

WITH MISSIONS accomplished, the friends tossed salads, and carried the goodies to the small table on the back porch.

"Yum, even when they're cold these mushrooms are good. I've been careful. I'm not sure what got into me today." Jennie attempted to look guilty.

"It's usually me who's the bad influence. Good thing I'm leaving for school soon."

The rest of lunch was filled with the casual conversation of good friends.

Marcy pulled into the drive and waved.

"Hey, perfect timing. Do you want to walk out to the barn to meet Riley and Stuffin, and, of course, Marcy?"

"Yeah, but then I'll need to get on home. Sam is coming over. He wants to show me a few videos of his more interesting clients. He has a new computer program that analyzes a horse's movement."

"Oh, you mean just-friends Sam?"

"You're getting mean in your old age." But Belinda was laughing, so the words were received with the same fun they were slung.

After introductions Jennie and Belinda walked to the ponies' pasture with Marcy.

"I didn't see your text until this morning, but thanks for going out in the storm to put my guys inside."

"You're welcome. I wouldn't be able to sleep unless I checked on them. They were fine, huddled under the roof overhang, but they also didn't mind a middle-of-the-night flake of hay."

"Riley and Stuffin never seem to mind a flake of hay. Hey, I'm going to get my marathon carriage and take a short drive. They won't lift their faces out of the grass unless I insist. Do you want a ride? They can pull all three of us."

"Maybe I'll stay a little longer." Belinda was confident Sam would understand.

Both girls still wore their church casual pants and shirts, but didn't worry. That's what washing machines were for—although Jennie was still taking her laundry to her parents' house.

While Jennie and Marcy rolled the carriage down the horse trailer ramp, Belinda groomed Riley. Both Belinda and Jennie found the harnessing and hitching process confusing, but interesting, and were impressed with how patiently the ponies stood. Marcy explained the importance of teaching a driving horse to

stand perfectly quiet until asked to move. This was an important skill for a horse being hitched to a carriage.

"This is a whole new world for me." Belinda was intrigued.

"Next time I'll teach you to drive, if you're interested."

They were VERY interested.

All three grabbed helmets. Marcy climbed into the front seat first, and when she had both reins and whip in hand, the other two climbed on back.

Marcy pointed her driving whip toward the mowed path in the pasture. "Is that path for me to use?"

"Yeah, I thought you could drive on the path and not worry about hitting holes or rocks."

"Smart girl. Thanks." Marcy approved. Jennie beamed.

Marcy gave a brief lesson on how to communicate with a driving horse versus a horse being ridden. Riders used their seat, legs, and reins to communicate with a horse. Since carriage drivers couldn't use their seats or legs like riders, they used voices and whips as well as the reins. The long whip was never used to whip a horse—not that the girls would do that, anyway. A driver used the long whip to touch or tickle the horse's flank, asking him to engage a hind leg, lift a shoulder, or move over. Excessive use of the whip was never permitted in carriage-driving competition and would be cause for elimination.

With slight encouragement, the pair moved up into a trot. What fun! Belinda and Jennie grabbed the bar behind Marcy's seat, held on tight, looked at each other, and grinned.

The ponies trotted several times around the pasture perimeter and then Marcy used the cut-through paths to change direction. Marcy alternated trotting with short walk breaks, finished with one entire lap walking, and drove the ponies back to the barn.

As Jennie and Belinda watched, Marcy unhitched and unharnessed the ponies. Eager to help, they led Riley and Stuffin to the wash bay for a quick spray of the hose, while Marcy rolled the carriage to her trailer.

"That was great. Thanks for the ride, Marcy." Belinda returned her helmet to the tack room. "I bet Sam is waiting, but he'll understand because he's a horse guy. I can't wait to tell him about my first carriage ride with a pair of ponies."

Jennie and Marcy led the ponies to the pasture. Still wet from his bath, Riley rolled in the dirt and scrambled to his feet looking like a mud horse. Stuffin found a nice patch of grass.

They carried camp chairs from the tack room, and sat in the barn aisle to wipe off the harness. Jennie filled Marcy in on her friendship with Belinda and Sam. She was chatty and also shared a brief history of what brought her back to Appleridge. Marcy seemed interested, asked questions, but she didn't offer to share any details of her life, and Jennie didn't pry.

"I think I'll spend some time organizing my tack closets, if that's ok."

"That's fine. Just enjoy this beautiful afternoon. I hung a white board in the tack room. It's for notes, in case you need to bring anything to my attention, but you can also call, e-mail, or text. You're welcome to come up to the house to use the bathroom. Let me show you where I hide the key to the back door."

"Thanks, Jennie. It feels good here." Marcy gathered her harness and grooming bag. She seemed anxious to start organizing.

"Thanks so much for the driving lesson. I guess I'll go up to the house now."

Although she would have loved to sit around and talk, Jennie didn't want Marcy to feel like she couldn't come out to the farm and have some private time. She pulled her phone out of her pocket and saw a missed call from her mom, and also a text inviting her to supper that night. Jennie returned the call instead of the text.

"Hey, Mom, it's me."

"Hi, sweetie, come on over. Your sisters and their families are coming tonight. It's just like before you went away to Chicago. We're having Sunday night supper together."

"I'll be there. What should I bring?"

"Don't worry about bringing anything. We'll have plenty of food."

Hmmm, my mom probably thinks I don't have anything to bring at such short notice.

Standing in front of the open pantry, she spotted an unopened package of gingersnap cookies. The cookies were a treat for the ponies, but since they were unopened, they would work just fine for tonight. She also had a box of snack crackers and a block of cheese. Perfect.

Family time was welcome. She wasn't quite so lonely after a day like today.

Chapter Fourteen

ear Equestrian,

Let's talk about clothing for horses. We don't like it very much. There may be some instances when it is acceptable, but not many. We don't get cold easily. At least not as cold as you two-legged creatures. We like cold. Ok, maybe not freezing cold, with rain and no shelter, but most of the time we are fine.

Most of the time, we don't need a blanket. Of course, if you decide to clip our winter hair, then we have nothing to keep us warm, and will accept a blanket. But there better be a good reason for clipping in the winter. Maybe we have too much hair during heavy training and competition season. In that case, clip away. It beats heat stroke.

There is one blanket we like in the winter. It's called a cooler or anti-sweat sheet. After a long workout or hard ride on the trail, it's nice to have a cooler to wick away the sweat during our trailer ride home. We don't like a chilled back from the open windows, and we have to have open windows to breathe. Yes, a cooler is a good idea, and hey, they don't cost too much.

If we are barefoot, we give the green light to hoof boots, especially on rocky trails. We don't like metal shoes, but we concede there are those times when we'll have a need for those, just don't expect us to like the whole nailing process. It doesn't hurt if the farrier knows what he's doing, so we tolerate it, but probably won't like it. Sometimes, like when we aren't working on pavement or rocks, we don't need shoes or boots. Yahoo!

Fly masks are interesting to wear. We don't exactly hate them because they are useful, but eliminating the flies by using fly

predators or fly strips would be another option. Fly masks are some-times used to protect our friends with white noses. Sunburned noses aren't fun. Flies in the eyes aren't fun, either. So I guess we will ac-cept fly masks—and maybe a little fly spray.

Leg wraps? Keep them on hand for injuries, but make sure you learn how to wrap legs properly. Quite a bit of damage can result by pulling on tendons or wrapping legs too tightly.

Let's talk about saddles, bridles, and harness. All the things you call tack. Why is it called tack, anyway? Not sure, but whatever you use, please make sure it fits comfortably. You don't like shoes or boots that pinch, rub, or twist, and we don't like saddles that do the same. Ouch!

Well, I guess that covers just about everything but remember you don't need to cover our body with everything.

Don't forget to buy carrots!

Your Favorite Horse

JENNIE SAVED her work and shut down her computer. She had just enough time to check on the ponies before getting dressed for the library. Some days words flowed out of her fingers as she tapped the keyboard. All in all, life was good. She earned enough to pay what she promised her grandpa, and was saving to start making actual payments on the farm. She was thankful.

Her *Dear Equestrian* letters were popular, and she sold a few other articles to small local publications, but so far, nothing per-manent magically appeared.

Her current project, writing stories for a small tourism guide, would bring a nice chunk of change for her efforts. The guide included information for new residents and places of interest for those visiting. Jennie had already logged several hundred miles traveling around the county for interviews, and fortunately, the project also came with a small travel stipend. The last two interviews were scheduled for later this week.

Riley and Stuffin nickered a welcome as she entered their paddock.

"Ok, you can each have a little flake of hay, but you're staying in the paddock. Your mom left strict orders to limit your grass buffet. Besides, I think she's planning on driving you later this afternoon."

Jennie scanned both ponies—looking for anything unusual. She took her role as caregiver seriously. She enjoyed her time with the ponies. She also enjoyed her time with Marcy. They were becoming good friends.

Jennie was anxious for Cassy Morton and her horse, Treasure, to arrive next week. She hoped the three of them would have many fun horse girl days. She was counting the days waiting for Julep to come home and join their little group.

MARCY'S TRUCK was parked next to the barn when she returned home from the library. She parked Blue Boy and walked to the barn.

"Hey, how were your guys this evening?"

"They were in good form, ready to work. I found a horse driving trial a few hours away and I need a navigator. How about you being my gator for the competition?"

"I have absolutely no idea what that is, but it sounds fun." Jennie laughed, and then she added, "I hope it isn't on my Saturday to work, but if it is, I may be able to trade with Suzanne. I've helped her out a few times and I think she'll trade with me."

"Don't worry, I can teach you the ropes. You'll help groom, harness, and then ride on the back step and balance the carriage.

That's all. Well, that and keep me on track so I get to each phase on time, and I've been told it's not an easy job." Marcy rolled her eyes.

"Ok, send me the dates and I'll get them on the calendar. When I have Saturday off, I usually get off at three on Friday. Will that work?"

"Yes, I'll load what I need and we can leave as soon as you get home. It should give us enough time to get the ponies settled and still have time for a course walk. I think the organizers are also having a cookout that night. It'll be fun."

"Cassy and Treasure arrive next week, so I'll need to make arrangements for the farm. That will leave Treasure here alone, and that may not be a good idea, but I'll work it out with Cassy."

Jennie paused for a moment. "Speaking of Treasure, I'll put her in the pasture next to Riley and Stuffin, so they can meet over the fence, and if that looks good, then we can think about two ponies and a horse together."

"I bet we'll all be here one weekend and give it a try. I know you'll have Julep soon, but have you thought about maybe getting another horse or pony? There'll be more than a few times when I take Riley and Stuffin away for the weekend, leaving Treasure here alone."

"I have thought about that, and you may not believe this, but I'm thinking maybe a driving pony."

Marcy jumped up. "I'm ready to help you look!"

"Yeah, but I don't have the money yet. And then there's the harness and cart—it could get expensive."

"You're right. I won't disagree. Maybe you could foster a horse? Or better yet, foster a potential driving partner." Marcy was on a roll.

"Or a youngster that needs time to grow. I've thought about that, also." Jennie walked over to the white board to erase her message to Marcy and Marcy's note in return.

"New day, clean slate," said Marcy, "and I better get home. I'm working a twelve-hour shift tomorrow, so I don't think I'll be out, but I'll pack some barn clothes just in case I need some pony time. Sometimes grooming ponies is just what I need after a tough day at the hospital." Marcy walked as she talked and waved as she reached her truck.

Jennie checked the ponies once more, turned out the lights, and walked to the house. She sat down at her computer, but not to write. Instead, she searched the internet with the words *horse driving trial, navigator, driving marathon.*

Chapter Fifteen

*I*t was a restless, sleepless, night. Her body didn't move but her mind was overly active.

Did I drive horses all night? It sure feels like it. Maybe I should be more careful about what I read before turning out the light. Better yet, maybe reviewing my interview notes would have been a good idea.

Today Jennie was driving to a large cattle operation to learn about Black Angus cattle. Apparently, the owner was well-known in county agricultural circles, and his farm was suggested for a feature article in the tourism guide. She recognized the name, although she didn't know anything about the farm. Maybe a little extra caffeine would make it a good day to drive to the other side of the county.

Rolling down Blue Boy's windows, Jennie placed her travel mug in the drink holder. It was a beautiful July morning, not too hot, with a slight breeze.

WOW, what an entrance—stone pillars, gate, and long, winding drive, flanked by four-board black fences—impressive. Huge black cattle grazed in the well-maintained pastures, and round bales of freshly cut hay dotted a large field on her right.

Mr. Gregory stood with his arms folded in front of his chest, immaculately dressed in cowboy attire; jeans, vest, boots, and hat. Jennie held back a giggle. He even sported a handle bar mustache. She didn't know Mr. Gregory's first name, but if it was something like Tex or Duke, she would be in serious trouble.

"So you're the young lady they sent. Come along."

Strange greeting, but she followed.

Mr. Gregory pointed out several buildings, each having a particular function. They stopped at an empty horse barn.

"I don't ride anymore. We use ATVs to move the cattle instead of horses." He motioned Jennie to follow him through the door he opened.

Jennie nodded and stepped inside the silent barn.

"I kept a few reminders."

The next door opened into a jam-packed tack room. He proudly showed Jennie several beautifully tooled western saddles, bridles, mohair reins, and numerous blankets. Everything was pristine clean.

Of course it stays clean with no horses on the place. Jennie thought.

"I bet you're one of those bleeding heart horse lovers."

"I'm not sure what you mean but, yes, I love horses."

"Well, let me tell you something. Horses need to be useful. Our last horse was a mare we had for twenty-five years. Taught my two sons and my daughter to ride and won most of those trophies." He gestured to a shelf of trophies and ribbons. "Yup, she was useful to the end. One day I waited until they were all gone and I called the kill dealer to pick up that old girl. The price per pound for horse meat was good and I made a few bucks. She was ready to go, anyway."

Jennie gasped. He laughed.

"Then I got on my back hoe, dug up a spot, and told them she died and was buried in the pasture."

Jennie swallowed and slowly backed out of the tack room, eager to get outside and feel the warmth of the sun.

Mr. Gregory noticed her reaction and laughed again. "I can see you ARE one of those bleeding heart horse lovers who don't understand that horses need to be useful, and they need to be useful right to the end. To live here you need to earn your keep."

"But don't you think you owed her a better end? The trip to slaughter isn't pretty. Why didn't you just ask your vet to humanely euthanize the mare?"

"That costs money, and like I said, I made money." His tone meant end of discussion.

Jennie no longer saw an immaculate farm. She saw a farm that probably held a lot of ugly secrets.

How can I end this interview quickly?

He was still chuckling as they walked out to the main cattle barn. Jennie listened politely while plotting her escape, pretending to write a few notes. Finally, Mr. Gregory motioned to the door. Jennie was eager to get outside, but in the corner she saw four or five kittens playing and stopped to watch.

Mr. Gregory saw what she was watching and commented, "I'm not so bad after all. I actually feed the cats on the farm but they better keep my barn mice free."

Before Jennie could comment, the large black dog that had shadowed them on the tour, charged the kittens, caught a tiny gray tabby by the neck, and shook. The other kittens ran, but one tiny gray body no longer moved.

"Oh, well, one less mouth to feed. They should know better."

Jennie gasped but didn't scream. Somehow she didn't run, either. She closed her notebook, looked Mr. Gregory in the eyes, and with a shaky voice said, "I will never understand people like you."

With as much dignity as possible, Jennie walked stiffly to her truck. She could hear his laughter but didn't turn around. Tears rolled down her cheeks before she cleared the farm gate. She still didn't know his first name but it didn't matter. There were plenty of names she could call him, and none were remotely nice. She wasn't writing his story; no way, definitely not. He was wealthy, and, quite likely, had some pull in the area, but if the county required a feature story about his farm, they would need to write it themselves.

Shaking, she drove a mile before she found a wide berm and pulled off the road.

Father, what is wrong with that man? My heart aches for his poor children and wife. I'm sure he made their lives miserable. I pray they never learn what happened to their poor horse. And, Father, please take care of all the creatures on his farm, especially the kittens. OK, now I guess I need to pray for him, too, but that sure is hard. How sad and pitiful his life must be. Maybe that's why he hurts everything around him. Bring someone into his life to save him from this darkness and lead him to Jesus. That man's world could use a little light.

She would never understand people like Mr. Gregory—never. What caused him to be so hard and cruel?

She felt ill when she thought about the sweet kitten shaken to death, or the faithful old mare being tossed away and sent to slaughter. She hoped the man's family never learned what really happened. Something was definitely wrong with that man.

Chapter Sixteen

The county directory project was finished. No one mentioned the omission of Mr. Gregory's farm. Maybe he wasn't so popular, after all? She wasn't worried about being asked to write anything she didn't want to write. Her bank account already held the fruit of her labor. What a relief. She wanted more projects, but at the same time, she didn't want to write what she didn't want to write.

It took plenty of effort to remain focused at the library. Cassy and Treasure would arrive later today. She was ready, and promised to pick up Grandpa for the big day. He hadn't been out to meet Riley and Stuffin, yet. Grandpa would enjoy getting his hands on that pair of ponies.

The circulation desk was quiet. It was a good time to shelve books. There was something about gathering the books, putting them in order on the cart, and then finding their places on the shelf she enjoyed. Her fellow workers thought she was crazy. They didn't like being away from the desk. No one complained when she disappeared into the book stacks.

She rolled the cart, loaded with what she thought was one hour's worth of work, and worked steadily. She finished, returned the cart, logged off the system, gathered her things, and rushed out the door five minutes after her shift ended. No sticking around to chat today.

Grandpa waited by curb, wearing his boots. Of course he would wear boots. When she was little, he always made sure she wore her boots in the barn.

"Hey, Jennie girl, it's a good day for going to the barn."

"Yes, Gramps, it is. Any day is a good day to spend at the barn, don't you think?" Jennie grinned.

"Well, as I get older, I don't think cold days are good days. I don't like those cold days anymore."

"Well then, good thing today is warm." Jennie teased. "Did you eat? I have some things to make sandwiches at the house. I don't expect the haulers to arrive until three or so."

"I ate lunch but a little dessert may be just the ticket."

"Hmmm, maybe I have a few cookies in the cookie jar. What would the farm be without cookies in Grandma's old cookie jar?" Jennie glanced over at her grandpa.

"I could be persuaded to try one of those cookies, I suppose." Grandpa tried to appear nonchalant.

"Peanut butter? Aren't those your favorite? But then, I don't think there's a cookie that you or I wouldn't like." Jennie glanced over at Grandpa again and they both laughed.

Grandpa found a seat on the back porch, and Jennie provided a plate of cookies and a glass of ice tea.

"I'll be back in a few minutes, Gramps. I'm just going to change my clothes. Enjoy your cookies and then we'll take a walk out to the barn to meet the ponies."

Jennie searched her purse for her phone, and saw a text from Cassy—*b there 3 treasure 4*

She sent a text. *Great, can't wait!* She still couldn't ignore punctuation and complete sentences in a text.

Wearing jean shorts and a T-shirt, she carried her glass of tea outside and sat down to enjoy a cookie.

"Hey, Grandpa, do you know Mr. Gregory with the Black Angus farm on the other side of the county?"

Grandpa hesitated. "Yes, I do. Why do you ask?"

Jennie proceeded to tell the whole story. "I couldn't include his story in the guide—I just couldn't."

"He's a little younger than me, but I've known him for a while. His dad was a mean one. There were three boys and they all grew up mean. I'm not sure why, but mean often follows mean."

"What about his children? I sure hope they never find out what happened to their horse."

"I'm not sure but I think only one boy stuck around. None help him on the farm. I guess that tells the story. They all stay away. Maybe he didn't fool them after all. Maybe he's the fool." After a pause, Grandpa continued. "I'm glad you went to prayer when you felt the need. Prayer is good for those being prayed for and also good for the person praying. I can't figure out why we don't do it more, can you?"

"No, Gramps, I can't." Jennie picked up another cookie.

"God always finds a way to take something bad and turn it into something good. I sure can't see the good in what you experienced, but your prayers pleased God."

"Praying sure helped me, but, I'll admit, I still get sick and then angry when I think about what happened to that little kitten. I guess I better keep on praying."

The cookie plate only held crumbs. It was time to for Grandpa to meet Riley and Stuffin.

The ponies were standing head to tail, under the barn overhang, swishing flies with their long tails, and enjoying the shade. They woke from their naps when Jennie called their names.

"Oh, my, what nice ponies you are!" Grandpa looked at Jennie. "Did you say they're driven as a pair?"

"Riley is the bay gelding and Stuffin is the gray mare. I was surprised, because I thought they needed to match in color, but they match when they move. I would show you the carriage but

Marcy keeps it in her horse trailer. I'm sure she'll give you a ride if you come out some weekend."

She shared what she knew about combined driving competitions and what her job as the navigator would entail. The ponies lost interest in the human conversation as soon as Jennie walked out with a flake of hay for them to share.

"The ponies stay here in the paddock during the day and go to the pasture at night. Marcy says the sugar and starch in the grass is lower at night. They have metabolic issues."

Grandpa found a seat on a bench in the barn and sat with his back leaning against the barn wall. They chatted until they heard Cassy's car. Grandpa remained seated, but Jennie got up to greet Cassy and lead her to the barn.

"I just heard from the driver. They're about twenty minutes out. I'm anxious to see Treasure. She usually travels well, but this is the first time she's been hauled without me tagging along with the driver. Someday I'm going to get my own trailer."

Jennie grinned. Cassy talked quite a bit on her first visit to the farm and today was no different.

"I'm sure she's fine, but I agree, it's nice to haul your own horse. I want to get a trailer for the farm." Jennie motioned for Cassy to come into the barn.

"Grandpa, this is Cassy Morton. Cassy, this is my Grandpa, Charlie Gantzler.

"Cassy, I hear you are getting ready to start college. Please forgive me for not getting up. These old knees are a little stiff."

"You're good. It's nice to meet you, and, yes, I'm ready. I'm so happy my parents are sending Treasure to college with me, and I'm so happy I found this place."

Cassy was bursting with the newness of everything. "Our agreement is that my grades need to be good or Treasure goes home."

Grandpa chuckled. "Sounds like you have smart parents."

It wasn't long before they spotted the huge trailer traveling slowly down the road. Cassy jumped up and ran down the drive, waving with each step.

Jennie explained the farm setup to the driver on an earlier call so they pulled past the farm then skillfully backed into the drive to reach the barn.

The driver approached Cassy to complete the paperwork. The other man opened the side door and lowered the ramp. Cassy squealed when Treasure's nose poked out the door, and was rewarded with a loud nicker.

"She traveled well, drank at stops, nibbled on hay while we were on the road, but didn't eat as much as I would have liked."

The driver continued his report as Treasure was led down the ramp. "She's a real nice mare. Thank you for your business. She was a pleasure to haul."

Looking at Jennie he added, "We have two horses on board. Would you mind if we did a quick cleanup of manure, offer fresh water, and just give them a few minutes of rest at this stop?"

"Go ahead and take the time they need. I'll get a muck bucket."

"Cassy, you can put Treasure in this small pasture to stretch her legs. She'll be able to see the ponies. We'll have to see how they get along, but I'd like to put all three together eventually."

Treasure was eager to see the ponies and there was a bit of squealing as they met over the fence. Riley didn't like Treasure getting close to Stuffin. He placed himself between her and the fence. Horses are fun to watch as they meet and greet, and it looked like Riley was going to take the lead in this small herd; at least for now.

After their break, the driver and his helper lifted the ramp, gave the trailer one more check, thanked Jennie for her help, thanked Cassy for her business, and began the next leg of their journey.

"Well, that seemed like a nice outfit," Grandpa said.

Jennie nodded. "I got their card while I was showing them where to put the manure."

"They came highly recommended." Cassy walked up holding Treasure's halter. "She pranced around the pasture for a while, but is now chomping on grass like crazy."

"Great. We'll keep an eye on her and make sure she's drinking. Will you be here for a while? I'll need to leave for a few minutes to take Grandpa to his apartment."

"I'll be here. My trunk is stuffed with Treasure's tack, blankets, and things to unpack. I may not finish, because I think it would be a good idea to check into the hotel before dark."

Jennie stopped quickly. "What hotel?"

"I can't get into the dorm yet, so I need a hotel. Mom and Dad are renting a little trailer and bringing all my stuff in a few days when the dorms open."

"Cassy, you don't have to stay in a hotel. You can stay here. I have two extra rooms, no furniture, but I can borrow a cot from my sister. They like to camp."

"That's nice of you, Jennie, but I don't expect you to put me up, too. I don't want to invade your space just because I'm keeping Treasure here."

Grandpa chuckled. "Cassy, my granddaughter wouldn't offer if she didn't want you to stay, and beware, she can be real insistent."

"I don't mind. Call your parents and check with them first, but I'm sure they checked me out thoroughly before they agreed to board Treasure here at the farm. After you call your parents, call the hotel and cancel. Do you think you'll get charged for tonight?"

"I'll call my parents, but I won't get charged because I didn't make reservations."

"Oh, ok, and tell them they're welcome to keep the trailer at the farm overnight. They'll drive up and arrive the day before you move into the dorm, right?" Jennie the organizer was now in full planning mode.

"That's the plan. They can't drive up and unload all in the same day, so they're making the drive one day, unloading and returning the trailer rental the second day, then driving home the third."

Cassy took her cell phone out of her back pocket and walked outside the barn.

"MY PARENTS like the idea of me staying with Jennie instead of in a hotel by myself, and they will gladly pay for my room and board. And, they think leaving the trailer at the farm the first night is also a good idea."

"Well, glad that's settled. I'm taking Grandpa home now, and then I'll stop at my sister's to see if I can borrow a cot or air mattress. I'll leave the house open in case you want to get something cold to drink or whatever. Make yourself at home and I shouldn't be long."

Before she left, Jennie showed Cassy the stall for Treasure and the tack closet with all its hooks and shelves. Cassy couldn't wait to empty her car into the closet.

"I don't think she'll miss me, Grandpa. She couldn't wait to get started." Jennie turned to look at her grandpa.

"Why are you laughing, Grandpa?"

"You're a good one, my Jennie girl." And with that comment he started walking to the truck, leaving Jennie standing in the barn aisle, wondering about her strange need to organize this somewhat messy world.

Chapter Seventeen

Cassy was a great housemate and considerate guest. Perhaps a little on the messy side, but she kept the mess more or less confined to her room. Cassy's parents arrived as scheduled, and although Jennie invited them to stay at the farm, they thanked her but chose a nice hotel bed over an air mattress. Jennie couldn't argue with their logic.

Cassy would leave the farm and move into her dorm, but she promised to stay at the farm while Jennie and Marcy were at the combined driving event.

"I love the idea of staying here at the farm, and waking up near her in the morning, and saying the last goodnight."

"I feel bad about taking you away from the campus just as you're making new friends and getting acquainted with college life."

Cassy just laughed. "I have four years to hang out on campus."

JENNIE ENJOYED meeting Cassy's parents, Joan and Tom Morton. She especially enjoyed their invitation to dinner at one of Jennie's favorite restaurants. Since it was in the small city of Richburg, where the college and hotels were located, Jennie drove Blue Boy and met the Morton family at the restaurant.

Stuffed with good food and conversation, Jennie drove back to the farm alone. Cassy packed a bag for a night at her parents' hotel. She suspected Cassy was a little tired of sleeping on an air mattress. She would offer Cassy the use of her bed when she came to watch the farm.

Jennie walked to the barn for a final night check, thinking about the beautiful evening with new friends. All three horses were in the pasture contentedly munching grass. She was tired, and didn't linger.

Headlights lit up the drive as Jennie put her key into the back door lock. It looked like Belinda's Red Roan. It was. And her dad was in the passenger seat. Why were they here so late? The horses were fine.

Belinda jumped out of the truck first—crying. Dr. Peterson opened his door and climbed out a little more slowly.

"I'm afraid we have some bad news. May we come inside?" Jennie had never seen Dr. Peterson so hesitant.

Jennie nodded, led them inside, and motioned to the kitchen table.

Dr. Peterson glanced at his daughter as he sat.

"We got a call from Megan tonight, and—and, I'm so sorry. She lost Julep." Belinda barely got it out before she started sobbing.

Lost? What do they mean?

Dr. Peterson finished, "Megan is at a competition in Georgia with JJ. The farm hands called and said she died before they could call the vet. Megan is beating herself up because she wasn't there with Julep. She's also very angry, because she thinks the farm hands are idiots."

Jennie sat silent.

Belinda whispered, "Jennie, are you ok?"

Devastated, Jennie put her face in her hands.

"I know." Belinda leaned over and hugged Jennie as they sat side by side.

"I'm lining up coverage at the clinic and driving down to South Carolina tomorrow to check on Megan, and I'm also going

to talk to this Johnson guy and get some answers. I know it won't bring Julep back, but I need answers, and I need to make sure my daughter is not being exposed to idiots."

Now that was the Dr. Peterson Jennie remembered; take charge Dr. Peterson.

"I can stay with you tonight if you want me to."

Jennie lifted her face. "No, I'm ok. Thanks, anyway." She didn't want to hurt her friend's feelings, but she felt numb. She couldn't even cry.

"Are you sure? I have a bag in the truck."

"Yeah, I'm good." Jennie wasn't good, but she stood up and did her best to pretend that she was fine. "Thanks for letting me know."

Belinda ached for her friend. It's so hard to know what to say in a situation like this. She wished Jennie would let her stay. She didn't look good.

Jennie watched the Red Roan turn around in the drive, and gave a little wave as they passed the back porch on the way out of the farm. Belinda waved back but Jennie couldn't see her from where she stood. Dr. Peterson lifted his hand briefly.

The house was dark, except for the light over the kitchen sink. Leaving it on, Jennie walked down the hall and slowly climbed the stairs to her bedroom. She sat on the bed near Beauty, her furry friend who offered comfort when good days turned sad. The cat raised her head and meowed softly.

The tears finally fell, and when they did, they wouldn't stop. Her face swollen from tears, her pillow damp, sleep finally came.

As dawn approached, she slowly opened her eyes and remembered. Julep was gone. Not just gone to South Carolina, she was gone forever.

She pulled the blanket to her face, catching a new tear slowly sliding down her cheek.

They promised to bring her home but, now, she isn't coming home.

Her mind said she shouldn't blame the Petersons, but her heart couldn't be rational in her grief.

Father, it's me. I hurt, and I'm angry, and I don't want to be angry. I know Megan would never let anything happen to Julep. It's not her fault. But, I'm still angry because they made a promise. I know that's not fair, but losing Julep isn't fair. Ok, I guess I shouldn't say that because you have given me so much. But, Father, I'm going to need your help in getting my heart to believe what I know to be true. Please be with Megan. I know she hurts, like me; maybe more. And, please take care of my sweet Julep. Maybe there's a kid in heaven for her to love. Thanks for listening. Amen.

Jennie ached for Megan, so far away from home, a dream turned bad. What would happen now? Staring at the bathroom mirror, she touched her puffy face with the wet washcloth.

I need to stop crying, or my face is going to scare the little kids coming to the library for story hour. And good grief, I'm still wearing the clothes I wore to dinner last night.

Riley, Stuffin, and Treasure waited for their breakfast, and that was a good reason for Jennie to get on with her day.

All three equines followed her into the barn and found their own stalls. She paused at the first stall on the left—Julep's stall. The stall she had all those years ago with Grandpa. Looking at the empty stall, the stall that no longer needed to be saved for Julep, Jennie said goodbye.

She rushed to the house to get ready for work.

I think I'll hide in the book stacks all day. It's worth a try.

JENNIE SURVIVED her shift at the library, but didn't avoid a visit from her mom and dad.

Her mom was first in the door and gave her a big hug.

"Belinda called. I'm so sorry, sweetie."

"Thanks, Mom. I was counting the days until she came home."

"I know, honey; you were excited about seeing her out in that pasture again." Ellen McKenzie looked out the kitchen window then searched her daughter's face. "Do you need anything? I have an appointment with a client in an hour, but if you want company, I can come back out later, or why don't you come have supper with us tonight?"

She didn't want company and she didn't want food. She wanted to be left alone. But, instead, she said, "Hey, before you go, do you want to walk out and meet Riley, Stuffin, and Treasure?"

"Sure, let's go." Jennie's dad was quick to answer and get up out of his chair. Her dad was ready to move on to something more pleasant than watching his daughter sit and cry.

All three equines trotted to the gate looking for treats, and Jennie explained that Marcy didn't feed the ponies treats out of her hand. She didn't mind if they were given treats, but the treats were placed in a bucket. Jennie found the special treat bucket and filled her pocket with gingersnaps.

"Dad, see how they're more respectful waiting for the treat bucket? The ponies become little terrors if they're fed by hand, especially Riley."

"That's smart." Jennie's dad moved to the fence to give Stuffin, who waited patiently for her treat, a nice stroke down her neck.

"Just give yourself a bit of time, but when you're ready, find yourself a nice horse. Not to take Julep's place, though, she'll always hold a special piece of your heart."

Jennie had never heard her dad speak like that, and he wasn't finished.

"These guys are nice, and I know you enjoy having them here, but your heart needs a horse of your own."

"Listen to your father, dear. He's a wise man. I should marry him."

In spite of herself, Jennie smiled. Her dad was right. She remembered a verse from the bible: *Weeping may tarry for the night but joy comes in the morning. Psalm 30:5.* Jennie was ready for her morning to come, but she was still in the night. She would be in the night a little while longer, but she could also see some light.

She waved as her parents drove away, then walked through her clean barn, the stalls filled with fresh shavings, the tack room organized, pastures freshly mowed, two ponies and a horse contentedly munching their breakfast hay. A little bit of thankfulness sneaked through the sadness. Being sad and thankful at the same time was a new feeling for Jennie. Julep was a great horse, and a good friend for a young girl growing up. She would cling to that thought.

I won't forget you, my sweet girl.

Chapter Eighteen

r. Peterson stowed his bag behind the truck seat and turned to his wife. "Susan, I'll call when I get to South Carolina. Megan won't be back at the ranch until tomorrow night, but I'm going to see what I can find out before she returns. I've already called a local vet. I'm going to his office around noon tomorrow and he's going to share a little bit of what he knows about this Johnson guy. I may bring Megan home kicking and screaming."

"Ok, Adrian. You be careful and drive safely. I'll stop in at the clinic to make sure they don't need anything."

"Bill's covering any emergencies for a few days plus his own appointments. I have a good staff and they'll move my appointments."

Remembering how much his staff loved food, he added, "Of course, they love anything you may want to make or bake."

Susan leaned in for a quick kiss on the cheek, then stepped back and smiled. He was a good dad—even if the girls thought he was unyielding most of the time.

With a ten-hour drive ahead, he had plenty of time to think about what he would find at the ranch, and how he would approach the situation. He wasn't known for being impulsive, but he didn't give fools much slack, either. And then there was Megan. Losing Julep was a huge blow and someone needed to be held responsible. Ok, maybe they couldn't have prevented the situation, but not calling the local vet was irresponsible.

Dr. Adrian Peterson soon grew tired of thinking and attempted to find a decent radio station. If ever there was a time for satellite radio it was now. Traffic was light and the weather good through West Virginia and Fancy Gap. One quick stop for fuel and a sandwich later, he crossed into North Carolina, and stopped at the Welcome Center to stretch his legs and use the facilities. It wasn't long before he was through Charlotte and crossed the Catawba River into South Carolina. Beautiful country, he thought, and found a local station to keep him alert for the last hour or so.

As he neared his exit, Adrian began to look for a hotel. It was only fifteen miles to Grayson Corners and the ranch, but there was no guarantee he would find a decent local hotel once he left the interstate.

Ranch, really? This Johnson guy liked to call the school a ranch, the Double J to be precise, but Adrian doubted it was a real ranch in the true sense of the word. Sure, there were working cattle ranches on the east coast, but with only thirty acres, JJ Johnson was exaggerating when he called his place a ranch. But then, it did have bunk houses and cows. Ok, maybe that made it a ranch.

Adrian called Susan. "Hey, I'm at my exit and checked in at a Holiday Inn Express. It's not too bad. I'm going to grab a shower, then have supper at a little place down the road."

He did exactly what he said—shower and supper. The local BBQ place was good—amazingly good. The coleslaw he found on his sandwich was a surprise. In Ohio coleslaw was a salad, not a condiment. It was quite tasty, so he didn't complain. He didn't have any complaints about the hush puppies, either. He even enjoyed the sweet tea. Satisfied, he went to bed early. He needed

to be fully rested to deal with whatever he found at the Double J in the morning.

THE HOTEL OFFERED a free breakfast, and he filled up, before climbing into his truck with a takeout coffee. It was a short drive to the ranch, farm, whatever. He found it easily, remembering most of the landmarks from their trip earlier in the summer, when he dropped off Megan and Julep.

It looked the same. Adrian parked by the horse pens and walked to the fairly new center aisle barn. Several young girls were inside cleaning the stalls, sweeping the aisle, listening to music coming from an old dusty speaker. They all stopped and stared when Adrian walked inside. An older woman looked up and walked over. That is, if you could call someone in her late twenties or early thirties older.

"Hey, can I help you?" She was at least ten years older than the rest of the crew in the barn. The others appeared to be teens around Megan's age.

Adrian resisted the urge to correct her English by saying, "I don't know if you can but you may try." Instead, he answered politely, "I'm Megan's dad, and I'm here to check on her after losing our Julep."

"Oh, I'm so sorry, Mr. Peterson. We're all sad about Julep. My name is Julie, and I'm in charge while JJ is on the road. Most of our crew should be back later tonight."

"It's Dr. Peterson. Why wasn't the vet called?" Adrian watched Julie brace and realized that he was being too direct. Susan always told him to be less direct, because it was rude to be too direct. He also noticed that the girls were now standing nearby, watching and listening.

"I'm sorry, Julie, it's nice to meet you. I'm sure you're all concerned about what happened. Is there anywhere we can continue this conversation in private?"

"Yes, I'm sure you're worried about Megan." Julie turned to the girls. "Finish the barn chores and start your assignments. We'll try to get most of our work finished before we break for lunch."

The girls scurried, and Julie motioned for Adrian to follow her to a small horse trailer, with a glass sliding door replacing the usual ramp, converting the trailer into a small office. Adrian found that interesting, but it wasn't a bad idea.

Once inside, Julie motioned for him to take a seat in one of two ancient office chairs.

"Like I said, DR. Peterson, we're all very sorry." Julie rudely emphasized the Dr. "I'm sure JJ will ask the same questions when he returns. Julep was fine before we went to the bunkhouses for the night. Our hired hands found her on the ground. They thought it was colic. I'm not sure how they found her, but I'm glad they did. It wouldn't have been good for our students to find her the next morning, after some animal tore her apart." Adrian thought Julie was too matter of fact as she described the scene.

"So you're saying she was dead when she was found?" Adrian leaned forward.

"No, I think she was still alive but died before they made the decision to call a vet."

"What decision? They should have called immediately." Adrian could see Julie felt attacked. "I'm sorry. My wife is always telling me I talk before I think. I'm not blaming you, but I'm a vet. I don't understand why people wait to call, and, of course, I want answers and these are the questions I'll ask Mr. Johnson tonight."

"JJ," Julie corrected.

"What?" Adrian was puzzled. "Oh, ok, these are the questions I'll ask JJ." He attempted a polite smile but it was more of a scowl.

"If you don't mind, Julie, I'll walk around a little before I leave. Thanks for your help." Adrian rose, shook Julie's rough hand, and left the trailer/office.

Julie walked out with him and climbed into a beat-up golf cart. "That's fine, Dr. Peterson. We have nothing to hide. Megan will return tonight, along with our horses and the rest of the crew, but I think JJ is staying an extra day to look at some new horses."

That was strange. Nothing to hide was a strange thing to say if you didn't have anything to hide.

Adrian watched Julie struggle to get the golf cart in gear and drive away, and then turned to climb the unusually large hill behind the barn. After being stuck in the truck all day yesterday, his body wanted to move, and he would have a good view of the Double J from the top of the hill.

He could see most of the ranch, but nothing looked strange. Well, except all the work being done by the young students. He saw a few guys but mostly girls, and they all looked to be in their late teens or early twenties. One was mowing the field with a huge batwing mower, several were weed trimming fence lines, and two guys were fixing fence. This JJ guy certainly had a good setup. He wondered if the two guys working on the fence were the two who found Julep. He also wondered if Megan did the same kind of work when she wasn't on the road. Not that she was afraid of hard work. She worked hard at home, and could drive a tractor and run a weed trimmer with the best, but she was supposed to spend the summer improving her horsemanship, not being a ranch hand. He remembered Megan talking about how hard they worked on the road grooming and taking care of the horses. He had to believe working with the horses was a better gig than this ranch work. He would learn more tonight. Megan would tell him the truth. She was strong-willed, and he often called her stubborn, but she was honest. She may fight to stay, but she wouldn't lie.

Walking down the hill and back to his truck, he glanced at his watch. It was time to meet Dr. Bobby Gray and get the scoop on this Johnson guy—one vet to another.

ADRIAN FOUND the equine clinic easily, noticed a sign on the adjoining building advertising a small animal clinic, and wondered how many vets were on board. Both buildings were painted with attractive simple scenes in bright colors. The equine building had a cream exterior, white trim, with silhouettes of moving horses in various shades of grey and brown. Interspersed around the horses were splotches of grass and flowers. Old wood pieces, representing a pasture fence, were attached to the outside of the building.

The small animal building was painted in a rich gray with white trim. On this building, silhouettes of small animals, birds, and reptiles were painted in shades of brown and black. Bright-colored flowers were painted next to each animal. The painting had a folk art charm. It was certainly eye catching. It was easy to identify the purpose of each building, but each also sported a wooden sign beside the door that read, Gray Veterinary Service.

Adrian went to the building painted with horses, walked inside, and introduced himself at the front desk. In minutes, a young vet walked around the corner and motioned for him to follow.

"Perfect timing; I'm Bobby Gray."

"Nice to meet you." Adrian followed Bobby to a surprisingly neat office.

Bobby laughed. "I can tell by your face you're surprised at my office. Yes, I'm a neat freak. A busy neat freak but I like to keep my office in good shape."

"No, I'm with you, but most of the vets I know love a good mess in their office. I'm impressed—and envious." Adrian liked this young vet. "I noticed the small animal clinic next door. Do you work out of there as well?"

"No, that's my dad and uncle. They used to do it all—equine, large animal, small animal. I now handle the equine side, and together they handle the small animal side. They give me a break when I beg for a few days off, and I help out with a few emergencies when I'm here and not doing farm visits. That's not often, though. I have a friend from vet school who's interested in buying into the equine clinic, and the help will be most welcome. We let the cattle side go to another vet who likes that work. There is a healthy cattle business in this area, which will keep him plenty busy, although he'll also care for horses and small animals when called. We all try to work together."

"Sounds like a good situation. I have a partner, but we do it all—horses, cows, dogs, cats, and whatever else gets brought into the office in a cage or on a leash." Adrian laughed. "I even have few box turtle clients and other reptiles."

"You must have a good staff." Bobby answered a knock on the door. "Come in."

An older woman carried a couple of lunch bags. "Speaking of good staff, this is the best office manager in the world. Martha, this is Dr. Peterson from Ohio."

"Flattery will get you lunch but that's all." Martha laughed as she dropped the bags on the desk, and held out her hand. "Dr.

Peterson, it's nice to meet you. Enjoy lunch and try to keep this youngster out of trouble for a while. But I warn you, it's a real big job. I've been working here since he was in diapers, so I know him well."

"Nice to meet you, too, Martha, and thanks for lunch. What a surprise."

Bobby and Adrian each grabbed a bag. One held sandwiches and one held chips and cookies. Bobby motioned to a dorm-sized refrigerator sitting on a table. "Grab a couple of sodas and we're all set."

Adrian looked where Bobby pointed and laughed. "You are young if that fridge is the same one you used in your dorm room."

"I'm not saying anything because it may incriminate me. Anyway, it's too good not to use, and I like grabbing a quick water or soda when I get a chance."

There wasn't much conversation while they ate their sandwiches, but once they were ready for the cookies, they came up for air.

"I'm sorry to hear about your daughter's horse, Adrian. We've been called out to JJ's ranch quite a bit. Nothing unusual, just the normal calls for cuts, scrapes, and an occasional colic. They keep most of the horses together and that's a nice environment, but there are the usual herd dynamics. JJ's competition horses are kept in the stalls. We pull Coggins, and issue health certificates and paperwork for the students traveling home."

"So nothing negative to report." Adrian took a big drink of his soda.

"Nothing much, except sometimes it's hard to get the bill paid. Right now he has a large outstanding balance. I'm not sure,

but he may have told his hired help not to call. Sometimes they call another clinic when they owe a large amount."

"Would you refuse to go out on a call since he owes so much?"

"No, I wouldn't refuse, especially if the call was for a student's horse. Heck, I wouldn't refuse to help any horse. We used to bill the ranch for all calls, even for the students' horses, but then we found out JJ was adding a little surcharge to our bill. Can you believe that guy? He was making money off a bill he wasn't paying." Bobby shook his head before continuing.

"The guy has some good horsemanship skills. I know he draws students like flies to honey. He can be real personable and not a bad guy, but I don't like him much. There's something about him that seems fake." Bobby bit into a cookie. "He claims to be this big horse lover, but he takes quite a few horses to the monthly auction, and not all of them find good homes."

"You mean kill buyers?" Adrian's cookie stopped its journey to his mouth.

"Well, it's not exactly a kill auction. It's a legitimate place to find good horses, but the kill buyers also pick up the horses that sell for meat prices. I'm not saying Johnson sells directly to the kill pen, but he doesn't put a reserve price on some of the horses he sells, so some do sell for kill prices."

"In my book, a horse lover would place a price reserve to discourage a kill buyer."

"My thought exactly, Adrian. Anyone selling a horse for less than a thousand is either clueless or he doesn't care. The kill buyers can make good money on a five-hundred-dollar horse."

"That's disgusting, but absolutely true." Adrian agreed. "So what Johnson is doing isn't illegal, but it lacks integrity, and he certainly isn't a true lover of horses."

"That pretty much sums it up. We go out to the sale occasionally to pull Coggins. The guy who runs the sale is honest and doesn't try to hide anything. Some of the buyers hide their true intent, but it's easy to figure out. Just watch for the buyers who fill big trailers with cheap horses."

"There is something strange," Bobby continued. "The cheap horses that end up on big stock trailers usually have huge chunks of their tails and manes cut off. Apparently, there's a market for horse hair."

"I've heard about that. We've had a few cases in Ohio with manes and tails stolen from pastured horses. No one seems real sure who's responsible. I know horse hair is used for things like jewelry, pottery, and violin bows, but they think most of the money is in fake horse tails for show horses."

"I know we cut some of the manes and tails for our clients when they need to euthanize their horses. Most of our clients ask for a lock of hair so we carry special bags for that purpose. There are legitimate businesses that will make jewelry out of the hair as a keepsake."

"We do the same. It seems to help if they have something to hold. I hate those calls. My wife, Susan, says I'm not a real sensitive guy, but I try to be when it comes to a client losing a horse, or any animal. I never know what to say. If they want a lock of tail, I try to be respectful when I cut it and put it in a bag. It's about all I know to do in that situation. I'm not a hugging sort of guy."

"I think having two daughters tests that theory on occasion."

Adrian noticed Bobby glancing at the time. "Hey, I better let you get back to your appointments. Thanks for lunch, and for the info. If you ever get to Ohio, stop by. We aren't too far from

Columbus. Do you ever get to the Quarter Horse Congress or Equine Affaire?"

"You're welcome and both Quarter Horse Congress and Equine Affaire are on our list of things to do. You just may get a call from me sometime." Bobby hesitated. "One more thing, Adrian, here's my private cell number; give it to Megan and tell her to call if she ever needs anything while she's here."

"Bobby, do you think she's in any danger?" He stopped mid-rise from his chair.

"No, I don't, but I also know how hard the interns work on the ranch, and sometimes they're asked to do things they aren't trained to do. Johnson is brilliant when you think about it. He gets paid to have free labor."

"I was thinking the same thing today while I was at the Double J. I plan on having a nice talk with Megan tonight. Our expectation with the girls has always been you don't quit once you start something, but in this situation, I'll make sure she understands quitting may be the best decision—and the safest."

Adrian shook hands with Bobby. "Thanks for the number. It will be good to know she has someone nearby to contact if needed."

"I'm not saying she'll need it, but I know you're ten hours away and I'm right here."

Adrian thanked Martha again as he walked through the reception area. It was still early afternoon and Megan wouldn't be back at the Double J until later. There was time to drive back to the hotel for a nap. He usually didn't need a nap on a working day. The long drive and worry about Megan were taking more out of him than he thought. His mind weighed everything Bobby shared. Although the information wasn't alarming, Adrian didn't think this JJ guy was someone he would choose to be his daughter's mentor. Talk about trying to close the barn door after the horse got out. Those thoughts should have occurred when she asked to participate in the program. But not one to beat himself up, he also remembered he was more than eager to support the idea. It was the first time Megan had ever been excited about anything remotely called school. Tonight they would have a very interesting conversation.

Chapter Nineteen

Grayson Corners, South Carolina

Adrian woke up and grabbed his phone. The room was dark. Where was he? What time was it?

"Hello."

"Dad, hi, it's me. Are you ok?"

"Megan. Yes, I'm fine. I guess I fell asleep waiting for your call. How are you?"

"I'm fine, but Dad, it hurts."

"Yes, I know. I didn't miss dinner, did I? Can I pick you up, and we'll get dinner and talk?"

"I'll get ready. It's not that late. Dad, the first thing I did when we got back to the ranch was check on Julep, and then I remembered she wasn't here anymore." Megan barely choked out the words. "I saw her grave."

"I'll be there as soon as I can. Where should I meet you?"

"By Julep's pen, I want to send her things home with you."

Adrian splashed water on his face, straightened his clothes, grabbed the room keycard, and went out to his truck. Each mile felt like forever. Finally, he pulled into the drive, trying to remember the location of Julep's pen. He didn't see anyone around to ask. The place looked deserted.

He spotted Megan just past the barn—waving. Climbing out of the truck, Adrian said a quick prayer. He wasn't a praying man, but he needed a bit of help tonight.

Megan threw her arms around his waist. "I'm so glad you're here, Dad."

"I am, too, Meggie Moo." He hadn't called Megan that name in a long time, but it just seemed right tonight.

"Let's go get something to eat. How about that place down the road you like?"

They walked to the truck, and in minutes were out the drive and heading down the road to the Fox & Hound. It was a neat little fox hunting-themed restaurant, a favorite of the local equine crowd, and happened to have great food.

"Ok, what was JJ's reaction to what happened and when can I speak with him?"

"Dad, JJ is still on the road. He sent me and two other girls back tonight with the horses. He said I was too—I think the word he used was distraught—to talk about what happened, but he would talk to me later, after he got more details. Other than not getting a vet out in time, he didn't think his help did anything wrong. He said Julep must have had something going on and I didn't notice. But Dad, I pay attention, and she was doing great."

"I know you pay attention. Yes, she could have had something that wasn't easy to see, but I'm concerned that they didn't call or even attempt to call the vet. I met with Dr. Gray today, and he said he would always go out on a call to the ranch, especially for an intern's horse."

"JJ said he would take action, but I'm not sure what that means. He also said I could work with one of the other horses here to be retrained."

"So are you saying you want to stay? I know they're working you hard. Is this what you want? Are you learning anything?" Adrian put his fork down and looked into Megan's eyes.

"Dad, it's not what I thought, that's for sure. I'm one of the lucky ones, because I get to travel a bit, and that's a learning experience. I'm not sure I want to stay after I finish my internship,

but I want to finish. I don't want to be a quitter. I'm angry. I don't think JJ is the horseman I thought, but I can play the game and finish."

Megan was determined. Most of the time he called her stubborn, but Adrian thought determined was a better word tonight.

"I'm willing to let you stay and finish the summer, but I need you to promise to be careful, and follow your gut if anything doesn't seem right. Ok?" Adrian waited for his daughter to respond with a nod. "Dr. Gray gave me his personal cell phone number, and you are to call him if you need help with absolutely anything. Will you promise to do that?" Again Megan nodded. "And will you promise to call me if you are asked to do something that doesn't feel right?" Megan again nodded her head several times up and down very slowly.

"And Megan, sometimes it's the right decision to quit, but I'm proud of how you're handling this loss and disappointment."

"I know Dr. Gray from his visits to the ranch, but I'm not sure if he remembers me, though."

"Well, he does. He said you seemed knowledgeable about horse care, and wondered why you didn't want to be a vet like your old dad." Adrian couldn't resist.

"Dad—and here we were doing so well." Megan smiled. It was good to see a smile, even a brief smile, he thought.

"Good meal. I ate too much. I'm not sticking around to talk to JJ tomorrow, but I'll give him a call. I need to get back to the clinic. Dr. Bill is supposed to leave for vacation with his family in two days, and I promised I would be back as soon as possible."

"You better not ruin his vacation, Dad. As a kid of a vet, I know how much we looked forward to getting away as a family, and I'm sure his kids do, too."

"Well, aren't you a wise one, Megan. You've grown this summer. I'm so sorry you lost Julep. We told Jennie."

"Mom said she was excited about Julep coming home. I'm so sorry we made a promise we can't keep."

"It's not your fault. We'll help Jennie." Adrian didn't know exactly how to help Jennie, but they would do what they could.

"I'm sorry this hasn't been what you expected. I know how excited you were to start this program. Sometimes you can learn from a bad experience, but I hope your last few weeks here are good. I know you'll do your best.

"Right now, your mom and I plan on moving Belinda to Florida, using the horse trailer. Then we'll pick you up and bring you home. I think that's what we worked out before."

"Yeah, we thought it was a perfect plan, but Dad, it's going home empty." Megan put her face in her hands. She had already cried out all her tears. All she had left were dry sobs and shaking shoulders.

Adrian reached for her hand and squeezed. "It's ok, cry when you need to cry. Stay busy. It will help, and that shouldn't be too difficult from what I noticed."

Adrian thought his comment would get his daughter rolling on a different subject—the subject of how hard they worked—and he was right. Adrian marveled at JJ's ability to draw students as free labor and also charge them for the experience. It was a brilliant plan, maybe not ethical, but brilliant just the same.

Chapter Twenty

Appleridge, Ohio

Her dad was right. Thinking about finding another horse did help. It made her feel good to think she would have a horse someday. There were moments when a random memory of Julep would cause her eyes to water, but looking for a horse helped. Jennie searched sale ads online, but most of the horses she found were expensive. In Marcy's mind, there were plenty of good horses in need of a home, and if she was patient, a horse would find Jennie.

The big question for Jennie was—should she look for a horse to ride or one to drive? Maybe she could find one that did both. Maybe a horse around Julep's size, about fifteen hands—horses were measured in hands, with a hand being four inches. Jennie wasn't too particular about the breed. Julep was a Quarter Horse/Thoroughbred cross, called a Quarter Horse Appendix, and she liked that cross, but she was also open to other ideas.

She logged off the library computer, went to the back room to get her purse, and after a few quick goodbyes, rushed to Blue Boy. Efficient Marcy would have the trailer packed and ready to leave for the combined driving competition. They would leave as soon as she hauled her suitcase out to Marcy's truck.

Jennie spotted Cassy's car parked near the barn. She parked her truck near the older barn, rushed inside the house, changed from library clothes into jeans and a polo shirt, and told Beauty to be a good kitty. Grabbing the handle of her small bag, and the hanging garment bag holding her riding jacket, she put on her paddock boots and walked to the barn.

"We're about ready to load the ponies," Marcy gasped as she lowered the bale of hay she was carrying. "Are you ready?"

"Yeah, I'm ready. I just need to get my helmet."

"We got it, Jennie," Cassy assured. "I sure wish I was going with you guys."

Marcy patted Cassy's arm and said, "I'll remember that, Cassy. I may ask you to be my gator, or we'll get you and Treasure into driving, too."

"You mean my Treasure?" Cassy asked.

"Dutch Warmbloods are excellent driving horses. For some, it becomes their second career." Marcy loved to recruit people into driving.

"Cassy, we talked about everything last night, but do you have any questions? Remember to feed Beauty, and don't be surprised if my mom and dad stop by for a visit. They'll want to make sure you're ok here by yourself, and will probably invite you to dinner or bring food."

"Cool. I welcome food, and I like your mom and dad. I'll take good care of Beauty and I'll be absolutely fine. I brought my laptop, and can you believe I already have a big paper due? I'm loaded with work. I guess that happens when they try to squeeze a semester of work into a short summer session."

"That will keep you out of trouble. Welcome to college." Jennie didn't envy Cassy's college assignments. Not one bit.

"Enough talk. Thelma and Louise need to hit the highway." Marcy was itching to get on the road.

Jennie carried her bag to Marcy's truck as Marcy and Cassy walked the gleaming ponies to the horse trailer. Marcy must have spent most of the day bathing the two munchkins.

She searched her backpack to make sure she remembered a notebook. Although she suspected there wouldn't be much free time, she wanted to write quick notes of everything she saw and learned. Marcy had both ponies loaded by the time Jennie pulled out the notebook. Wow, this girl was quick. Climbing into the passenger seat, Jennie waved to Cassy as Marcy started the engine. Let the adventure begin.

Marcy was thirty years older than Jennie, but the two of them had a lot in common. Jennie told Marcy about writing the county guide, and her experience at the Gregory Black Angus farm.

"What a terrible person. I went to school with one of his sons. He was nice but shy. He didn't seem to have many friends and didn't participate in many school activities or play sports. I think he worked on the farm most of the time." Marcy kept her eyes on the road as she talked.

"I bet you were active, Marcy."

"Not as much as you would think. I've become a lot more extroverted as I age, and I think driving a pair of ponies in competition has helped my overall confidence in life."

"Well, I'm impressed. And you drive this rig like a pro, too." Jennie was impressed.

"Hey, have you heard from that boy with two first names recently?" Marcy teased.

"Well, yes, Jeremy called last week, and Belinda, Sam, and I met him for lunch. Belinda and I tried to apologize for being little 4-H brats. He seemed embarrassed, so we let it drop. Jeremy asked me to go with him to a movie next week. It's a special documentary about horses."

"Did he ask as a friend or as something more interesting?" Marcy raised her eyebrows.

"Well, I hope it gets more interesting, but I'm not sure for now. Did I tell you he was going to seminary in the fall?"

"Yes, you did, and I can totally see you dating someone going to seminary, and I can also see you as a pastor's wife." Marcy noticed that Jennie blushed, but didn't mention that she noticed.

In an effort to remove herself from the hot seat, Jennie asked, "What about you? Tell me more about your life."

"Well, my divorce was finalized last month. My two boys are both newly married. No grandchildren yet, but I'm hopeful." Marcy smiled. "I love my job, I'm glad I moved back to Appleridge, I love my ponies, end of story."

"Ok, I'll let you off the hook for now, but I want to know more; when you're ready."

They pulled onto the horse show grounds before dark, and settled the ponies in nicely bedded stalls. After unloading the carriage and other equipment, they moved the truck and trailer to their assigned camping spot. Marcy demonstrated her expertise as she unhooked the trailer from the truck, and hooked up the water and electric. She called it glamping instead of camping because they had power and water.

The trailer had one bed in the gooseneck, but it was large and they didn't mind sharing. Jennie hoped she didn't do anything embarrassing like snore, or worse. The trailer also had a little bathroom and tiny kitchen space all in about five feet. Jennie couldn't help but think maybe she should have gone to nursing school instead of getting a degree in journalism. The pay seemed better and jobs more plentiful. Then immediately she chastised herself. Marcy worked hard for every dollar, and it was wrong to be envious.

They rushed to the show office for the competitors' meeting with minutes to spare. Marcy seemed a little bored as the rules

were reviewed, but everything was brand-new for Jennie. The meeting broke up and they climbed into the rented golf cart to map the course. At each obstacle they discussed their strategy. Each obstacle contained a series of gates marked with letters of the alphabet—A through E. Marcy needed to drive the ponies through each gate in the correct order, and it would be Jennie's job to help keep track of each gate and help keep her on course.

"I'm getting nervous. I'm not sure if I know enough to do this." Jennie motioned to the obstacle they just finished walking.

"Don't worry. I could do this by myself if needed. It's a safety requirement to have another person on the carriage." Marcy realized how her comment must have sounded and quickly added, "But I welcome another pair of eyes, not to mention, help balancing the carriage. I won't hold you responsible for a mistake. Just have fun and do your best."

JENNIE AND MARCY dressed quickly and walked to the barn in the pre-dawn. Dressage and cones were scheduled for today, and the marathon tomorrow. Dressage competition required braided manes and the ponies groomed to perfection. Fortunately, the ponies had long manes that they braided into tight French braids along the crests of their necks, instead of little individual button braids. Jennie was skilled in both braids, but the French braid was definitely easier.

Next on the list was a final swipe of the towel on both the carriage and the harness before returning to the trailer to change into their show clothes. Jennie changed into her breeches and riding jacket left over from a brief attempt to show in English hunt seat classes. Her attire wasn't exactly correct, but Marcy thought it fine for a show at this level. Marcy wore a beautiful navy jacket, matching navy and cream plaid driving apron, and a gorgeous hat. The entire turnout—carriage, ponies, driver's attire—needed to look good together. Marcy was challenged with two different color ponies, but her look and presentation was attractive, and pleasing to the eye.

Riding on the carriage during the dressage and cones phases, Jennie was not allowed to talk or assist the driver. She couldn't smile, either, and that was a challenge because Jennie was having a great time.

Marcy drove well, and the ponies were willing partners. They ended the day in third place. Marcy was pleased.

"I'm so happy with these two," Marcy said as she groomed Riley and Jennie groomed Stuffin.

"They are troopers. I couldn't believe how calm they stayed after that other pair caused such a commotion in the dressage warm-up arena. That was scary." Jennie was impressed at how calm Marcy and the ponies remained.

"I felt bad for the driver but he drives with rough hands and a busy whip. Those poor horses; no wonder they objected."

They were both silent for a moment—thinking.

"You did real good, thanks for the help."

"It was my pleasure. I pray I'm ok on the marathon."

"You'll be fine. I realize your first trip around a marathon course will be during an actual competition, and that's a lot to ask, but, you'll be fine." Marcy was confident. Jennie had such a calm demeanor around horses and she was very athletic.

"I'm going to take the braids out tonight. Riley will rub his out, anyway, and ruin his mane in the process. They don't need to be braided for the marathon, but I may do a quick French braid to keep their manes from getting tangled in the harness while we set the course on fire." Marcy felt great.

Both Jennie and Marcy were famished after feeding and set-tling the ponies for the night. They were either too nervous—Jennie, or too busy—Marcy, to eat much lunch. They changed out of their show clothes and into jeans and polo shirts, grabbed folding camp chairs, and walked to the chili supper hosted by the local driving club. It was fun eating chili with friends around a campfire. The party broke early. Marcy had one of the early start times. That meant another pre-dawn start. The group doused the campfire and a few walked to their trailers, and others left for hotels. Jennie and Marcy checked on the ponies one last time and followed the small group to the trailers. Sleep came quickly.

Up by six, they ate a cold breakfast. They had an 8:25 start time in the marathon. Since the marathon involved driving through obstacles, sometimes including water and mud, the po-nies didn't need to be perfectly polished. Today Jennie and Marcy dressed in black jeans, polo shirts, and helmets. Comfort and safety were the attire rules for marathon day.

The ponies' efforts paid off with a second place in the mara-thon—good enough to clinch the reserve championship for their division. Marcy was beaming, and Jennie was hooked. She was ready to find a driving horse—or pony. Julep would have been a great driving horse. She was willing and had the right tempera-ment—but not now; Julep was gone.

Stop it; this is time to celebrate with my friend and not get all weepy about something I can't change.

"Let's head over to the awards ceremony." Marcy was run-ning on adrenaline and Jennie quickly caught her mood. The ponies munched hay, quite content and pleased with them-selves. The carriage and equipment were already loaded and an enterprising young boy was paid to clean the stalls after they loaded the ponies.

Smart friend, Marcy.

They would pull out as soon as the awards ceremony was finished.

The awards ceremony was brief but fun and included a picnic buffet. Marcy chatted with a few of the other competitors, and Jennie enjoyed listening to them talk about various competitions, teasing one another as they ate. It was a friendly group, and they were full of tall tales and comradery.

MARCY KEPT GLANCING at the reserve champion sash lying on the dash of the truck, and Jennie was thrilled she had a part in the win. They arrived back at the farm around 9:30, unloaded the ponies, and led them to the pasture. After rolling in the dust to erase any evidence of their beautiful gleaming show coats, they settled into a much-deserved night of grazing. Treasure nickered and greeted them at the gate.

Jennie held a flashlight to help guide Marcy as she backed the horse trailer into its parking spot, and, again, helping Marcy unhook the trailer from the truck. Marcy didn't stick around long. Their beds called.

The light was on in the kitchen. Cassy sat at the table tapping away on her laptop, surrounded by papers.

"Hey, Jennie, how was it?"

"It was fun and Marcy won the reserve championship."

"Awesome! Treasure and I had a great weekend...and your mom and dad invited me to their house last night for supper...I met your sister, Sallie, and her little boy—they are so cute! Hey...I think we'll need to find a friend for Treasure when the ponies are away...she paced the fence line whinnying most of the day yesterday...and, by the way, I didn't sleep in your room... I slept in what I now think of as my room...you look beat and your

bed is calling...and I'm ready to wrap this up tonight...we can talk later...I have a morning class tomorrow and you have work, right?" Cassy finished in a rush.

Jennie laughed. Cassy must have missed talking during the weekend. "Ok, I need to be at the library by nine, so yeah, talking later sounds like a good plan. I'll see you in the morning." And Jennie climbed the stairs to her comfy bed.

Chapter Twenty One

ear Equestrian,

Let's talk about competition. We like to have a purpose, so competition is good because we're working on purpose. Most of the time training for competition makes you, our human, happy. But sometimes you forget we can't be perfect, and then you get unhappy. Sometimes you forget we need help to understand what you ask. Don't forget that competition is a journey, not just one day.

We will always try to do our best, but we need to be prepared. We can't do our best if we haven't had time to practice. And sometimes, we can't do our best because we aren't physically able. Please take the time to help us prepare mentally and physically, then we'll have a great time.

And, Dear Equestrian, don't forget it's hard to travel. Please make sure our trailer is safe and not scary. We don't like to be hot. We need good ventilation. Don't hang all sorts of things on the walls that make a lot of noise. It makes us anxious, and it's annoying. Provide plenty of hay and water on our trip. We may not choose to eat or take a drink on a rest stop, but please give us the opportunity. A rest stop every three hours would also be appreciated, because that gives us time to relax without moving and balancing. And talk about balancing—be a good driver. Be careful when you turn, accelerate, and stop. A good trip helps us arrive in good shape, and ready to be good partners in the competition.

We want to do what you ask, and show the world how much we have learned. We want to win those things with tails that can flap

in the wind, because they make you so happy. We heard you call them ribbons. Sometimes we do our very best, and we don't get ribbons. Please don't think we didn't try. Or when we do win ribbons, please don't see only the ribbons. Our reward is working hard and doing something fun. We want that to be your reward, too.

Wishing us many years of doing our best together,

Your Favorite Horse

JENNIE COULDN'T WAIT to tell Jeremy all about the driving competition. Was this a date, or just two friends getting together for a movie? She wasn't sure, but she hoped she would know more after tonight.

Eager, she dressed early, too early, and walked outside to sit on the back porch to wait. She barely sat down before Jeremy pulled into the drive followed by Marcy. He parked on the side of the gravel drive to allow Marcy to pass—which she did with a grin and a wave. Oh boy, thought Jennie, I'll get the third degree tomorrow.

"Hey, Jennie, hope it's ok that I'm a little early."

"That's fine, I'm ready." Jennie thought maybe they were both a little eager. "Come on out to the barn and meet Marcy and the horses."

"Sure, but I know Marcy."

"You do?" Jennie stopped walking.

"My nephew fell off his bike last week, of course on my watch, and we spent a few hours in the ED."

"Is he ok?" Jennie reached out to touch Jeremy's arm.

"He'll be fine. Broke his arm but didn't need surgery."

Jeremy called out, "Hi, Marcy, glad to see you again."

"Well, hi, how is that little nephew of yours?"

"I was just telling Jennie about the battle of the bicycle, but he's fine. It ruined the rest of his summer for baseball, but he attends the games, fills his mouth with bubble gum, and misbehaves in the dugout." Jeremy paused. "I'm not sure what my sister ever did to deserve such an active little boy."

"I'd say she's done something right, because he sure is a cutie. I'm not his favorite person, but hopefully, he'll remember choosing a prize from the treasure chest." Marcy thought a moment. "Hey, bring him out to meet the ponies and then I'll be his most favorite person in the whole world."

"I may just do that, if it's ok with Jennie."

Jennie smiled. *It's more than ok, especially if it means another maybe sort of date.*

"Well, we better go. I have a surprise for Jennie before the movie starts." Jennie was afraid to look at Marcy, her cheeks were hot. She hated how easily she blushed.

Jeremy opened the passenger door of his small SUV and smiled at Jennie. She smiled back as she wondered about her surprise. She didn't wonder too long because it was a short drive to the old restored movie theater in Appleridge, and as soon as they parked, Jeremy reached behind the seat, and pulled out a small cooler. He had a goofy smile on his face.

"I thought we could have a little picnic in the park before the movie. Nothing fancy, I just picked up a few things."

"Wow, ok, but does this mean I can't have popcorn? Remember you promised popcorn when I agreed to this movie."

"You'll get your popcorn. I wouldn't think of making you sit through a movie without popcorn. As I recall, I also promised butter on the popcorn."

"Yes, you did. Wow, look at those salads! I thought you were going to pull out a baloney sandwich. You certainly know your

way to a girl's heart." As soon as those words escaped her lips, Jennie wished she could take them back. *Why did she say heart? Yikes.*

Jeremy turned away when he noticed Jennie's red cheeks. "This bench looks like a good spot."

Jennie was glad Jeremy pretended not to notice her embarrassment. He was comfortable to be with and he liked salad—win, win.

They talked easily. Jeremy shared his excitement about starting seminary in a few weeks. Jennie shared a little about her writing, and about her experience at the driving competition.

"This summer has been both good and bad—I've had happiness and disappointment."

Jeremy stopped eating. "What do you mean?"

"Well, when I look at my move back home, and getting Grandpa's farm, working at the library, getting a few writing projects, helping Marcy at the competition—all are good. My experience at the Gregory farm and losing Julep are bad. I've had more good things happen, but I seem to remember the bad things the most. Why do we focus on the bad instead of being thankful? Even small good things are better than large bad things."

"Very insightful, Miss Jennie, and I do hope that having our paths cross again is listed in your good column."

"Yes, you are in the good column—well, at least for now." Jennie tried to hide a smile without success.

"I'm trying to be good, but to answer your question, bad things hurt and sometimes the hurt tries to hide what's good. Look for the good all the time. I know, sometimes it's hard. I'm not sure why something happened to Julep and I don't know why people, like Mr. Gregory, seem to enjoy causing pain. But I do know, if you dig deep, you'll find most people who cause pain are hurting badly themselves. Prayer is always the answer—as you discovered with Mr. Gregory. There is plenty of bad happening in our world, and if you don't pray, you'll only find anger. And when you choose anger, it will grow until hate will soon follow." Jeremy paused before adding, "I'm so sorry, I didn't mean to preach. I want to share the beautiful message of grace, but not preach."

"You're going to be a great pastor, Jeremy. I feel the grace in your words."

"Well, then, it's about time for the movie, and your popcorn waits."

Jeremy reached for Jennie's arm as they walked down the sidewalk to the theater. She didn't object. They waved to a few people and spoke to others. The news would be all over the small town of Appleridge by tomorrow—Jennie McKenzie was at the movie with Jeremy James, the boy with two first names. Now she was being silly and it felt good.

Chapter Twenty-Two

*D*r. Adrian Peterson threw his phone down on the desk. Apparently JJ screened his calls and never returned messages. Who did this JJ guy think he was, anyway? Adrian vowed to call every day until Johnson returned his call. He didn't expect a satisfactory conversation, but he did enjoy pursuing what evidently Johnson expected to be uncomfortable. He spoke to Megan often, and didn't worry, except for the fact that her teacher didn't appear to be a person of integrity. Adrian would be glad to get her home and this situation behind them both.

His cell phone vibrated on the desk, and he checked the display. "Well, hello, Dr. Gray."

"Hello, Adrian. I just wanted to touch base and say I'm glad to know you're using microchips at your clinic."

"What? Well, yes, we do chip dogs and cats when asked but..."

"Oh, and by the way, you owe me seven hundred and fifty dollars, friend, and I take checks."

"What are you talking about, Bobby? I owe you money for what? I'm not following." Adrian searched his memory, but came up with nothing, wait—something was starting to come to mind. "Bobby, did you find a dog or cat with a microchip from our clinic?"

"You're smarter than you look, old man. Wait—that wasn't a very nice thing to say to my older vet friend, was it?" Bobby was enjoying himself. "I didn't find a dog or cat, but I did find a certain bay horse, called in the microchip number, and found her owner of record listed as a Miss Megan Peterson."

"Bobby, are you saying you found Julep?" Adrian motioned to his staff to give him a few more minutes.

"There was a horse auction last Friday and I decided to take my microchip scanner out to check a few horses, especially the ones without a reserve. Megan's mare didn't even go through the sale. I found her with a known broker, huge hunks of her mane and tail missing. I offered the guy six hundred, but he wouldn't take it. He finally went for the seven hundred-fifty. I didn't want to seem too anxious and make him suspicious, so I made up some story about how she reminded me of my childhood pony. Man, I didn't breathe until my wife brought me the cash, and you should know she had to dig deep to find that much cash. After I sealed the deal, I took Julep out of the pen, walked her to a secluded corner, and waited for Mary to return, this time with the horse trailer."

"I can't believe this! What is Johnson up to?" Adrian lowered his voice when he noticed several clients glancing into the hall where he now stood. "Where is Julep now? Does Megan know yet?"

"The mare is at our place, and other than missing some hair, she seems fine. And, no, I didn't call Megan. I'm still trying to sort this all out and didn't want to let anyone know that the horse was found. I probably ruined any chance of bringing whoever is responsible to justice when I paid for Julep and removed her without contacting the sheriff, but I'm sure the broker would have loaded her into the trailer and run before I could get help. I'm sorry it took me several days to call. I couldn't get my head around what needed to be done next, and I wanted to have more answers. I wanted to tell you someone was in jail."

"Bobby, oh man, I'm glad you got her out. I know you're right. She would have been loaded and gone before the sheriff arrived."

"I've been nosing around, and I don't think Johnson is involved, but he sent a load to the auction with those two ranch hands. There were six horses listed in the sale. No one could tell me how many horses were in the trailer when it arrived. They don't check the trailers or match papers at the gate. Like I said, the owner of the auction is legit, so things may change, but I'm not sure. I think those two thieves added Julep to the load, and snuck her in to do a backdoor deal. They may have a side business that Johnson knows nothing about, or they could all be crooks. Like I said, I'm not sure."

"Bobby, how many other interns have lost their horses?" Adrian's thoughts were flying.

"Yup, I checked that, too. None have died. Several sold horses to Johnson when he promised to find them good homes."

"What a creep."

"I agree, buddy. Even if Johnson isn't involved with horse theft, his reputation is about to get tarnished. Well, at least if anything can be proven." Bobby paused. "I have friends in the right places. One is a lawyer and one is a sheriff deputy in another county. I'll try to get some advice."

"Ok, what do you need me to do? I can drive down this weekend and pick up Julep. I'll pick up Megan, kicking and screaming, but I've had enough."

"Let's do nothing for now. I think it would be a good idea to keep this quiet. Julep is fine with us. She's a real nice mare, and she's getting along fine with our two horses. We need to do some thinking about how to handle this. I don't think we have much evidence, but we may be able to flush out something."

"Ok, I agree, although it'll be hard not to tell Megan. Losing Julep stole a bit of her spirit. If we need her help to snoop, she's good at keeping secrets. Of course, there's always a chance she wouldn't be able to stop herself from ripping old JJ Johnson to shreds, and then picking him up and hauling him to jail, all by herself. I like that thought—old JJ in jail-jail." Adrian couldn't believe he was getting silly at a time like this. He was never silly.

Adrian and Bobby agreed on a plan, and both hung up to attend to their patients. What a crazy, sad world, but he also couldn't help but feel elated about Julep's resurrection.

Chapter Twenty-Three

ennie jumped when her pocket vibrated. It was Belinda. She quickly hid in an alcove behind the circulation desk and answered her phone.

"Hey, Jennie. Do you realize I leave for school in less than two weeks and we haven't done much together this summer?"

"Hi, girlfriend, I know. You've been busy getting ready to leave and I've been working. What are you doing now?"

"Right now, I am driving to town because I know you get off work at two, and I thought maybe we could visit over a snack at the Bake & Shake. Mom sent me to town to pick up a short list at the grocery. I just need to be home by five, because she needs what I'm picking up for making supper."

"Sure, I'll walk down and meet you there around two-fifteen. We aren't busy today."

JENNIE LOGGED off the computer and grabbed her purse for the short walk to the Bake & Shake. Belinda was already at a high-top table and looking quite smug with a banana split.

"Are you sharing the love or do I need to get my own?" Jennie waited for the answer before she sat down.

"Oh, sit down, I'll share. No, wait. Why don't you get us two pops to go with this deliciousness? Ice cream always makes me thirsty."

Jennie went to the counter for two drinks. "Here you go, madam soon-to-be vet student." Jennie loved teasing her friend. "Now, move your spoon so I can get some of that, too."

Jennie and Belinda chatted as good friends always do. Belinda grilled Jennie about the evening she spent with Jeremy, but Jennie only shared just enough to make Belinda happy, but not enough to make her feel like she was being unfair to Jeremy. It was hard because she loved and trusted her friend, but she also wanted to protect what she thought was a developing relationship with Jeremy.

"How's Megan? I've thought about her a lot. I know she'll feel like she let me down in some strange way."

"She seems fine, a little guarded. It's my dad who seems weird. He doesn't seem as angry as I thought he would be about the whole situation." Belinda took a drink. "Ok, vanilla is gone. Now let's attack the chocolate."

"Oh, oh, brain freeze, but if I slow down, you'll take all the chocolate." Jennie put her spoon down to hold her head. "No fair! Put your spoon down."

"I think, dear friend, next time we'll need to get our own cups of ice cream." Belinda put down her spoon and waited.

They laughed and finished splitting the banana split. Belinda enjoyed hearing about Jennie's first driving lesson with Marcy and the ponies, and Jennie enjoyed hearing about Belinda's attempt to pack everything she owned.

"Well, at least you won't need many winter clothes."

"No, not like here, and I won't want to come home for Christmas—not even a white Christmas. I'll want to stay in the warm, sunny south."

"You better come home or I'll come spend Christmas with you for some fun in the sun." Jennie was only kidding—a little.

"That would be great, but I can't imagine either of our parental units agreeing to that idea. At least not the first year you're home, and the first year I'm so far away."

"I don't know, Mom and Dad are thrilled with the grandkids, and I don't think I would be missed."

"You have a point." Belinda wiped up the ice cream she dripped on the table and threw the crumbled napkin into the now-empty bowl. "I better get going. Mom needs me to bring home the bacon."

"Let's get together a few more times before you leave, ok?" Jennie didn't want to say goodbye.

"Sure thing—maybe you and Jeremy can meet Sam and me for dinner or something before I leave."

"Hey, isn't the county fair next week? I haven't been to the fair in years."

"Oh, poor old Jennie, you mean maybe the four years you were away at school and didn't bother to come home for the summer?" Belinda couldn't resist the dig.

"Yes, friend who just happened to choose an instate school and was home the entire summer and working at her dad's vet clinic."

"You make me sound so perfect, but I guess it can't be helped." Belinda tossed her hair, pretending to be sassy.

"Ok, you win. I never could out-sass you." Jennie gave a fake sigh and, with that, they said goodbye, at least for now.

Jennie waved as Belinda and the Red Roan relinquished the parking place conveniently located in front of the Bake & Shake. She was eager to get home and start an afternoon of writing. As she climbed into Blue Boy, Jennie noticed the sky was darkening in the west and grabbed her phone to check the weather. Change of plans. No stop at the grocery store to pick up a few things; instead, she turned toward the farm to beat the approaching thunderstorm. The ponies and Treasure had access to the barn overhang for shelter, and they usually chose to get under it in bad weather, but she liked to be on the farm during a thunderstorm, if possible. Jennie had a healthy respect for wind and lightning.

The first heavy drops of rain hit the ground as Jennie pulled into the farm drive, following it to the barn where she could see the ponies and Treasure without getting out of the truck. Just as she predicted, they were huddled underneath the six-foot overhang of the paddock side of the barn. She resisted the urge to put them in their stalls. They were happier being together outside, but would be even happier with a little hay.

She made a quick run to the barn and then back to the truck, but enough exposure for Jennie to get soaked. She turned Blue Boy around and drove to the house, parked as near to the back porch as possible, and ran through the rain again. Grabbing a towel from the downstairs bathroom, she wiped her face, then wrapped it around her wet hair like a turban. She changed into dry clothes, then unplugged her laptop, and carried it to the kitchen table. Battery power was her choice until the storm moved through the area. And, she could watch the barn from the kitchen window.

Her phone sang a song. She looked at the display and saw Kyiko's name.

"Kyiko, hi, how are you?"

"Jennie, take a breath," Kyiko said with a laugh. "I have Kate here with me, and we both have news."

"Good news, I hope," Jennie said, but she could tell from Kyiko's voice it was good.

"We need your help. Kate and I have been chosen to dance with a group that uses horses in their choreography. Sometimes there's a rider on the horse and the rider guides the horse.

Sometimes the horse gets to choose and the dancers match the horses' movement. It's cool."

"Wow, I've read about this and thought it was a lot like our contact improvisation classes."

"Yeah, I guess it is, but we sort of told a little fib on our applications. It asked if we were comfortable being around horses and we both said yes."

"Where and when?" Jennie was intrigued.

"We have to be in Pennsylvania in three weeks and we wondered if we could take a little detour to your place to learn about horses. Then by the time we get to the dance workshop, hopefully, we really will be comfortable with horses."

Jennie heard Kate add, "Then it won't be a lie."

"I'd love to have you both. I'll ask my boarders if we can play with their horses, but I have some bad news to share about Julep."

She didn't want to end on a sad note, so after she told them about Julep, she also shared a few good things—and there were plenty.

"I'll need to work at the library while you're here, but I'll make sure you have some fun things to do."

"That's good, don't worry. We just want to relax and read a few good books."

Jennie wasn't sure how Kyiko could say that without laughing. She didn't believe that for one moment, because both Kyiko and Kate loved to be active—all the time.

"How are you traveling? Will you fly? There's a train that may work." Jennie was trying to think where she would pick them up if they chose to travel with Amtrak.

"We're renting a car and going to see the USA. Well, at least, we'll see a part of the Midwest, anyway."

Now Kate was on the phone and she could hear Kyiko laughing in the background. "I'm driving. Kyiko doesn't have a driver's license."

"I can't imagine you two in the car together for seven hours, but drive safely and I can't wait to see you."

Jennie hung up and started to plan. Where was her notebook, anyway? She needed to start a new list. She hadn't started a new list for a while now, and it was time. She needed to borrow air mattresses from her sister and some sheets from her mom. Maybe she should think about buying a used bed. It would be nice to have an extra room furnished for guests. What a great surprise to have Kate and Kyiko here at the farm to learn about dancing with horses!

She remembered how she and Julep could dance together while playing at liberty.

Stop it. Remember the good times with Julep. Always remember the joy she brought to your life. She deserves to be remembered with happiness.

Beauty came out of her thunderstorm hiding place and wrapped herself around Jennie's legs. "Hey, sweet Beauty, I'm glad the storm is over, too. Guess what? Our old roommates Kate and Kyiko are coming for a visit and we need to get ready." Beauty meowed and jumped into Jennie's lap.

She couldn't wait to see Kate and Kyiko again, and show them Appleridge, and teach them about horses. Boots, they need boots. Ok, time to make a list of things they would need. She could picture Kyiko showing up with flip flops. Not a safe idea around horses, unless you wanted smashed toes. Jennie was certain no dancer would welcome that possibility.

Maybe I could host a little picnic at the farm for my family and a few others. Maybe Jeremy would like to meet my friends.

Maybe that would be a good way to touch base with Jeremy without seeming too anxious. Maybe I should stop being so stupid about my relationship with Jeremy. Maybe I should stop having conversations with myself and a cat. Maybe I could go out and talk to the horses, instead. MAYBE, I should stop saying maybe. Funny, Jennie, very funny, you need to get a life.

Now she was even scolding herself in a conversation with herself. She definitely needed to get outside and do some physical work. The storm was over and it would be a good idea to walk the property and make sure there wasn't any damage.

IT TOOK about an hour to walk the fence lines checking for downed limbs and broken fence boards. Fortunately, there was no damage this time. She hauled sticks and small branches to the burn pile and had an idea. Instead of a picnic she would host a campfire gathering.

Ever mindful of her budget, campfire hotdogs would be budget friendly and fun. She would try to talk her mom into making her special potato salad, and maybe her sisters would bring something.

An idea for making invitations popped into her head. No one did that sort of thing anymore because it's easier to send an e-mail invitation, but definitely not as creative. Maybe Mom had some neat bandana-type material or something rustic she could tie around a rolled-up invitation.

Now for the guest list: Kyiko, Kate, Belinda, Sam, Jeremy, Mom, Dad, Sallie and family, Connie and family, although she wasn't too sure about her toddler nephews around a campfire, but she'd let her sisters work that out. She would ask Marcy and Cassy, of course, and she couldn't forget Grandpa and Belinda's mom and dad, although Dr. Peterson rarely did that sort of thing.

It was getting to be a crowd—nineteen including herself and her nephews, bumped up to twenty if Cassy brought a friend.

A few bales of straw covered with old blankets would serve as seating, and she would also ask her guests to bring camp chairs. This would be her first party at the farm—very exciting!

Dear Equestrian,

Let's talk the weather. We don't mind all sorts of weather, but it's always nice to have a little shelter in bad weather.

We aren't big fans of getting wet in extremely cold weather. That's why it's nice to have a roof to go under, if needed. You see, Dear Equestrian, our winter coat fluffs up when it's cold, and it acts like an insulator. When it gets wet, it can't do its job. We don't mind being wet, and we don't mind being cold, but we don't like being wet and cold at the same time.

We don't mind wind, either, because we know how to stand so the wind hits us behind, and not in the face. We aren't too crazy about thunderstorms. We know horses are often struck by lightning during a storm. We try to hide in a thunderstorm, but it seems lightening likes to strike trees, too. A thunderstorm would be a good time to have a shelter, if possible, maybe one that's grounded, but that will be your job to figure out, Dear Equestrian.

On the rare occasions that the weather is too out of control for anyone to be safe, we just do our best. We understand and accept the force of nature better than humans. You can't protect us from everything, Dear Equestrian, so please don't worry about a little rain, a little cold, or a thunderstorm. We're thankful for your care but, after all, we're worth it, right?

May our days together always be sunny,
Your Favorite Horse

Chapter Twenty-Four

Grayson Corners, SC
The Double J Ranch

Megan finished grooming Starlight, the new horse assigned to her care. She was a sweet little mare, but young, and she didn't know too much yet. JJ purchased four new horses on his last trip, brought them to the ranch for training, and assigned the smallest, a bright chestnut with a white star, to Megan. She was starting to figure out JJ's game. To his adoring fans, it appeared he had a magic touch with horses, but she noticed he bought and sold horses until he found the ones that were easy and made him look good. The difficult behaviors were shipped off to who knows where, and the horses that were willing and learned quickly, or already knew quite a bit, were used in JJ's demos to entertain future devotees.

She played her own game of pretend—being a devoted student of JJ. She wasn't exactly sure why she felt the need to stay. It would be easy to say goodbye, and call her dad for a ride or flight home, but it also felt like there was still something to accomplish before she left. She was learning a few things. Maybe not what she expected to learn, but sometimes, learning what not to do was also important. She wanted to have a career with horses, just not a career with JJ. Maybe a few more weeks away from home would help her figure out some things. That alone would be worth her time here on the ranch.

Megan didn't understand why she seemed to be the only unhappy student at the ranch. It appeared the others worshipped

JJ. She supposed it was like most things in life: once you make a choice, you don't want to feel totally stupid if it's a bad choice, so you pretend it was a great decision. Megan felt totally stupid.

Pete and Jeff, the two ranch hands, drove by in the ranch truck—windows down, leaning their elbows on the door frame as if they owned the place. Megan called them Pete and Repeat, because Jeff followed Pete like a shadow and copied every move he made. Her mom would scold her for making up those names. She would say, Megan, don't be ugly. But her dad would laugh, and call them Mutt and Jeff, because whenever he thought someone was being clueless, that's what he said. Megan never understood the reference or why her dad thought it was funny.

Pete and Repeat turned away and pretended not to see Megan as they passed the barn. Maybe they felt guilty for not calling the vet. Well, they should. They acted like they were better than the students just because they were getting paid for their work. She noticed they seemed quite friendly with Julie. But then, Julie was also being paid to supervise the interns and work on the ranch.

Megan finished grooming Starlight and lifted the saddle to place it gently on her back. "Easy, Star, it's ok, sweetie." Megan wondered what was done to this sweet girl to make her so skeptical of everything. At least she was getting more confident during grooming, and allowing Megan to lift her feet to check for stones or debris caught in her hooves, especially the thorny balls that fell from the sweet gum trees at the ranch.

Before she mounted, Megan did a few exercises from the ground to make sure Starlight was comfortable with the saddle and ready for a ride. She mounted and turned the horse away from the barn and arena. Her plan was a quiet ride around the perimeter of the ranch. In her mind, Starlight wasn't ready for

serious training. She needed to become confident with Megan on her back first.

Starlight blew air out between her lips several times and dropped her head, a good sign that she was getting more relaxed. Megan picked up a trot and the mare responded at a nice pace, ears forward. Relaxing herself, Megan blew out air to match the mare. She felt a little tight and that wouldn't help this young horse. After years of riding true-blue Julep, Megan wasn't as comfortable riding a new horse, especially a young new horse. It was one of the reasons she wanted to get a young horse to train herself, maybe one like Starlight. The young mare seemed willing, if you gave her time to think. She hated to think about all the horses sold and thrown away because of behavior problems. Why couldn't people understand behavior problems were caused by inappropriate human behavior and not the horse's fault?

They approached a small wooded area, halfway around the perimeter, on the far side of the ranch. Megan silently asked Starlight to walk and smiled as she responded smoothly. Walking into the woods was a good test of the horse's confidence in a tighter area. What Megan called woods was a small grove of trees only about an acre in size. Following a narrow path through the trees, Megan found a small cleared area, roped off to make a small corral. It looked like a couple of horses had been in the corral recently, but she couldn't imagine what it was being used for, or who was using it so far from the barn. She would ask Julie about it tomorrow.

Leaving the small grove, she asked Starlight to trot again, following the fence line until they completed the entire circuit, and returned to the barn. It was dusk and a nice time for a ride and she was pleased with Starlight. What a nice horse. Megan wanted to help her as much as possible, so she would end up in a nice home. Her size was perfect. The mare was small enough to be comfortable for a child but large enough for an adult. She wouldn't be outgrown like so many ponies. Megan always thought it was sad when families couldn't afford to keep outgrown ponies and also buy another larger horse. Sadly, it happened a lot.

She thought about her 4-H club and felt a little stab. Next week would be the county fair at home, and all her friends would be there, camping, riding, hanging out in the barn and on the midway, eating all that great fair food, and ending the week with the annual 4-H horse show. She and Julep would have had a great show this year, but maybe Julep would have died at home, just like she did here. Somehow she couldn't imagine anything getting by her dad. In her mind, he would have saved Julep. Megan carried a lot of guilt for taking Julep away after they promised her to Jennie. She needed to call Jennie and tell her she was sorry. Tonight would be the night.

Megan untacked and groomed Starlight before turning her out into the pasture with the rest of the ranch mares. It was dark by the time she walked to the building used as a dining hall. Long past the dinner hour, the hall was empty. Megan didn't miss eating with the other interns because they weren't particularly friendly, but she didn't like being in the hall alone. Hunger won and Megan went inside, turned on a few more lights, and hunted for leftovers or something to make a sandwich. Oh, well, peanut butter and jelly would have to make do, again tonight. There never seemed to be an abundance of food, even when she was on time, but being late meant there was never anything left to eat.

Chewing her sandwich, Megan thought about 4-H again, and realized horsemanship skills and knowledge she possessed came from 4-H, and from the times she tagged after Belinda, Jennie, and their friends. She hadn't learned anything new while working at the Double J.

Walking to the bunkhouse, Megan whispered the 4-H pledge, *I pledge my head to clearer thinking, my heart to greater loyalty, my hands to larger service, and my health to better living, for my club, my community, my country, and my world.*

It was a good pledge. Maybe she could practice more patience and kindness during her remaining time on the ranch. She wasn't being the person she wanted to be these last few weeks. She was angry most of the time. Megan stopped walking.

Father, this is Megan. Thank you for the love and support of my family during this crazy summer. Please help me through this terrible anger. I can't show your love to everyone I meet when I'm angry. I don't know why Julep had to die, but I trust you will help me through this sadness, and I guess I should thank you for the four years I did have with her, so thanks for that, too. Amen. And p.s. thanks for the great ride on Starlight tonight.

Megan took a deep breath, and pulled her phone from her back pocket to make the call.

"Hello, Jennie, it's Megan."

"Oh, sweetie, I've been thinking of you so much. Are you ok?"

"I'm fine, but I miss her, and I'm so sorry."

Jennie could hear Megan choking back tears. "Why are you sorry?" She chose her words carefully; Megan needed kind words. "Losing Julep wasn't your fault. You took good care of her. I'm very thankful you wanted Julep when I couldn't keep her. I knew she would be loved, and she was. I'm sad she's gone, but I'm happy her last years were with you. You believe that, don't you?"

"But we promised you could have her back this summer, and now you can't, and I feel terrible." Jennie heard Megan's voice crack. If Megan started crying, she would have trouble holding it together herself.

"It's going to be ok, and it isn't your fault. I'm not mad. I'm sad like you, but I'm not mad. I'm so glad you called, because I've been thinking about you and praying you're ok."

"Thanks, I'm doing ok. I don't like it here, but I'm going to finish. It's nothing like I thought it would be, but now I think maybe I only wanted to get away from home this summer, and only saw what I wanted to see."

"Wow, you sound so grown up. I think the things you're learning this summer may not be what you wanted to learn, but they're exactly what you were ready to learn. That has happened to me before, fairly recently. I finally figured out, God has a plan for each of us, and it's always a good plan."

"I think God spoke to me tonight. He's just about my only friend down here, but he's a good one, right?" Megan's comment made Jennie smile.

"I can't wait to see you again. Did you hear I bought my grandpa's farm? Well, I'm living here, and hoping to start paying for it sooner rather than later."

"Dad mentioned it when he was down here, and he also said something about you driving ponies."

"Yup, one of my boarders drives a pair of ponies and she's teaching me a little." Jennie stopped herself before she added the part about how she'd hoped to teach Julep to drive. No need to go down that road, especially when they were now on a happier path.

"I will definitely come over when I get home." Megan promised.

"This may be too soon to ask, but will you get another horse? I can't imagine you without a horse. I know you wanted me to have Julep because of traveling with that Johnson guy, but if you don't stay, what will you do? I've been looking at horses online and it makes me feel good."

"I'm not sure what I'm going to do but I'm giving it a lot of thought. I'll go back to Appleridge High for my senior year, but I also want to get an early start with college courses. After Belinda lost Sugar, it was just Julep and my old pony. When he died, Julep was all alone and that wasn't good. That's part of the reason why we wanted you to have Julep again. Well, that and because I planned to travel with JJ. I don't think Mom and Dad will want me to get two horses and then take off for college, but I can't imagine not having horses in my life, either."

"Hey, I was thinking, I have three horses boarded and five stalls. So when I find a horse, there would still be room for one more. If you want to keep a horse here, I wouldn't charge you board, but you would need to pay for everything the horse ate or needed. Of course, maybe we could bargain and your dad would trade some vet services for board. Hey, I like that idea." Jennie was such a planner, although she was aware that some people would call her a schemer.

"I would love to have a young horse to train. Julep already knew everything, thanks to you. I've been assigned a little mare to train while I'm here. She's a sweetheart, and learns quickly when you give her time to think and respond. I've just started working with her. I've been holding back on her, not wanting to give her my heart yet, and I think she knows I'm holding back."

"They always do read us better than we read ourselves, don't they?" Jennie was now enjoying their conversation.

"They do. Hey, it's been great talking with you, and thanks so much for making me feel better, but we have a curfew, and I need to get a shower before lights out."

"Wow, they run a tight ship on that ranch."

"Well, I don't know how tight it is, but it's definitely a strange ship that sails each day."

Both Megan and Jennie were laughing as they said goodbye.

Father, thank you so much for giving me the right words for Megan, because I know I couldn't have done that by myself. Thank you for taking away my anger, and for so many good things in my life. Amen.

Several states away, Megan said a similar prayer. They shared a loss, but they also shared a friendship—and that felt good.

Chapter Twenty-Five

Appleridge, Ohio

Jennie scanned her list. The campfire menu was all set. Good all-beef hotdogs were on sale at the market this week, and she picked up plenty. She was sure most people would want at least two hotdogs, and some maybe more. The ever-popular and fun-to-make s'mores would be their dessert. Maybe peanut butter cookies, too, if she had time to bake. Her mom was making potato salad, her sister Sallie was bringing baked beans, and Connie was still undecided, but was leaning toward bringing a snack tray of veggies, cheese, and pickles. Jennie still needed to buy buns and condiments, and something to drink.

She had a blast creating the invitations. They were finished except for tying little strips of fabric around them once they were rolled like a scroll. Her mom was working on a big project today but promised to set aside time to help Jennie. She thought about her mom's ability to stay focused on her work—unlike her daughter. It wasn't anyone's fault but her own, but if Marcy asked if she wanted to drive ponies, or if Belinda stopped by for a visit, Jennie found herself easily persuaded.

Her mom turned from the counter as Jennie opened the kitchen door. She was studying a pattern while she ate a sandwich. She's such a multi-tasker, thought Jennie.

"Hi, Mom, that looks good—do you have more?" Jennie used her hungry face as she eyed her mom's sandwich.

"You'll find a bowl of tuna salad in the fridge." Ellen handed Jennie a plate and two pieces of bread. "Help yourself."

"Where's Dad?" Jennie added a slice of ripe homegrown tomato to her sandwich and put a handful of potato chips on her plate.

"He's out in his shop. I think he's looking for a few things you may be able to use at your party."

"Like what?"

"Oh, extra chairs, campfire forks, and he thought we still had a few of the camp plates and cups we took to the horse shows—the blue enamel plates and cups?"

Jennie pulled out a counter stool. "Oh, yeah, I remember. I hope he can find them."

Ellen finished her sandwich and walked over to a plastic container of fabric sitting on the counter.

"I found some calico and bandana print. You can pick what you want. For the strips, just tear the fabric. Here are my pinking shears. I thought you could cut squares for napkins and maybe something for the tables. You'll be happy to know your dad found the camping tables. The big one is large enough for the food, and you could use the smaller table for drinks, cups, plates, and forks. By the way, your dad and I have been trying to get rid of a few things, so keep the tables if you want."

Jennie stopped eating to look through the box. "This is great, Mom, and yeah, I'll keep the tables. Thanks."

"Well, I need to get back to work, but you can cut what you need here at the counter, and then just put what you don't want back in the box. And Jennie, Susan Peterson called, and I just want to say I'm so proud of you. Megan called her mom and shared what you said."

"Geeze, Mom, I didn't say that much. I feel bad for Megan. And she was worried that I would blame her for losing Julep."

"I know, honey, but she told her mom that you thanked her for taking such good care of Julep after you left for school."

"Well, Mom, Gramps set me straight on that—when I was griping about Dr. Peterson and Megan taking Julep to South Carolina after they promised I could have her back this summer. He said Megan and her parents did me a huge favor and I was too selfish to see the truth."

"Well, that certainly sounds like your grandpa. He's good at seeing the truth. But I think you're pretty good at seeing truth, too." Ellen gave Jennie a hug and headed back upstairs to her workroom.

Jennie spent the next half-hour tearing long strips and cutting squares for napkins and table decorations. She threw away the scraps, then folded the remaining fabric and stacked it back in the box. She rolled an invitation, tied it with a fabric strip, and left it on the counter for her parents to find. One delivered and only about ten more to go. She also put her lunch plate in the dishwasher and wiped the counter clean. She stole two cookies from the cookie jar and wrapped them in a paper napkin for her dad. He was tinkering in his garage and didn't keep a strict schedule like her mom. He would welcome an unexpected visitor.

"Hey, you're just in time. I've got a few things to load into your truck."

"Hi, Dad, Mom mentioned I could have the tables. What else did you find? Great, I see you found the camp plates. I always loved that stuff. But remember, you can't drink hot chocolate from the cups. I still remember burning my lips and hands."

"I remember—you poor girls. All three of you were in tears. I wonder how the cowboys drink their coffee from a metal mug."

"I guess that's why they grow mustaches. You know, so the hair protects the upper lip." Jennie smiled. "Thanks for finding all this stuff. It all brings back good memories."

"Those were good times. We didn't have a lot of money for fancy vacations, but we had fun on those camping trips."

"We sure did. I better get going. I haven't been home since early this morning."

Jennie waved to her dad as she backed out of the drive. She was anxious to get home to roll and tie the rest of the invitations. Jeremy, Belinda, and Sam would get theirs tonight when they picked her up for the county fair. Belinda could give one to her parents, and Jennie would leave Cassy's and Marcy's invitations out in the barn. Let's see, that left only Grandpa and her sisters. Tomorrow would be a good day to take him to lunch. That is, if he was available. Then she would also drop off invitations for each of her sisters. Kyiko and Kate's invitations would be on their pillows, waiting for their arrival on Wednesday.

This is going to be so much fun!

Hey, Partners
Mosey on over to Fawn Song Farm
For a Campfire Hotdog Roast
S'mores, too, you bet!
See y'all Saturday at Dusk
Bring a camp chair
You won't go thirsty, partner, we'll have water & ice tea
Not strong enough? FYI—BYOB
Come meet the dancing cowgirls from Chicago

Chapter Twenty-Six

Grayson Corners, South Carolina

Megan saddled Starlight for another ride around the perimeter of the ranch. Her curiosity led her to the little paddock hidden in the trees. Megan never asked Julie about the paddock. She had a gut feeling she shouldn't say anything—at least not yet.

She was starting to feel like a little sneak, as she glanced around to see if anyone was watching. Yesterday, she hid and watched Pete and Repeat, but saw nothing unusual. She was counting the days until she could go home. She wouldn't miss anything about the Double J, except Starlight.

She didn't ride directly to the woods. Instead, she worked on canter circles in the pasture, gradually moving in that direction every time she changed direction on the circle. She came back down to a trot and then a walk before entering the small group of trees.

Well, the paddock looked the same. Whatever the paddock was used for, evidently it wasn't needed now. She dismounted from Starlight and gathered the rope, unwinding it from the trees used as fence posts. It was the same rope used for other things on the ranch and didn't look old. What a waste to leave it in the woods.

Gathering the rope into a nice coil, she tied it to her saddle, then found a log, and asked Starlight to position her body so she could use the log as a step. The mare was small enough to easily mount from the ground, and Megan was athletic enough to get back up without a step, but she thought it was better and more considerate to the young horse's back to use the log. She finished her ride around the perimeter of the ranch at a walk, cooling down Starlight as they gradually returned to the barn.

The sweat was dry on Starlight's body, except under the saddle pad. A quick hose off at the wash bay would be a good treat for the horse on this hot South Carolina morning. Starlight would love a good roll in the sand after being wet from the hose. Horses loved that sort of thing.

JJ rode up on his stallion while Megan scraped the excess water from Starlight's coat. Dismounting, he handed the reins to an intern, and walked over to Megan.

"Megan, I talked to Julie last night and I have to say I'm very disappointed in you." JJ stood with his arms folded across his chest, feet in a wide stance.

"Sir?" She could sort of follow where this was going.

"She met with you for a status update. What's this about not being interested in continuing with my program as an apprentice?"

"Well, sir, if you're offering me an apprenticeship, I certainly thank you for the opportunity, but I don't think this is the best path for me." She fought an urge to say more.

"I thought you had real potential until you lost your horse, and then your emotions got the best of you. You need to be tougher than that, girl. Horses come and horses go. Say goodbye and get on the next ride."

Did JJ have a smirk on his face? Megan hated confrontations, but she wouldn't run away from a fight, either.

"No, I don't think so, JJ. Horses are much more than the next ride and I think that's what most true horse lovers think. They

think horses are much more." Megan copied JJ's stance and didn't move an inch when he pressed into her space.

"I expect complete loyalty from all of my students. My students never question my leadership or what I say—never! And anyone who turns down an invitation for an apprenticeship isn't being loyal in my book. If you don't want to stay, you need to leave. I want you off this ranch just as soon as you can get yourself gone. Let's say two days—gone. Do you understand?"

"I understand perfectly, JJ," Megan answered and after JJ stormed away she added defiantly, "I understand more than you think."

Taking a few deep breaths to get control of her anger, Megan waited before approaching Starlight. Horses didn't understand the crazy emotions that humans carried. Starlight wouldn't understand Megan's anger at JJ. She would get worried.

"It's ok, sweet girl. Let's get you back to the pasture and your friends. It's a great afternoon for a good roll in the sand, and then a nap under a couple of trees." Starlight couldn't understand her words, but talking soothed them both.

Geeze, getting kicked off the ranch was crazy. She didn't mind leaving early, but she hated to be kicked out of anything, and certainly hated leaving Starlight in this crazy place. Well, there wasn't any reason to report to her afternoon jobs. In essence, she, as free labor, had been fired. Why bother showing up? Instead, she grabbed a cup of water from the dining hall and walked up to the top of the hill to call her dad. It was usually the only place she could get decent cell service.

"Megan, are you ok?" Megan's dad answered quickly. He must not be with a critical patient, and since she never called during clinic hours, he must have been worried when he saw her name pop up on his phone.

"Yeah, Dad, I'm fine, but you won't believe what just happened." Megan told her dad the entire story with a few of her own embellishments, of course.

"I don't want you there one more night. I'm calling Dr. Gray. I'll ask him to pick you up and give you a room for the night. Then we'll make a plan, ok?"

"Ok, I'll get packed, and Dad, can we talk about the little mare, Starlight? I hate leaving her here. I told you about her last week, remember?"

"I don't know. We weren't going to buy any more horses. First you were going to leave home for the apprenticeship, and now you'll leave for college in another year. Your mom and I hope to retire from farm work."

"I know, Dad, but Jennie said I could keep a horse at her place. I mean I haven't talked to her about it again, but when we talked about losing Julep, she asked if I would ever get a horse again, and it sort of became our plan."

"We'll talk about it some more, but first let's get you out of there. Starlight will be ok for a few days." Adrian didn't exactly believe that and wondered when the next auction was scheduled.

"Ok, I'll start packing. Let me know what Dr. Gray says. Love you."

"Love you, too, Meggie Moo." Adrian hung up and punched Bobby's number.

Bobby didn't answer, but he would call back as soon as possible. He returned to the examining room and apologized to his client, explaining he needed to take an emergency call from his daughter. The client, of course, understood as most people do when it involves someone's child.

When Bobby called back, Adrian was with another client. It was a routine exam and he was able to step out of the room for a few minutes. He explained what had happened to Megan, and waited for Bobby's response.

"What a creep. You bet, Adrian, I'll pick up Megan. Just tell her to send me a text when she's ready. No, wait, I'll ask Mary to pick her up this afternoon. I can't get there until around six."

"Thanks, friend, I owe you a lot."

"Hey, don't forget we have Julep. How is this going to play out? I talked to my sheriff friend, and he doesn't think we have much to go on, no proof that JJ was involved. The two ranch hands lied and then took the horse to the sale. That's horse theft in my book, plain and simple, but my friend doesn't think you'll get an arrest or any real satisfaction without more proof to pin it on them. You could possibly file something for damages from JJ. Now that Megan is leaving his program, maybe you could hold his boots to the fire. I'm not thinking blackmail, but unless he pays up, you could put a little tarnish on his reputation. You do have some facts. You were told Julep was dead and then she was sold. Fraud, theft, lack of integrity, whatever. I'm sure he wouldn't want Megan's story to get out to his adoring fans."

"You're right, Bobby. Thanks for all your help. You're darn smart for a vet still wet behind your ears. I guess I'll have to treat you with more respect now. You sure worked the whole thing better than this old man."

"Just you wait, I'll figure out a way you can pay me back. But first, what's the plan? I can't do all the work." Bobby's voice revealed that he was mostly teasing but he still needed a plan.

"I'll call Megan and tell her to text you when she's ready to leave, and your wife, Mary, will pick her up. I'm also going to say you and Mary have a very nice surprise at your place, and then

I'm going to ask her to forgive me when she discovers the secret we kept from her, and not to be angry until I have a chance to explain. When I do get a chance to explain, I'll pull out my trump card, and tell her that you saved Julep's life. She'll love you forever. Megan has a very long memory."

"That sounds good. I'll let Mary know she can explain the situation whenever and however she thinks is best. She's better at that sort of thing. I'm going to guess Megan will be riled when she finds out about us hiding Julep."

"You're correct. That's my daughter. She'll demand to know why I didn't trust her and why I didn't share the plan. I'll make sure to say a little prayer for you, friend."

"Thanks, I'm a praying man and I welcome all the prayers anyone wants to send my way."

"Please tell Mary I owe her big time. It seems I am racking up more debt to the Gray family."

"You bet and we'll collect." Bobby hung up, pleased with his wit.

Adrian hadn't met Mary, but he had heard good things about her from both Bobby and other people in the horse world. He could also Google fairly well. At one time, Mary was a very well–known competitor in the horse world. She also was a talented artist. She was certainly an interesting lady. Megan would enjoy her short time at the Grays'. Well, once she cooled down enough to enjoy the situation, anyway. Adrian thought it wouldn't hurt to say a prayer for himself.

Chapter Twenty-Seven

Megan finished packing. She was doing her best to hold back tears. She wasn't sad about leaving, exactly, but she was experiencing the sadness you feel when something you dreamed about for a long time turns out to be an unbelievable disappointment. She also hated to leave Starlight. There was something about that little mare that captured her heart. Megan felt a huge connection with Starlight. Surprising, since it had only been a few weeks since she arrived with a load of other horses.

Megan was relieved when she heard the ping of a text and saw it was from Mary Gray. They would meet for the first time today.

On my way!

ready thanks

Walking to the dining hall to wait for Mary, she saw Julie.

"I'm leaving this afternoon. I'm all packed and waiting for my ride."

"I'm sorry to hear that, but since you aren't interested in staying, I guess it's good that you go sooner rather than later."

"Well, it doesn't feel good. I'm sure my dad will be in contact with JJ. I'm being asked to leave before my time is finished. He'll want some of my room and board money returned. He isn't happy about this situation."

"It's non-refundable. Just tell your dad not to bother JJ." Julie wasn't being exactly nasty but she wasn't friendly, either.

"You don't know my dad. He won't let this drop." She had a feeling he would do more than not let it drop. He would demand much more.

"Whatever, Megan, I have work to do. Too bad you're going home with nothing—no recommendation, no awards, no friends, and oh, yeah, no horse." Julie sneered and then walked away.

Now that was just plain nasty. You're right, Julie. No horse, and that's the worst crime of all.

Megan felt like chasing after Julie to tell her this wasn't finished yet. She had faith in her dad. He would take that sneer off both JJ's and Julie's faces. Before she could continue that thought, Megan saw a silver truck traveling slowly down the ranch drive. The driver was a young woman, maybe in her thirties. She waved, and the driver stopped and rolled down her window.

"Megan?"

"Mary?"

"I'm so sorry we're meeting under these circumstances." Mary smiled. "Is there someplace we need to go to pick up your things?"

Megan opened the truck door and climbed up into the passenger seat. "Yeah, up at the girls' bunkhouse. It isn't far."

Mary followed Megan's directions, and parked at the bunkhouse. There wasn't much to load into the truck. Megan traveled light.

"We just need to make a quick stop at the barn for my tack. I sent most of Julep's things home with Dad, but I kept my saddle and a few other things here to use when I rode other horses." Megan pointed out where they needed to head next.

"Nice saddle, Megan. I like its weight." Mary opened the back door of the double cab. "Let's put your saddle inside. We're going to stop someplace for an early supper. Bobby won't be home for a few more hours and I'm starved. Ok?"

"That sounds good. Thanks. With everything that happened today, I didn't eat lunch."

They climbed into the truck and drove down the ranch drive to the road. Megan didn't turn around for one last look. She only wanted to look forward and put the Double J behind.

Mary stopped at a local deli. "They have fresh salads and unusual sandwiches here."

"I'm so hungry I could eat just about anything. Good food is a bonus."

The sat at a small table and both ordered big salads and Cokes. While they waited, Megan asked, "Do you ride, Mary?"

"I have a little Arabian and we have fun. I've done a few competitive trail rides and hunter paces this year."

"You both must be fit. I mean you look fit, and I'm sure your horse is in great shape. Is your horse a mare or gelding?"

"Gelding, and yes, he's fit. I ride a lot to stay in shape. I love riding. Never liked training in an arena very much, but we love to hit the trails and just enjoy being together."

"Have you done much training in an arena?" Megan was interested.

"No, not now, but I've competed seriously in dressage and earned my silver medal. Now, I just need riding for balance in my life—no pun intended." Mary smiled. "Well, I guess it helps my physical balance along with my mental balance."

"Do you have another job?" Megan was always interested in what people did for a living.

"I paint barns and signs." Mary looked over at Megan mischievously.

"You paint barns, like--you mean the entire barn?"

"No, I don't like painting the whole barn, although I've done it a few times. I paint signs for barns. Folk art, farm signs, or the barn quilts, and some Pennsylvania Dutch signs. They're called hex signs, but I don't like that word much, so I don't use it. I try to say folk signs. And I help out at Bobby's office when his staff needs an extra hand."

"You're so busy, and here I am stealing your time." Megan suddenly felt awkward.

"Now, don't you worry, I'm enjoying my afternoon. Are you interested in art?" Mary had sensed that Megan had something to share.

"Yeah, I love to draw and paint. I try to get an art class of some type on my schedule every year. Since I'm going back home for my senior year, after all, I think I'll try pottery. But I'm not as talented as you, Mary."

"I don't know. It sounds like you have a good background in all sorts of media. Have you done any photography?"

"I've played around a little. I like getting unusual shots and angles, and I like getting good nature pictures, especially of horses." Megan was feeling comfortable again. "How did you get started with your painting, Mary?"

"I've always messed around with art, but majored in graphic design in college, working mostly with websites and computer stuff. Then one day, I was looking online for design ideas. I needed something for a farm website, and I saw the neatest quilt sign on a barn and fell totally in love."

"Oh, I know what you mean. I've seen them in Ohio." Megan felt a little twinge of homesickness. Ohio had beautiful old barns.

"Have you seen the bi-centennial barns in Ohio? Each county has one barn painted to celebrate Ohio's bi-centennial year."

"No, but I would love to see them. I'll look it up." Mary was interested. "I've painted huge advertisements on barns. It's a lot of work and a lot of ladder climbing, but also fun. I love being outside, either painting or riding." Mary was finished eating and leaned back in her chair. "I have a little studio in the loft of my barn and can usually see the horses as I work. It's a neat set up."

"So you like painting signs and barns instead of creating your art on a computer?" Megan liked both. "Do you think it would be important to get a degree in graphic design if someone wanted to do what you're doing?" Megan's dad would be surprised that she seriously thought about these things.

"I don't know, but that's definitely a discussion for another time." Mary shifted in her seat, and then leaned forward with her elbows on the table.

"Megan, I have something I need to tell you before we get to my place."

"Is it bad?" Megan's stomach suddenly felt queasy.

"No, it's good. But you're going to be angry with me, Bobby, and your dad. Please let me finish my story before you form an opinion, ok?"

"My dad? Now what did HE do? This feels scary serious."

"I'm just going to come out with it—Julep didn't die. She's at my house."

Megan was stunned. Then the tears started. "Why do you have my Julep?"

Mary could see Megan's face turning red. The tears stopped and anger would follow. Mary needed to quickly tell the whole story—she told Megan about Bobby finding Julep at the auction, how he asked her to bring money, Bobby staying with Julep until she returned with the horse trailer, Megan's dad and Bobby keeping it a secret because they were trying to get some answers—all the way up to today, and Megan being asked to leave the ranch.

Megan sat stunned. "They could have trusted me. Why didn't my dad trust me?"

"Yes, your dad said he could trust you, but it wasn't about trust. He thought you would be able to figure out what was happening at the ranch easier if you didn't know about Julep. That's why he was so agreeable about allowing you to stay."

"I found a hidden corral on the back side of the property, and I bet that's where they hid Julep until the sale. But why take Julep?"

"I'm not sure, but she has big hunks of her mane and most of her tail missing. Your dad and Bobby think there's a black market for horse hair."

"My poor baby! Her gorgeous mane and tail are gone?" Megan felt sick. It was bad enough to think about Julep being sold to a kill buyer, but to know someone stole Julep just for her mane and tail was hard to digest.

"What kind of person does something like that, Mary? Is she ok, was she hurt?"

"She's healthy and still gorgeous, a nice mare. I've gotten quite attached to her." Mary stood up. "Let's go, she's waiting for you."

They returned to Mary's truck for the short drive to the Grays' farm and Mary continued to share all the information they had gathered from the last few weeks.

"Unfortunately, because Bobby took Julep away from the sale before he called the sheriff, it's going to be hard, if not impossible, to press charges. We can't prove JJ was involved. All we know is you were told she died and she ended up at the sale."

"Those dirty, lying sneaks. I thought they were up to something." Megan told Mary about calling them Pete and Repeat. "I followed them but couldn't catch them doing anything to report. I have their rope, though."

"What rope?" Mary pulled onto her farm.

"I found a rope tied around the trees. They must have hidden Julep in the trees until they took her to the sale. It isn't much proof, I guess, but I know that's what they did. I tied it to my saddle and it's still there."

The truck stopped and Megan jumped out and ran in the direction Mary pointed.

"Julep, Julep!" Julep lifted her head, whinnied, and cantered to the gate.

This time, Megan was crying big tears of joy.

Chapter Twenty-Eight

Appleridge, Ohio

*S*am offered to drive his new double-cab truck to the fair. He planned to pick up Belinda first, and then meet Jeremy and Jennie at Jennie's place around five. Jeremy called Jennie and asked if he could come by early—around four. He wanted a chance to talk to her alone, and to visit with all the four-legged creatures at the farm.

Jennie was fine with that idea, but since she worked until three, she rushed home to get changed from her work khakis and polo shirt into navy capris and a navy and white striped T–shirt. She thought it looked fresh and cute, although she wasn't a fashionista by any stretch of the imagination. She pondered what shoes to wear and chose her L.L. Bean sport sandals. Fairs required a lot of walking, and since they were all former 4-H kids, they would visit all the barns. The sport sandals would protect her feet almost as much as jogging shoes. Anyway, her only other choices were barn boots or dress flats, with maybe a tennis shoe or two thrown in for good measure.

She finished putting her hair in a messy bun, and ran down the stairs when she heard Jeremy's small SUV drive past the house, opening the back door before he knocked.

"Hey there, come on in. I'm ready but thinking that maybe I shouldn't have gotten ready before feeding the horses. I'm not sure I can get within ten feet of the barn and still stay clean."

"Well, hello to you, too. Yeah, all it would take is one snort from a sassy pony to dirty that nice outfit."

"I know. What was I thinking?" She was only thinking about looking good for Jeremy, but she sure wasn't going to say that.

Jeremy stepped inside. "Remember how we always covered our show clothes with a large shirt or apron until we were up on our horse and ready to enter the show pen? Do you have an old apron or anything?"

"I do. Good idea, but don't laugh."

Jennie went to the pantry and pulled out an old bib apron belonging to her grandma. It had lots of ruffles on the edges and a pattern of large red flowers printed across the fabric. It even had white rickrack trim on the pockets.

Jeremy bit his lip to keep from laughing. "Somehow that wasn't what I expected but it will work just fine. It's very retro of you, Jennie."

"Actually, it's the real deal, not a copy."

Jennie put on the apron and hammed it up, pretending she was a model.

"And to add to my fashionable presentation, I will take off my shoes and put on my good old barn boots."

"Good idea. I wouldn't want you to get those pretty toes smashed."

Jennie kicked off her sport sandals and thought, pretty toes, yikes! She was very glad she gave herself a pedicure last night.

They walked out to the barn, still laughing. Jennie and Jeremy led Treasure and the ponies inside to eat their evening meal.

"I put them in their stalls to eat because Riley scarfs his food and then wants to chase the others from their food. They each get something different, so he doesn't need to get his nose into Treasure and Stuffin's buckets. Riley doesn't need anything extra. Marcy calls him her little air fern."

As they ate, Jennie carried fresh hay out to the run-in area, making several piles in different spots. Riley liked to move Treasure and Stuffin from their piles until he was sure he had the best hay. When he was satisfied, they could all claim a pile to eat.

The water tub needed filling and Jennie turned on the spigot, letting it run while she ran to the tack room to write a note on the white board.

"Are you sure that's a good idea? I don't see a bell."

"I'm a big girl now, and I shouldn't have told you that story."

When Jennie was a kid, she forgot to turn off the water so often that her grandpa installed a bell that rang while the spigot handle was up and the water running. Before the bell, on many occasions, the forgotten water ran so long it caused the well pump to shut off. That never made Grandpa or her grandma very happy.

"Sorry, I couldn't resist. It's funny." Jeremy walked to the paddock and turned off the water. He pointed at the water over-flowing the tub.

"It's your fault. You distracted me." Yikes, why did she tell him that? It was too close to the truth.

"I'm happy to serve as your distraction." And he was.

The equines finished eating and Jeremy collected the buckets and sprayed them clean with the hose while Jennie led Treasure, Riley, and Stuffin to the paddock and their evening hay. Jennie glanced at each horse to make sure they didn't have any new bites or scrapes that needed attention. Everything looked fine.

"Thanks for your help overfilling the water tub. Maybe you need a bell."

"Glad to be of service." Jeremy enjoyed Jennie's humor.

"Somehow we both stayed fairly clean. Although I'm sure I could have found you an apron as stylish as the one I'm wearing."

"No offense, but I was willing to take the risk. Are we done?"

"Yeah, let's hurry and get back to the house before Sam and Belinda get here. If Belinda sees my outfit she'll tease me forever."

"Ah, I think you're a little too late." Jeremy nodded to the house where they could see Sam and Belinda climbing out of Sam's truck.

"Yikes. Well, at least I can get this apron off. The boots Belinda will understand."

Jennie pulled off the apron, folded it into a small square, and tucked it under the counter in the barn. I'll get that later. I'm not going to be doing any cooking or baking tonight."

"Oh, I'm so disappointed. Are you sure?" Jeremy teased.

"Yes, sir, we are going to the fair, and eating crazy delicious fair food and you won't be a bit hungry later tonight."

"Sounds good but I'm hungry now. Hey, guys, good timing. We just finished out at the barn." Jeremy stepped up to shake Sam's hand and give Belinda a hug.

"I'll just get out of these boots and be back out in a minute." Jennie motioned for Belinda to follow her inside.

"What's up, girlfriend?" Belinda looked great, also in capris but with a sleeveless shirt and cute sandals.

"Oh, I just wanted to ask if you thought I looked ok. I was rushed getting home from work, and I hurried to get ready before I fed the horses, because I didn't want Jeremy to see me in my old barn clothes, and then I had to be careful not to get dirty."

"Jennie, stop and take a breath. You look fine, and it isn't as if we haven't seen each other in stinking, dirty, stained barn clothes before." Belinda laughed. "Oh, I get it. Jennie McKenzie likes Jeremy James, the boy with two first names."

"I just want to look nice, and yeah, I do like him. I just don't know how much like yet."

"Let's go, then. Our dates are waiting." Belinda led the way back outside.

The four of them chatted and joked on the ride to the fair. They parked in the pasture that turned into a parking lot during fair week, and walked through the grass to the main gate. Jeremy stepped up and bought Jennie's ticket into the fair.

They walked the entire length of the midway, looking for something to eat, stopping for roasted corn, followed by corn dogs. Jeremy and Sam grabbed bratwurst sandwiches, Jennie wanted a candy apple, and Belinda went for cotton candy. They washed it all down with large Cokes.

A visit to the 4-H barns was next, especially the horse barn, where they said hello to several of their former 4–H advisors. There were also a few familiar parent faces, as well—those parents who had children their age, plus younger children currently in the Silver Spurs 4-H club. The foursome recognized several of the older 4-H kids who were junior members when they were in the club, but were now all grown up and the club's senior members. Several asked Belinda about Megan. She was missed. Several said the club just wasn't the same without her. They were also very surprised and sorry to hear about Julep.

After enjoying the meet and greet at the horse barn, the four friends strolled through the commercial displays before they closed for the evening. The fudge booth was in the largest commercial building, and the aroma led the way. The girls made getting the sweet treat mandatory and the boys didn't complain.

Standardbred race night at the fair lured them to the grandstand to grab seats, rest their legs, and enjoy a bite of fudge.
Jeremy disappeared and returned holding four bottles of water
from the concession stand.

"Is anyone thirsty?"

"I'm thirsty. You'll have to roll me back to Sam's truck. I can't
believe how much I've eaten tonight." Jennie offered Jeremy the
last piece of fudge but he declined.

"Save it for breakfast," he whispered.

"There was a time when I would have considered that a great
breakfast. But, hey, I'm visiting my grandpa tomorrow, and I'll
save it for him. He loves fair fudge."

"Good idea." Jeremy gulped his entire bottle of water. "Sorry,
I was dry."

The races stole their attention. They didn't bet but played a
game of picking who would win. Sam seemed to choose the most
winners.

"Not to brag, but I think those horses must have a talented
farrier." He grinned, and then confessed that several of his picks
were also clients.

Belinda squeezed Sam's arm. "Well, based on their performance, I bet you're correct."

"Hey, Sam, are you coming out to the farm next week?" Jennie asked.

"All three are due for their trims on Tuesday."

"I'll remind Cassy and Marcy to leave checks if they can't be
at the farm. I'll be there in the morning, but I have to be at work
by three."

They stayed seated after the races finished for the evening as
they waited for the grandstand crowd to thin a little. Back on the
midway, all four voted to ride the Ferris wheel but to forego the

twirly-swirly carnival rides. At eleven o'clock they started the long trek back to Sam's truck for the trip home. What a fun evening. They hated to see it end.

"Sorry I can't stay out later, but I have early shoeing clients tomorrow, and need my rest so I can be the awesome farrier I proved to be tonight." Sam winked at Belinda as he helped her into the truck.

They didn't talk as much on the trip home. They were winding down just like the evening.

"Thanks for the ride, Sam. Bye, Belinda. See you guys later." Jennie climbed out of the truck and looked at Jeremy.

"Do you want to come inside, Jeremy?"

"Yes, I do, but I can't. I need to get home. I promised Mom I would take her to visit her sister and she wants to leave early. That means before breakfast. She loves to stop for breakfast at a little diner on the way."

"Well, make sure to tell your mom hello from one of the girls who beat her son a few times at the 4-H shows. Jennie frowned. "No, wait, just say hello. I don't think she would laugh at my little joke. I don't suppose it's her favorite memory."

"No, I don't think she would laugh at the joke, but not because she's still angry. It's mostly because there's a lot she doesn't remember."

"I didn't know. I'm so sorry." Jennie was truly sorry.

"I haven't mentioned it because I've just started to notice her memory isn't as good as it used to be, and when I told her I was going to the fair with you tonight, she said she would love to meet you some time, and she had never gone to a fair."

"Has your sister noticed anything?"

"I haven't had a chance to talk to her about it, but I will soon. Maybe Mom just had something else on her mind, and wasn't listening. I'll know more after being with her all day tomorrow. And now, I need to get going." Jeremy stepped a little closer to Jennie.

"I had a nice time tonight, Jeremy James, the boy with two first names." Jennie didn't know what should happen next so she fell back on her stupid humor.

"I had a good time, too, Jennie McKenzie. I guess you were right—no need to cook tonight. Or for the next couple of days, either. And by the way, I'm glad my parents didn't name me James, because then you'd call me James squared." Jeremy leaned over, gave her a hug, and kissed her on the cheek. Before Jennie could respond, he waved, and was in his SUV with a huge grin on his face.

Smooth, Jeremy, very smooth, Jeremy.

His gesture was sweet, but not assuming, friendly, with just a hint of something more.

Chapter Twenty-Nine

*S*aturday morning and Jennie didn't have to get up for work, but for some strange reason, Beauty was on the bed, kneading her paws into Jennie's side.

"Beauty, it's only six o'clock, I don't need to get up so early." Just as the words left her mouth, Jennie tossed the covers and sat up. Oh no! She didn't open the gate to the pasture last night. She was so focused on Jeremy she totally forgot to go back out to the barn.

After throwing on a pair of jean shorts and a tank top, Jennie grabbed a clean pair of socks, and ran downstairs. She would turn them out now, and give them a few hours to graze, maybe until mid-morning.

Oh no, I have to tell Marcy and Cassy I forgot to turn the horses out last night! What will they think?

They would think she wasn't taking her responsibility seriously. Maybe they would be right to think that, too. After all, she had one date, and then forgot about the horses in her care.

All three nickered as she approached the barn. Jennie brought them inside for their breakfast. They were agreeable to that idea. After they licked buckets clean, Jennie opened the gate, and they happily trotted to the green grass, Riley leading the way. Jennie checked the water tub and filled it a couple of inches. The sides of the tank were looking a little green. She would dump it and clean it with a touch of bleach later today.

Back inside, Beauty wove between Jennie's legs. "Well, Beauty, I guess I should apologize and thank you for getting me

up early. Riley, Stuffin, and Treasure would like to thank you, also. They'll get a few bites of grass time this morning to make up for missing last night."

Finishing her toast, Jennie called her grandpa. He was an early riser so she didn't worry about the time.

"Well, hello, Jennie girl. You're up early." Grandpa seemed in good spirits.

"Hi, Gramps. I'm calling to see if I can come for a visit later this morning, and take you out for lunch. Nothing fancy, I don't want my landlord to think I'm rolling in dough."

Grandpa chuckled. "Your landlord would love a hotdog, all the way, complete with Coney sauce, down at the Bake & Shake. Throw in some chips and you have a deal."

"Great. What time?" It would be before noon. Grandpa ate lunch early.

"I'll look for you at eleven, Jennie girl."

Jennie could only smile. It was too late to teach Grandpa to say goodbye when he ended a telephone conversation.

Jennie looked at the clock. Wow, breakfast over, Grandpa called, and it wasn't even eight o'clock. She walked through the house.

I think it's time to rearrange a few things.

The desk in her bedroom wasn't working as an office. She thought it would be better to keep her work separate from the room where she needed to sleep.

There were two more small bedrooms upstairs. Cassy stayed over occasionally in the smallest room she called her bedroom, and Jennie wanted to keep the other room ready for occasional guests, like this week when Kyiko and Kate came to the farm. The house wasn't huge, but it had the three small rooms and a full bathroom upstairs, and a large kitchen, two medium-size rooms downstairs, and a little half bath tucked under the stairs.

Her grandparents always used the room next to the kitchen as a dining room, then a TV room. Maybe she could turn it into her office. She didn't need a separate dining space, and right now it was completely empty. Walking into the living room, or what her grandma used to call the front parlor, Jennie realized it would be more private for an office, and it could be closed off from the rest of the house with the original double glass doors. Jennie was glad Mrs. Jerome wasn't the type of person to modernize everything by taking out the doors to open up the space.

Jennie went to work moving newly purchased Ikea chairs, her old tack trunk she used as a coffee table, and several other small items into the former dining room, creating a new living/media room. She pushed and shoved the furniture using a blanket to protect the refinished old wood floors. Jennie didn't want to make fresh scratches.

Whew! Jennie was sweating from her work. Her new living room looked great—cozy. Maybe she could talk Jeremy or Belinda into helping her move the desk and bookcase downstairs after church tomorrow.

With the ponies and Treasure tucked back in their paddock with the appropriate number of hay piles, Jennie returned to the house for a quick shower. If Grandpa said eleven he meant a few minutes before and it was already 10:15.

Jennie dressed quickly. Her sport sandals were still at the back door, where she kicked them off last night. Perfect. She opened the pantry door to get her purse and headed outside.

Oh no. Where's my phone?

Retracing her steps, she found the phone on the kitchen counter.

She noticed a text from Kate. *Can't wait to see you! Have boots will travel.*

Jennie responded quickly, *Good job, cowgirl.*

Grandpa met Jennie at the curb as Blue Boy rolled to a stop at 10:55.

"Hey, Jennie girl, it's good to see you all bright-eyed and bushy-tailed on this fine morning." Grandpa had a little difficulty climbing into the truck, but an offer to help would be quickly rebuffed.

"I was very busy on this fine morning, so maybe the bright you see is me glowing from exertion. But don't worry, I showered."

Jennie filled Grandpa in on her morning's work as they drove to the Bake & Shake. It was early for the lunch crowd, but the place was buzzing with the Saturday morning donut crowd. They found a small table and Grandpa sat down.

"I'll go to the counter, Gramps, I know you want a Coney dog all the way and chips. Do you want anything to drink?"

"I do believe I would like a root beer, and don't give me that look. I can handle all three. I have the stomach of a twenty-year-old man." Grandpa leaned back and patted his round stomach. "Ok, maybe not the same size as it was when I was twenty, but it still works fine."

"I wish I could say the same, Grandpa. I think I'm going to leave the chili off my dog and maybe the onions, too. I challenged my stomach with a large array of fair food last night.

"Oh, before I forget, I saved a piece of fudge for you." She sat down to dig into her bag and found the little box. "It's chocolate peanut butter."

"I never met fudge I didn't like." Grandpa opened the box for a peek at his treat. "How was the fair this year? I'm going on the senior citizens' bus tomorrow. I volunteered to push a friend's wheelchair."

"It was good. We had fun and watched a few races. Sam was thrilled several of his clients won their races. But hey, Grandpa, be careful pushing a wheelchair around the fair. That's a lot of walking and pushing."

"Jennie girl, the staff from the senior center will keep an eye on me. I can't get away with anything. Hey, are you going to buy my lunch or let me waste away to nothing while we talk?" Grandpa looked longingly at a mother carrying a tray of hotdogs to her children at the next table.

"Yes sir, coming right up. Grandpa, get ready to start your stomach." Jennie got in line behind two other people at the snack counter. The Bake & Shake's menu was simple and orders were filled quickly. The line was a lot longer at the bakery counter.

"Here you are, sir, your lunch is served." Jennie made a show of removing the items from the tray, and presenting her grandpa with his lunch. She returned the tray and sat down.

Grandpa reached for Jennie's hand, and they bowed their heads for a prayer.

"Father, I thank you for this food. It's fun food and food should be enjoyed. I also thank you for this time with my Jennie. Time with those we love is so precious. In Your name, the One who gives us this joy."

Jennie joined in on the "Amen."

"So, you seem happy. Life is good?" Grandpa was careful not to drip chili on his shirt.

"Yes, Gramps, sometimes I think my life is too good." Jennie put her sandwich down on the paper plate.

"Why in the world would you say that, Jennie?" Grandpa put down his hot dog and reached for his chips to open the bag.

"Do you believe that God wants us to worry about what will happen next or thank him for what is happening now?" Grandpa looked right into Jennie's eyes. His blue eyes had aged and were a soft, reassuring blue, and right now they revealed concern.

"Not worrying, so I think thanking is the right answer." Jennie wasn't trying to be humorous

Grandpa smiled. "You're correct. In good times and in bad, don't let anything or anyone steal your faith and God's joy." Grandpa picked up his hot dog for another bite, and then ate a few chips.

Jennie didn't know what to say. Her grandpa was extremely good at making a point without causing her to feel like she was being judged, but why did he feel the need for a lesson on joy?

"Gramps, I choose to celebrate joy, and be thankful. I admit, I do sometimes wonder why I've been blessed while others have so little. And sometimes, I think life is too good and it's only a matter of time before something bad happens." As soon as those words were out of her mouth, she understood what Grandpa meant.

"I had a tough time when I returned from fighting in Korea. I couldn't understand why I came home to my wife and family while several of my friends came home in boxes. I carried a lot of guilt, that's for sure. Your grandma was patient, and put up with me for a good while, but then one day she said, 'Charlie, the question isn't why, it's what are you going to do with the gift. Are you going to honor God or throw his gift away?' Grandpa paused and then continued.

"Well, I had to think about that for a while. I admit, when she first said it, I was angry. She didn't know anything about what I went through. She didn't know what it was like to be in a war.

They called it a police action, but it was an ugly war, and I don't care what the history books say."

Jennie had never seen her grandpa so serious. He was reliving the painful past.

"It's ok, Gramps. I understand." Jennie reached for his hand.

"I'm fine, but I need to finish, it's been on my mind lately." He sat back and continued. "When I could think clearly, I thought about what your grandma said. She was right. Your grandma was always right." Grandpa managed a smile. "And I told her she was right. She deserved a husband who would help her live in joy, not steal her joy."

Jennie saw her grandpa's body relax as he talked about her grandma. Grandma was still bringing him joy.

"We had a good marriage. A lot of bad things happened in those years, but we made sure we looked for the good things. I made it my mission to thank God for everything, even the bad. If I believed God loved me, and I was precious to him, I had to believe I would survive all the bad things life threw my way, and be better for having the experience."

"Grandpa, I didn't know. I mean, I remember being told you were in Korea, but I didn't know how much you struggled after coming home."

"When you see men killing men, you get a good taste of evil. When you see innocent women and children murdered, you stare evil right in the face. When you kill a man to save a friend, you still feel the evil. I can't possibly think of any reason to feel justified for taking a life. Even killing to save someone else should feel wrong and it did."

Her grandpa, one of the wisest and kindest men she had ever met, lived with the memory that he had killed. Oh, oh, oh, Jennie's heart ached for him.

"I did what I had to do, in a time when it had to be done. I saved several lives, including my own. I wasn't a hero. I'm not sure anyone should be called a hero in time of war. It's what happens after the war that defines a real hero. If you survive, will you honor God by living a life that honors him, or will you allow the experience to steal your joy? Your grandma set me straight, and I chose to honor God."

"What did you do, Gramps? How did you honor God?"

"Most people think that means you become a missionary or pastor, but I chose to honor God in my everyday ordinary life. That's much harder, don't you think?"

"Well, yes, and that's what prompted this conversation, isn't it? I forgot to honor God. I suppose I seem like a spoiled child right now." Jennie took a drink of her water.

"No, sweetie, you don't, but please remember, it doesn't matter what trials you have in life. There isn't a contest to see who has the most challenges. Anytime you worry, you're in a dangerous place. It's like you leave the door cracked open for evil to steal your faith. When you worry, that's Satan, the devil, whatever you want to call it, trying to steal your joy.

"Evil surrounds us in our normal, everyday lives. But we know how it turns out, right? God wins. Enjoy your life. Don't be worried about what may or may not happen, because I promise you bad things will happen. But I also promise that nothing is too big or too small for God. Stick with the Savior, Jennie girl."

Jennie smiled. "Grandpa, you would make one good pastor."

"We're all called to pastor others. We're called to share what God has done for us, and to tell others what he wants to do for them. I just chose to do it at my work, with my friends, and with you, instead of behind a pulpit.

"There's a verse I like, Jennie, it's from Luke 12:48: *From everyone who has been given much, much will be demanded; and from the one who has been entrusted with much, much more will be asked.*

"Jennie, you've been given much, so, of course, much will be asked. You will face trials, but you will also have the King of Kings ready to fight for you."

Jennie sighed. She noticed Grandpa wasn't going to finish his chips or his root beer.

"Gramps, thanks for loving me so much that you shared something that I know you'd rather not think about. I'll remember that living a joyful life isn't something you earn or that you deserve. It's a gift from a wonderful Creator, and I want to make sure I appreciate the gift."

Grandpa smiled. "By golly, I think you got it, Jennie."

"Hey, Gramps, I think I would like a root beer now. Do you want me to get you a fresh one to go?" Jennie looked around and noticed the donut breakfast crowd was gone, the hot dog lunch crowd was thinning, and the ice cream baseball and softball crowd was arriving.

"That sounds like a great idea. This one's getting a little flat."

While Jennie went to the counter for two root beers to go, Grandpa cleaned up the table, and threw away the trash. Together, they went outside and found a shady bench on the sidewalk.

"Grandpa, do you remember Jeremy James from when I was in the 4–H club?"

"I sure do. Nice young man. His mom was quite a pill though, wasn't she?"

"She was, but she sure raised a nice son."

"Oh, I see. Are you interested in this nice son?" Grandpa picked up on her interest right away.

"Yes, Grandfather, I'm very interested. You've always been a good judge of character, and I'm interested in what you think. He'll be at the campfire. Oh wait! I haven't given you the invitation to the campfire." Jennie dug into her bag again and pulled out the smashed scroll with the bow also smashed but still intact.

"Grandfather? My, oh my, that is a serious word. Let me read this scroll and then we'll talk about Jeremy James."

Grandpa set his drink down on the cement and opened the invitation. "Well, that certainly sounds like fun. I'll be there but I won't stay late. I'm sure one of your sisters will bring me home." He chuckled. "Those little boys can't stay up too late, and neither can this old boy."

"Great! You'll get to meet my college roommates because the party is for them. I want them to meet my friends and family while they're visiting."

"Ah, yes, I've heard your mom and dad speak fondly of them. But back to another friend, your friend Jeremy. I always liked Jeremy. His mother had a sharp tongue, but he always tried to mediate and soften the bite. She embarrassed him but I never heard him refer to her with anything but respect. That's good character in my book—to honor your mother, even when she has faults that make life difficult."

Grandpa turned and pointed a finger at Jennie. "You, on the other hand, young lady, as I recall, you and Belinda used to make fun of his name."

"Guilty as charged, but when I tried to apologize, Jeremy just laughed and said I did it because I secretly loved to say his name out loud. I'm thinking I may be guilty as charged with that offense, too. That makes me double guilty." Jennie couldn't believe she was sharing this with her grandpa.

"I'll look forward to meeting Jeremy again next Saturday, and will make sure I put my chair next to his, and we'll have a nice little chat. But now, sweet Jennie, I'm full of good food, depleted from our emotionally charged but rewarding conversation, and ready for my afternoon nap."

Jennie drove her grandpa back to his apartment, and watched as he walked with some difficulty. Getting out of the truck to help him as he walked to the door would be refused, so she didn't offer.

As Jennie watched, she thought about their conversation. Her comment about things being too good and waiting for something bad to happen sure struck a nerve with her grandpa.

Jennie drove to each of her sisters' houses to deliver their invitations. She didn't stay long at either place. Connie was right in the middle of weeding her flower beds, and Sallie was sewing. The things they both enjoyed. Jennie didn't want to take them away from their projects. Her sisters always tried to make good use of toddler nap time.

Jennie's brothers-in-law usually helped with the boys on Saturdays, but today they were playing golf with two other friends from church. She couldn't help but wonder where Jeremy would fit into the family—if they would happen to become a couple.

Chapter Thirty

oth Marcy and Cassy were at the farm when Jennie returned. She changed into her boots, and walked out to the barn. It was confession time. She would need to confess about forgetting to open the pasture gate last night, and cheating the horses out of their evening grazing.

"Jennie, don't worry, one missed night of grazing won't hurt my two. They had access to water, and I'm sure they had enough hay because you always give them plenty. Don't beat yourself up, girl." Marcy was speaking but Cassy nodded her head in agreement.

"Thanks, guys. Oh, before I forget, here are your invitations to the campfire. Please bring someone if you want." Jennie held out the scrolls.

"I can't wait. I'm bringing my roommate, Sandra. She doesn't have a car and hasn't left the campus yet." Cassy untied her ribbon. "These are very cute."

"Nice touch with the ribbon. Maybe I should save it for my hair." Marcy slid the bow off her scroll and pretended it was a hair decoration. "I don't think I'll bring anyone. I'm still making friends at work, and I'm quite comfortable with your family."

"Great, I think it'll be fun. I'm anxious for you both to meet Kate and Kyiko. Thanks so much for sharing your ponies for their lessons."

"You can play with Treasure, too." Cassy offered.

"Thanks, but I was hoping you would play with Treasure, and maybe ride. Kate and Kyiko need to get comfortable with someone riding near them while they dance."

"I wonder if they've ever used driving horses with dance." Marcy always promoted driving.

"Not sure, but maybe we should experiment. Let's try to get some good video of you driving them as a pair, and Kate and Kyiko could share the video at the workshop."

"Just tell me when," Marcy volunteered.

"Are you available Monday afternoon? We could experiment a little, and I can give you both a quick liberty 101 lesson."

"I could be here both Monday and Wednesday afternoon. My classes are in the morning." Cassy was eager.

Marcy pulled out her phone. "Sorry, I work all day on Monday but I'm off Wednesday evening and all day Friday."

"Cassy and I can get started on Monday, and you join in when you can. This week is my Friday off, too, so we'll plan that as our big video day. I'll put them to work feeding, grooming, and leading. The ponies will be gleaming by Friday."

Jennie hesitated. "Could I ask one of you a favor? When you're finished in the barn, could you help me move my desk and a few other things downstairs into my new office?"

"Sure, I can help." Cassy made a gesture showing off her arm muscles.

"I'm so sorry, Jennie. I was called in to work at the hospital for a few hours, and I need to go home for a quick shower. They need me to be there by 5:30 and its 4:00 now."

"That's ok, I understand." Jennie added, "Oh, before I forget, Sam will be here Tuesday morning to trim."

"Great, I noticed the ponies were getting a little long in the toes. I'll leave a check tomorrow. Bye." Marcy rushed to her truck.

It didn't take them long to get Jennie's desk and bookcase down the stairs, and into her new office. Cassy also helped Jennie move the sofa from the old living room to the now new media room.

"Wow! Thanks so much. What do you think?" Jennie sat on the arm of the sofa scanning the new room.

"I think I like it and I also like that you didn't turn my bedroom into your office."

"I couldn't run out my sometimes roommate, could I? Are you staying any of the nights Kate and Kyiko are here? If not, could one of them stay in your room?" Jennie was seriously asking for permission.

"You're sweet to ask, when I don't even pay rent," Cassy laughed. "I'm not staying. But, just so you know, I'm thinking about paying for that room. I wouldn't mind getting out of the dorm next year."

"Would you miss campus life?" Columbia College didn't have dorms so Jennie didn't live on a college campus while she was in school.

"I don't think so. I've made some friends, but I'm not the sorority type, and my idea of a fun party is the campfire you're having or a day spent with Treasure."

"My grandpa thinks your parents were extremely smart to allow Treasure to come with you to school."

"My parents are brilliant, but I'll deny saying so." Cassy made her way to Jennie's back door. "I've got to get going—Sandra and I are going to catch a movie. Is that offer to meet you at church still good?"

"It sure is—I always go to the 9:30 service."

"Wow! That's a bit early for me on a Sunday, but I'll try to make it. After church I want to ride. We love the paths and jumps you made. We're having a fun time pretending we're on a cross–country course."

"It looks like fun. And you and Treasure make it look easy." Jennie meant every word. Cassy was a beautiful rider.

"Thanks, Jennie. Treasure makes it look easy. Need to run." Cassy waved as she jogged to her car.

"Bye. I'll see you tomorrow, either in church or after." Jennie prayed a little prayer that it would be in church. Her church had a great worship band and young adult group, and maybe Cassy would enjoy both.

Jennie had a rare free evening. It was a perfect time to finish arranging her new office and give it a trial run. Jennie was happy, and life was good. Grandpa was right—bad things will happen, but she needed to be thankful. The Lord of Lords and King of Kings had her back.

Dear Equestrian,

Let's talk about being happy. Yes, horses like to be happy, and we find it easy to be happy. We don't mind doing what you ask us to do—things like jumping, running, sliding, turning, even pulling a cart. Well, we don't mind if our human is happy. When our human is happy, everything becomes easier.

Now, I suppose you think it's up to the horse to make the human happy, but we don't agree. If it's the human's idea to ride, the human should be happy to ride. If it's the human's idea to groom, the human should be happy to groom. If it's the human's idea to jump, the human should be eager, and it should feel like fun. Everything we do together should feel like fun, Dear Equestrian, and shouldn't cause

you fear, frustration, or anger. If it does, maybe you aren't ready to ask from us what you aren't ready to ask from yourself.

Sometimes it feels like the human isn't happy about what she asks us to do, and that feels bad. Sometimes the human gets tight and stiff, and then can't understand why we get tight and stiff. Dear Equestrian, please understand that your feelings are directly transported through your body, especially through your hands.

But remember, Dear Equestrian, happiness has a feeling, too. When you are relaxed and soft, we can then be relaxed and soft. When you are eager and happy to ride, to groom, to do anything with us, we can enjoy our time together.

So yes, Dear Equestrian, your horse wants you to be happy. Please make sure everything you do with your horse is something you want to do, and not something you feel obligated to do. Your horse doesn't want to be an obligation.

Dear Equestrian, you are our advocate. You don't have to follow the latest trend or ride a certain number of hours each day, or groom only because you think it's required. It's permissible to say, "No" to a trainer, a friend, a barn owner, and simply do what you think we would both enjoy. Over time, we'll figure out what we enjoy doing together, and we'll both be happy.

A desire to learn is healthy and important. But remember, learning can only happen if there is freedom to learn. Horses like to be free, and we think you'll enjoy spending free time with your horse. It's your choice.

See you soon, friend, and let's have some fun together,
Your Favorite Horse

Chapter Thirty-One

ennie slid into the pew beside Belinda.

"Hey, girl, how did you manage to get to the early service?"

"Well, if you're insinuating that I don't like to get up early, please note who got here first, Miss Jennie."

"Oh, aren't we grouchy this morning. Those who like to get up early are usually cheerful in the morning." Jennie sat down and scooted over to Belinda. "No offense, Miss Sunshine, but don't you usually feel obligated to attend the late service with your parental units?"

"If you must know, I told them I wanted to meet you, because we haven't seen nearly enough of each other this summer, and I will be leaving soon, although I can't imagine why I thought of that now." Belinda wasn't mad but she was choking on a laugh.

"Oh, that's too sweet. I guess I'll have to call you Sunshine Unicorn Cupcake Sugar." Jennie leaned away, pretending she was ducking out of Belinda's reach.

"Funny, Jennie, very funny. I guess I'll need to call you Funny Jennie."

That's fine, just make sure you spell it F U N N I E with an *ie*. It's a family thing, don't you know."

"Well, Jennie with an *ie*, I dislike happy people in the morning, just so YOU know." Her friend fought a smile.

"I know." Jennie looked around and saw her grandpa at the far end of the pew behind theirs. She gave him a little wave and he waved back with a little grin. Jennie hoped he hadn't heard

the little exchange between friends. He enjoyed teasing her about misbehaving in church.

Jennie loved seeing her grandpa at the early service, swaying with the latest Christian music. Not many older people came to this service with the worship band of guitars, keyboard, and drums. He certainly enjoyed life, and he enjoyed this type of worship. Jennie's parents preferred the traditional service with the old hymns and pipe organ.

The worship band walked to the front. The service was about to begin. Belinda nudged Jennie, motioning for her to turn around.

"Yes, Mom," Jennie couldn't resist teasing. She sighed when she realized Cassy wasn't going to attend the service and prayed silently, *I planted the seed, God, and I trust you will do the rest in your perfect time.*

Grayson Corners, South Carolina

Megan woke up and looked around the room. It wasn't the bunkhouse, it was a much nicer room, and she was alone. She was at the Grays' little farm and she loved this little room, and knowing that Julep was outside in the pasture. Megan stretched and looked at the time. It was only 7:30. She had plenty of time. The Grays invited her to attend their church, and their church didn't begin until eleven.

Megan heard noises in the kitchen, threw on a pair of shorts and a T–shirt, and went out to investigate. Mary was sitting at the table drinking a cup of coffee and Dr. Bobby was frying eggs. Megan didn't feel comfortable calling him Bobby, and he said Dr. Gray was too formal, so they agreed on Dr. Bobby.

"How about having an egg sandwich on white bread for breakfast? I call them the Bobby special, complete with Duke's mayo, and a large slice of ripe tomato fresh from our garden."

"Sold, sounds great." Megan walked over to the kitchen French doors to look outside.

"She's still there, Megan," Mary said kindly.

"I know, but it's still hard to believe."

"It's too hot to ride after church today, but how about riding early tomorrow morning? We'll trailer over to a state trail. It's supposed to stay in the mid-eighties, a cool spell for August in South Carolina."

"That sounds great." Megan pulled out her chair to sit, just as Dr. Bobby placed her egg sandwich on the table.

"Thanks, Dr. Bobby, it looks..."

"I know—it's great." Bobby smiled and sat down with his own coffee and egg sandwich.

Megan blushed, something she didn't normally do. She liked Dr. Bobby and didn't mind being teased, but being corrected was embarrassing.

Mary scolded Bobby. "Bobby, please don't tease Megan, today IS great. Megan is here and she has Julep. It doesn't get much better. Amen, sister?"

"Amen, Mary. Do you want me to take care of the horses this morning?"

"That would be great," Mary laughed. "I'll just linger over my coffee while Bobby takes his shower, then I'll take my turn, and we'll try to save some hot water for you."

"Great!" they all said in unison and laughed.

Megan finished her breakfast and went out to the barn. All three horses gathered around Megan at the gate, Julep with Mary's Arabian, Windward, and her rescued pony, Twinkle. All

were ready for their morning feed. Megan gave them each a bucket in their stalls, and then put several flakes of hay out in the paddock. Mary's routine was similar to what she liked also, and it was easy to remember.

As Megan waited for the three to eat, she thought about everything that had happened in the last few weeks, and especially the last few days. Her time at the Double J was a disappointment, losing Julep was heartbreaking, finding her again was unbelievable, and the last two days with Dr. Bobby and Mary were awesome. She wasn't in much of a hurry to get home. At home she would need to figure out what she wanted to do with her life, and she didn't have a clue.

Chapter Thirty-Two

Appleridge, Ohio

Jennie drove back home to the farm after her shift at the library. She was meeting Cassy for an introduction to playing with horses at liberty. Sunday evening, Jennie used temporary poles and rope to section off a small part of the pasture near the barn. They would use the area for their liberty play. It was large enough for the horses to feel like they could leave if they chose, but not so large to make it difficult for the humans to reconnect with the horses.

Cassy was already at the barn when she arrived home. Jennie changed her clothes quickly. She found Treasure tied in the aisle and enjoying a nice grooming from Cassy.

"I'm sorry I didn't make it to church yesterday."

"Cassy, please don't feel pressured. You're welcome anytime."

"Thanks. Doesn't Treasure look great? She shines. She's happy here, Jennie, and I am, too."

"I love having you both. Are you ready to play? I think you're going to love how liberty play will connect you with Treasure." Jennie led the way to her temporary play paddock. Let the fun begin.

"Cassy, Treasure doesn't have to be obedient at liberty. She has the freedom to choose how she wants to respond. That's why it's called liberty, she's at liberty to obey—or not."

"What if she runs away?"

"She'll leave at first, because she doesn't understand the game. Don't worry, that's what makes it fun."

Cassy removed Treasure's halter. She stood with Cassy for a few seconds, and then wandered off to eat a little grass.

"Cassy, here are the rules to the game. Liberty isn't about obedience, but every game has rules, right?"

"Right–o." Cassy held out the halter. "What should I do with this?"

"Unsnap the lead line, and I'll take the halter. You keep the rope." Jennie reached for the halter.

"The first thing I want you to do is teach Treasure how to catch you instead of you catching Treasure. I guess that sounds strange, doesn't it?"

"Well, she'll always come up to me in the pasture, so she's catching me, right?"

"Yes, she's catching you. Right now she's eating grass, and we want her to catch you instead. She's wondering why she's in this small area separate from the ponies. She doesn't seem worried, but she's thinking, you can be sure."

Cassy was intrigued. "She's eating grass, but I can see her watching us while she's eating."

"Yes, good observation. So, she has two choices. She may move away from you, or come to you. She can't eat grass. To get her attention, swing the rope a little. Good. Since she's looking at you, invite her in by moving backwards, and use your hands to ask her to come toward you, like this, just like you were asking a person to come in your direction. Stay soft because she's being soft. Always match her energy."

Treasure took a few steps toward Cassy and then stopped. She didn't know this game.

"Ok, just for fun, send her away, swing your rope with your right hand, and use your left arm to point left, and ask her to move to the left at a trot. Good, that's it."

Treasure trotted away, with a toss of her head. She kept one eye on Cassy, but continued trotting until she made a complete circle of the play paddock, then she stopped and turned to face Cassy.

"Great! Invite her to come to you."

Cassy invited Treasure to come to her using the body language from Jennie's demo. Treasure walked to Cassy and waited. "Good girl, Treasure."

"That was really good. She's very connected to you. What I want you to do now is start walking and ask her to follow. If she doesn't, you can use body language to influence her and she'll do one of two things—leave you or stick with you. If she decides to stick with you, try to increase the challenge. Can she run with you, stop when you stop, turn when you turn? If she leaves you, keep her moving. She can't stop and eat grass. If she looks at you, invite her to join you again."

"I think I understand—Treasure can choose if she wants to stay with me or leave me, but if she leaves, she has to keep moving. If she looks at me, I invite her back, and then we can do some more fun things together."

Jennie nodded and smiled. "You catch on as quickly as your smart girl. Some days are easy, and then there will be days when she'll test the game. But always remember it's a game—a game that builds connection and you both get to test your communication."

"I love this. Can I try again?" Cassy stroked Treasure's neck and then walked, asking her to follow, which she did. But when Cassy started to run, Treasure trotted a few steps, squealed, and

took off running in the opposite direction. Cassy swung her rope, adding energy to Treasure's idea, and then she waited. After ten seconds, Treasure looked at Cassy while she continued to trot.

"Cassy, invite her in at the trot. You don't have to wait until she stops if she's looking for you," Jennie called.

Cassy invited her in and Treasure trotted directly to Cassy, stopping within touching distance, but she didn't invade Cassy's space.

"Perfect! Not bad for your first session." Jennie walked over to Cassy with the halter. "I think that's enough for today. Liberty can be mentally challenging for the horse—and you, too! Try to keep your play fresh and fun."

"Wow! That was fun! Thank you."

"First sessions don't usually go that well. You two are superstars." Jennie closed the temporary gate. "I don't think these three will bother the play paddock tonight. Well, all except maybe Riley. He's a curious pony." Jennie looked over at the handsome pony. "But then, he rarely lifts his head out of the grass."

Grayson Corners, South Carolina

Megan and Mary loaded the horses into the trailer for their trip to the state forest trails. Twinkle wasn't too happy at being left home all alone, but when she realized Mary was leaving the pasture gate open, she happily trotted into the grass for an unexpected day of grazing. Mary usually kept her in the smaller paddock during the day. She was weight challenged, or in horse owner lingo, an easy keeper. Twinkle thought grass was a little more interesting than carrying on about missing her pasture friends. She was old and wise, and understood they'd be back. She just wanted to raise a little fuss for Mary's benefit.

"Instead of parking at the usual trailer lot, Bobby and I have a friend with property bordering the state park. He lets me ride his trails, and I can also reach the equestrian trails on state land from his place. You may have noticed we're going in the general direction of the Double J."

"I thought so. I thought JJ's place was near the state park, but I didn't think he had access to the trails from his place. At least no one told me about it if he did."

"I don't think he does. I think our friend Toby's place is between the Double J and the state park." Mary pulled into a drive and continued past a large barn and riding arena.

"Wow, nice place! What does your friend do?" Megan was impressed.

"Well, he's a lawyer by day, and loves to compete in endurance on weekends. He's the one who started me down that trail, so to speak. Good guy and college friend of Bobby's."

"Does he know JJ?" Megan wasn't sure why that mattered but asked anyway.

"Yes, and let's just say, JJ wouldn't be welcome to cross this property to have access to the state park."

"Enough said. I noticed that the neighbors on the other side of the Double J weren't friendly with him, either. For a man who has bluffed his way into a devoted following, he sure isn't liked much by his neighbors. I can't believe he fooled me."

"JJ can be quite entertaining, but he can't bluff his way all the time. People down here have seen the real man and they don't like him much." Mary parked the trailer behind the barn.

"Hey, Mary, that's a cool sign on the barn. Is it one of yours?" Megan pointed to the barn.

"Yes, Toby was one of my first customers."

Megan and Mary pulled their saddles and bridles out of the trailer tack compartment, then unloaded the horses. As Megan saddled Julep, she felt herself getting a little emotional. It would be the first ride on Julep since her return from the dead.

Mary was saddled and up on Windward, waiting for Megan to mount.

"Sorry, I was having an emotional moment."

"It's ok, kid, I understand. Julep and I spent some time together and she's lovely."

"Thanks. She's taught me a lot." Megan used Mary's little stool to mount. "I usually use a stool, too. I think it's better for their backs."

Mary nodded her head in the affirmative. "I agree. Out on the trail if I can't find a log I can mount from the ground, no problem. But I use a mounting block or stool if one is available."

It was a beautiful morning, not too warm. They followed the trail into a small woods still on Toby's property. Megan realized where they were heading the same direction as the backside of the Double J.

"Are you taking me here on purpose?" Megan called.

"I was thinking the wooded area you described must be near Toby's property line and I thought maybe we could spy a little." They were getting closer and Mary was whispering.

Megan asked Julep to move up beside Mary and Windward. "Do you think we'll find anything?"

"No, I don't think so. Bobby checked around and he couldn't find anyone else who lost a horse like you did. Several sold or gave their horses to JJ, and they were sold at the auction, but none just came up missing."

"He wanted me to sell Julep. He said he would find her a good home. I just want to rip him apart. The cheat," Megan spit out the words.

"Well, he is a cheat and a creep, but we can't find any evidence that he's a horse thief."

"He didn't need to be because he took horses given to him and promised to find good homes," then she added, "that makes him a liar, too, then." Megan was sure she could add a bunch of other descriptive words to JJ's résumé.

"Hey, right there, see those trees? That's where I found the rope." Megan pointed as she stood up in her saddle stirrups. And saw nothing.

Chapter Thirty-Three

Appleridge, Ohio

*J*ennie wasn't supposed to look at her phone while she was working, but since there were no patrons at the circulation desk, she stepped back into a small office to remove her phone from her pocket to take a peek. It was from Kyiko.

2 hours out C U soon

Before putting her phone away, she looked at the time. She had one more hour before she could leave, and it was going to be a very slow hour.

Two staff members sat on stools and chatted between assisting the patrons. Jennie was happy shelving books and the hour passed quickly. Five minutes after her shift ended, she grabbed her purse and drove straight to the farm. She didn't need to make any stops. She was ready with borrowed air mattresses, sheets, and pillows from her sisters and mom. Kate and Kyiko liked to eat simple things so she didn't plan any dinners, except for the cookout.

Jennie quickly changed clothes and ran out to the barn to check on the horses. All three were standing in the shade of the overhang dozing. Riley raised his head and nickered as she approached.

"Yes, Sir Riley, a few flakes of hay coming right up."

Jennie also checked their water and added fresh. With those simple chores finished, she walked back to the house to wait on the back porch with a glass of ice tea. Sitting quietly only lasted a few minutes. Restless, she walked to the mailbox. Not much today, except a few sale flyers for the recycling bin. She thought junk mail was certainly better than unexpected bills, and congratulated herself on being so positive about receiving junk mail.

A small blue compact car drove slowly down her road. She had forgotten to ask Kate about their rental car, but a honking horn confirmed it was them. The car pulled into her drive and Kate rolled down her window.

"I can't believe you're here!" Jennie hunched down so she could see Kyiko in the passenger seat."

Both talked at the same time. "It's so good to see you...we had so much fun driving here...do you like our car? Where should we park? Kate drove the entire way...I don't have a license. It was scary getting out of Chicago, but then ok...we stopped at a roadside rest for a picnic...wait until you see what Mrs. Samuelson packed for us and for you."

Jennie started jogging up her drive and then motioned for Kate to pull the car beside Blue Boy.

"Is that your truck, Jennie?" Kate was out of the car and stretching her arms overhead.

"Yup, I'm a farm girl, and a farm girl needs a truck." Jennie put her fingers on her chest pretending they were under suspenders.

All three ran together into a big three-person hug.

Jennie stepped back. "I miss you guys, I want to hear all about everything you've done this summer."

"We've been doing a lot of dancing." Kate looked at Kyiko. "And we both needed some extra cash so Mrs. Samuelson schedules us for a few hours at the deli each week."

"That's funny. Well, not funny that you need extra cash, but funny you're working at the deli."

"We like working at the deli. They take good care of us." Kyiko pulled a cooler out of the backseat. "And I have the goodies as proof."

Jennie looked at the cooler. "Wow, I love them!"

With arms full, all three went into the house. They didn't stop until they climbed the stairs and could dump the luggage on the floor in the extra room.

"I apologize for making you sleep on air mattresses. I think I have a lead on a bed, though. My sister, Sallie, has a friend who's getting a divorce, and moving from her house into an apartment. She may give me a bed and a few other things."

"Good for you, but bad for her, I guess." Kate looked around. "But don't worry, this is good."

"Meow."

"Oh, there's our Beauty. How are you, sweet kitty?" Kyiko sat down on the floor and Beauty climbed into her lap.

"Now don't you put your claws into our air beds, Miss Beauty, or we may need to have a discussion." Kate reached down to give her a scratch under the chin.

"That's why we'll keep the door closed." Jennie picked up Beauty.

The three walked back downstairs to get a few more things from the car.

"Do you want me to empty the cooler?" Jennie opened the lid.

"Ha, ha, you can't wait to see what Mrs. Samuelson sent. Go ahead; Kyiko and I only have a few more things to carry in. It's great traveling by car, because you don't have to squeeze all your stuff into one bag. I don't think our boots would fit in the same bag as our clothes. Hey, wait until you see our boots."

Mrs. Samuelson had included all of her favorites—potato salad, deli pickles, sliced salami, an assortment of cheese, and my, oh my, even her favorite tuna salad. She would find something nice to mail to the Samuelsons as a little thank you. Maybe some Ohio maple syrup or something made locally.

Kate and Kyiko returned, and both were wearing cowboy boots with their shorts.

"You're styling!" Jennie loved the boots. Kate's were pink and Kyiko's were red.

"Horses! We want to meet the horses," they pleaded in unison.

"Ok, cowgirls, let your lessons begin." And with that, Jennie slid her feet into her own boots, and led the journey to the barn.

Grayson Corners, South Carolina

Megan absolutely loved staying with the Grays and riding with Mary. They saw nothing unusual at the Double J when they checked again yesterday, so they wouldn't waste their time spying. Whatever the corral was used for, it wasn't being used right now. Megan had trouble thinking she didn't sense Julep was still on the property when she returned to the ranch. She wondered if they purposely assigned extra chores to keep her busy. She remembered she didn't get a chance to ride those few days.

Both Mary and Megan suspected that Pete and Jeff aka Repeat used the rope corral to hide Julep until they took her to the horse auction. So far they had nothing to link JJ or anyone else to her disappearance. At least not enough to get an arrest, let alone a conviction. Even if convicted, the punishment wouldn't be much.

Today, they took the short trail from Toby's into the state park. Megan followed Mary at a fast trot. They flew down a fun

trail that led down to a creek where they stopped to give the horses an opportunity for a nice drink.

Megan had ridden more in the five days with Mary than during her whole time at the ranch. Being a Double J ranch hand, or working as a roadie, didn't allow much time for riding. Strange, thought Megan, especially since the internship was sold as an opportunity to improve her riding and horsemanship skills.

Riding together gave them a chance to talk, and Megan found Mary to be a good listener. She still didn't know what she wanted to do after she left South Carolina, but Mary shared a few observations that helped. She told Megan to stop beating herself up about her decision to spend the summer with JJ.

"Hey, I need to work on a few signs tonight. Are you interested in giving me a hand?"

"I'd love to, thanks." Megan was eager to help out. "Hey, Mary, do you think I could try to paint a sign for Jennie's farm?"

"That would be a great project, and maybe you could do some stall signs to match."

Mary was aware of the Jennie and Julep story.

"When you get back home, are you going to keep Julep or give her to Jennie?" Mary was trying to figure out if Megan felt any obligation to give up Julep.

"Mom and Dad don't want to have horses again. If Julep went to Jennie's, I could see her whenever I wanted."

Mary felt she needed to pursue this more. "Do you think that would work out—I mean for you and Jennie to share?"

"Well, I think so. Jennie is a good person and she would take good care of her. Julep is getting older. She'll be sixteen this year."

"That isn't old and she's in great shape." Mary didn't understand Megan's reference to Julep's age.

"I know, but I'm thinking that after this year, and then my four years in college, Julep will be twenty-one, and it wouldn't fair to ask her to do whatever I decide to do when I get back into horses. I love competition. I love to have goals. That's why the opportunity with JJ appealed to me." Megan sighed. "I wanted to learn from a master. I just didn't know he was a master liar."

"Don't you go and start blaming yourself again. JJ owns whatever he's up to, not you. You came in good faith." If there was one thing she accomplished before Megan left, Mary prayed that she would help her work through the JJ garbage.

"Jennie doesn't even know Julep is alive. Dad wants to keep it a secret until he picks us up. That seems sort of mean."

"Like Bobby said last night, your dad doesn't want JJ to know because he's going to use losing Julep as a bargaining tool. Bobby still hopes someone will slip up, and say or do something revealing. I don't think so, do you? I think maybe somehow Julep got mixed up in the rest of the group going to the auction, and after they cut her mane and tail they panicked, and hid her with a few other horses, and made up the whole story."

"If it was Pete and Repeat, I think you're right. They're not the sharpest crayons in the box." Megan wanted them to pay for what they did to her and Julep.

"They're doing something illegal, that's for sure. Bobby has a sheriff friend checking them out. If they're stealing manes and tails, or doing anything else, they'll get caught eventually."

"They didn't think twice about sending my horse to slaughter? What kind of person does something like that, Mary? What's wrong with people?" She guessed the cheats didn't lose much sleep over the things they did.

"I'm not sure. I'll never understand people like that, either." Mary shook her head.

"Hey, let's pick up a trot, and when we get to that straight stretch, let's give them their heads for a nice gallop."

Mary took off at a good trot, and Megan and Julep followed.

Oh boy, thought Megan, *Mary and Windward could fly. Hang on tight, Julep, hang on, girl.*

AFTER MEGAN'S favorite supper of hamburgers and fresh corn on the grill, she sat with Mary and Bobby on the back porch, watching the horses graze and the sun slip behind the trees.

"I talked to your dad today. He wanted to know if he should pick you up this weekend or if you could stay until he takes your sister to Florida next week. I told him to wait. Is that good with you?" Bobby stretched his legs, careful not to bother their dog, Rainy, lying at his feet.

"That's fine, I mean as long as I'm not wearing out my welcome." Megan hoped not because she wanted to stay.

"Ha, I told him we started our own internship program here, and Mary is making you work."

"Megan painted a sign background today so I guess that's true. It's great having unpaid staff."

"I'm such a bargain! You aren't even charging room and board. At least I don't think so, anyway." Megan thought maybe she should give them something to cover her stay.

"No worries, your dad already offered. I just told him he could repay the favor when we plan a trip to Ohio."

"You'd like Ohio. I like South Carolina, but Ohio is a little cooler in the summer. I'm not real crazy about the winter, though."

"Well, then, you'll just have to spend the winter with us. Right, Bobby?" Mary teased them both.

"My sister, Belinda, is going to vet school at the University of Florida. She doesn't like cold weather, either. And, contrary to what Dad may think, we may never get her back in Ohio again."

"That's my school and a good choice." Bobby made a gator chomping motion with his arms.

Megan and Mary laughed at Bobby being silly.

"Anyway, your dad has been trying to get JJ to take his calls. I'm going out to the Double J tomorrow for some routine work, and I'm going to nicely suggest JJ return his calls. I'm not sure what I'm going to say, exactly, but I'll think of something all friendly-like."

"Good luck. I saw a side of JJ that wasn't so friendly-like when I crossed him. My dad won't put up with his attitude, but I don't know what my dad will do, other than threaten him, and Dad's too smart for that—I think." Megan prayed her dad would find satisfaction over the phone. She didn't want him to confront JJ in person.

Mary spoke up, "Well, not allowing you to finish your internship is grounds to get some of your money back, unless there's a non-refundable clause."

"I don't remember signing anything. It's not about the money, though. I guess it's more about Dad making some sort of point."

"Well, my money's on Adrian." Bobby stretched out again. "And I think the most valuable commodity JJ has right now is his reputation, and he won't want any of this stuff to hit Facebook."

"Funny when you think about it, his reputation, I mean. It's not his reputation he needs to worry about. It's the truth he needs to hide." Mary was sitting in a porch rocking chair, and the more she talked about JJ, the harder she rocked.

Bobby answered, "I didn't say he needed to protect his good reputation."

Megan also rocked. She loved listening to Mary and Bobby. She also loved hearing the respect for her dad in their voices.

"Hey, what do you two have planned for tomorrow while I'm slaving away at the Double J doing things I'm never going to get paid for? Wow, I guess I'm one of JJ's unpaid interns, too." Bobby frowned.

"Megan and I have perfected our routine. We ride in the morning and paint in the afternoon." Mary's rocking was calmer now. "Right, Megan?"

"Right. And I'm also trying to figure out what I'm going to do for the rest of my life."

"One day at a time. Take one day at a time." With that all three got up and walked into the dark house.

Chapter Thirty-Four

Appleridge, Ohio

Adrian finished his last client for the day and dialed JJ's number again. He would call every day until the man had the decency to answer or return his call. This time, he wasn't paying attention, because he didn't expect JJ to answer. He was waiting for the message to play so he could leave another voice mail message.

"What do you want?"

"JJ, is that you? I thought maybe you were on the run." Adrian jabbed.

"And what is that supposed to mean, Dr. Peterson?" JJ wasn't pretending to be friendly.

"Whatever you want it to mean. I can keep this conversation civil, if you can." Adrian just couldn't resist. He could hear his wife, Susan, scolding him now.

"Of course, I have no reason not to be civil. Now, whatever is so important that you feel the need to harass me with your daily calls? I'm sure Megan told you why her internship ended. She chose not to stay for an apprenticeship, so there wasn't any reason for her to continue her internship. I think that's all the explanation you need."

"Well, JJ, I need more. We paid for an entire summer and so I believe a refund for the last few weeks is fair. And then, there is the issue of Julep. I need a better explanation of what happened than what I got from Julie." Adrian closed his office door to prepare for battle.

"The loss of Julep was unfortunate, but we are not liable. We are not responsible for Julep's unfortunate demise, and we don't give refunds for interns who leave early." JJ's voice was firm, but Adrian noticed a little doubt and he was going to jump on it quickly.

"Megan didn't voluntarily leave the program. You sent her away, and the loss of Julep was a little bit more than unfortunate. Your staff didn't call a vet, they didn't notify me or Megan immediately, and Julep was buried on your property without our consent. There are a lot of things that were wrong with the entire situation, but I've just named a few."

"Oh, come on, Dr. Peterson, you can't mean the boys should have left Julep lying there all night, or until Megan got back to the ranch." JJ gave a strained-sounding chuckle.

"They should have called the vet clinic, and then called us to make a decision. It wouldn't have taken all night." It was time to end this silly conversation and move on to the truth. "But actually, JJ, I'm going to lay a little truth on you, so you can make a better-informed decision. My friend and colleague, Dr. Gray, happened to scan a few horses for micro-chips at the last auction, and he scanned a certain little bay mare with a chip that's registered to a Miss Megan Peterson." Adrian heard JJ suck in his breath. "I wonder how she got out of the grave and found her way to that auction."

"I had nothing to do with anything. I was out of town." JJ was scrambling.

"Yes, I know you were out of town, and I also know that a load of horses went to the auction from your ranch, and some were sold without reserves—to kill buyers." Adrian could practically hear the wheels turning in JJ's head.

"Maybe you don't know what happened to Julep, but maybe you should ask your boys why they lied, because you're responsible whether you like it or not. And furthermore, you're in the business of buying and selling horses, and you don't seem to care where they end up in the process." Adrian was struggling to keep his voice clear of emotion.

"I don't know what you think you know, but I don't deal in the killer trade. There's nothing wrong with buying and selling horses." JJ didn't sound so confident.

"You may not deal directly with kill brokers, but you don't put a reserve on the horses you sell and you don't seem to care if they go for meat prices. I'm not so sure those are the actions of a horse lover. Somehow it doesn't fit the image you present to your adoring fans. I sure would hate for this story to ruin your stellar reputation."

"Are you threatening me, Dr. Peterson?"

"Nope, just saying the truth can be very revealing." Adrian sensed that JJ would now be willing to deal.

"I think we can come to some sort of arrangement about a refund. It won't be much." JJ was trying to give the appearance of control.

"Well, actually, JJ, I was thinking more like the entire amount refunded. That money was part of Megan's college fund, and since she isn't going to pursue a career in your organization, she'll need the money to start college. I know you won't want to quibble over the amount of a refund, especially since we still have the fraud concerning Julep to discuss." Adrian was beginning to enjoy the conversation. And he especially enjoyed emphasizing JJ in a condescending voice.

"I'll have Julie issue a refund. It will be worth it just to get rid of your daily calls. But like I already said, I don't have any

information about Julep, and anyway, if she was found you don't have a leg to stand on if you think you're going to get anything more out of me." JJ was trying his best to save face.

"Now, JJ, you're responsible for what happens on your ranch, whether you're there or not. And, I'm going to guess you need current and future students to believe their horses are safe on your ranch. You sure wouldn't want them to think their horses could just disappear off the Double J when you aren't there. No, that wouldn't be good. When you give this some more thought, I'm sure you'll agree."

"What do you want?" JJ asked with defeat.

"I heard that another load of horses ended up at your ranch and Megan was assigned to a certain mare named Starlight. Now, JJ, I sure would hate for Starlight to disappear, or worse, end up at the auction. That just wouldn't be right. I think you'll agree that maybe Starlight should find a nice home with Megan. I mean you did put my daughter through a lot this summer, and I don't take kindly to anyone who hurts my daughter. Of course, if you were to show some concern for her, and wanted to help her feel better about this experience, we could put this unfortunate situation behind us both and move on."

A few moments of silence then JJ exhaled a deep breath. "Ok, fine. I would love to gift Starlight to Megan." The words were correct, the sound of JJ's voice wasn't, but Adrian didn't care.

JJ couldn't resist adding, "That mare isn't much anyway, and I wouldn't mind getting all the trash off my ranch."

"Well, I've heard one man's trash is another man's treasure. Maybe you should keep cleaning. You've probably buried a lot of trash on the Double J."

Adrian pressed the off button on his phone thinking good riddance to bad rubbish. Now all he had to do was get Starlight off the ranch. He was going to be in so deep with Bobby that he would never be able to repay him for his help. Adrian hated to be indebted to anyone, but he was humble enough to know that, without Bobby, this situation would have gone from bad to worse to unbelievable. Susan was always telling him that he needed to value help from friends, and not to perceive it as weakness on his part. She was a wise woman. He loved her, but didn't appreciate her enough. He couldn't wait to share the conversation he had with JJ, and break the news they were in the horse business again. But first, he needed to call Bobby and ask for his help one more time.

Chapter Thirty-Five

Appleridge, Ohio

ennie sat down on a bench in the barn aisle. "I'm pooped. You guys are wearing me out."

"What's the matter, have you gotten a little soft on us?" Kyiko was still full of energy. "May we go out to the pasture and get the ponies, Marcy?"

"You two are pooping me out, too!" Marcy motioned to the pasture. "Go ahead, you and Kate can groom them, and then maybe we'll hitch up Riley and give each of you a driving lesson."

"That would be awesome. I'll go get Kate. I think she's just sitting out there in the pasture with Treasure and the ponies." Kyiko ran out of the barn.

"They can't get enough, can they?" Marcy motioned for Jennie to scoot over, giving her a place to sit.

"Thanks so much for sharing your ponies." Jennie was sincere.

"Well, you can thank me by helping to remove the pole on my carriage, so I can drive Riley as a single." Marcy got up and motioned for Jennie to follow.

It had been quite a week. Kyiko and Kate spent every day with Treasure and the ponies. Cassy demonstrated playing with Treasure at liberty, and then Kyiko played with Riley while Kate played with Stuffin. Marcy impressed Jennie by playing with both ponies at the same time. Cassy rode Treasure while Kate and Kyiko danced, using the horse's movements to create their own. Thursday evening, Marcy drove the ponies as a pair, giving Kate and Kyiko rides on the back of the carriage. They took turns jumping off the carriage in a little dance and jumping back on as Marcy passed. Jennie caught most of it on video, and she was sure the directors of the Horses in Dance workshop would find it intriguing.

Even Jeremy enjoyed some good pony time with the ladies, and took a turn handling the reins of the pair. Marcy thought he did well, especially since he had never driven a single, let alone a pair. She teased Jennie later, saying, "That boy has good hands."

Today Cassy gave both Kyiko and Kate a lesson, as they took turns riding Treasure, and then Cassy did a demo riding Treasure in the pasture, taking all of the log jumps. Cassy was not only a beautiful rider, but seemed to have a natural gift to teach. No wonder she chose elementary education as her major.

Having made the adjustments needed on the carriage, Jennie and Marcy rolled it into the barn aisle and harnessed Riley.

"Do you also drive Stuffin as a single pony?" asked Kate.

"Sometimes, but I thought Riley would be the better teacher today. Stuffin has been moving a little stiff, I want to keep an eye on her and give her some time off." Marcy loved her ponies.

The lessons went well accompanied by a lot of laughter.

"It's much harder than it looks, isn't it?" Jennie asked her friends.

Kyiko was the first to respond, "It sure is, but I love it."

"I was scared but Marcy said she wouldn't let anything happen." Kate wasn't quite as enthusiastic.

Jennie helped Marcy unhitch Riley and rolled the carriage back into her trailer, while Kate and Kyiko gave him a quick bath. With everyone helping, they fed all three equines and returned

them to the pasture for a well-deserved night of grazing. The girls were invited to the McKenzies' house for dinner.

"Well, we better start the shower rotations for us humans. Marcy, are you joining us at Mom and Dad's?" Jennie hoped so.

"Yes, thanks, I'll go home to shower and change, and meet you there around six. Was that the time?"

"Yup, see you then. Come casual and comfortable, and bring your appetite. My mom always cooks enough to feed an entire army." Jennie was looking forward to the meal. Mom was making her famous meatloaf and garlic smashed potatoes.

Grayson Corners, South Carolina

Bobby had one more farm call but he needed to stop at home first. After an interesting conversation with Adrian last evening, he needed to bring the horse trailer on this farm visit. It would be hitched and waiting, because he asked Mary to keep it hitched when she and Megan returned from their morning ride.

"Hey, someone just left with the truck and trailer." Megan got up to look out the window.

"It's Bobby. Sometimes he takes it on a farm call." Mary hoped Megan didn't ask why. She didn't. Instead she went back to the sign she was painting for Jennie.

"It looks great. *Fawn Song Farm*, I bet that name has a story."

"It does, but I don't remember the story, I just remember it has something to do with Jennie's grandpa. It was his farm and I think his father's farm." Megan finished and started to close up the paint.

"I just want to tell you this week has been the best week of my summer, maybe my whole year." Megan wanted Mary to know how she felt.

"Oh, sweetie, I've had a GREAT week, too. They both laughed when Mary emphasized the great. Maybe you could come down for a few weeks next summer. I'll make you work for your room and board. I may even hire you as my helper. I get busy in the summer, and the projects are always big projects."

"I'd love that. I think I'm getting the hang of all this, and I'll even paint the whole barn." Megan couldn't believe she made that promise. But she would paint a barn to help Mary.

"Now that you bring it up, we have a barn project next week that will require us to paint the entire side of the barn for an advertisement. I tried to get someone else to do the preparation, so I would only need to paint the design, but that didn't work out." Mary stepped back to look at her work.

"I'm game—I painted our barn one summer." Megan didn't like the job, but she thought working with Mary would be different.

"Too bad school is starting soon, or I would try to keep you for a while." Mary loved having Megan's help and a good riding buddy to boot.

They continued to work until they heard the truck and trailer return and pull alongside the barn.

"Hey, let's go down and see if Bobby needs any help."

Megan thought that was strange, because Bobby never seemed to need help, but she put her brush in a glass of water, and got up to follow Mary who was already halfway down the stairs.

"Well, hello ladies, you're just in time to see what I found today." Bobby opened the trailer door to untie a horse—a horse that looked familiar—a horse with a chestnut face and a white star on the forehead.

"Starlight, my sweet girl; how did you get Starlight?"

"I'm just the delivery man. Your dad had a nice conversation with JJ last night, and funny, he couldn't wait to get Starlight on my trailer today, and he couldn't have been more pleasant about it, at least with me." Bobby loved telling the story.

"According to your dad, he wasn't so pleasant last night, but since I'm the local vet, he needs to keep up his charismatic horse whisperer routine."

"Did Dad buy her?" Megan vowed to never doubt her dad again.

"JJ felt it his duty to gift her to you for all your pain and disappointment." Bobby's attempt to look serious failed.

"It was all I could do to play along, thanking him for his generosity and compassion, knowing all along that your dad held his boots to the fire."

"You mean he doesn't know I have Julep?" Megan asked.

"Oh, he knows now. Your dad mentioned it last night. JJ acted like he knew nothing today. I don't think he realizes that your dad and I are in cahoots." Bobby untied Starlight as Mary and Megan opened the back trailer doors and pulled down the ramp.

Mary hadn't said much as she stood watching the mare back off the trailer. "Wow, Megan, she's nice! What will you do with her?"

"I'm not sure, but we just seemed to connect. I think she has a lot of potential." Megan stepped up to hold her hand out for Starlight to sniff. "Hey, sweetie, I missed you."

"Yes, I totally understand." Mary motioned to the barn paddock. "Let's put her in the paddock so she can have a little meet and greet with the others before we turn them all out together."

"She'll have to get Twinkle's permission before she joins the herd." Twinkle was small but ruled the herd.

"She was toward the bottom of the pecking order at the Double J, so I don't think she'll challenge Twinkle or the others. She'll mind her own business until she gets invited, but I like your idea about letting them meet over the fence."

"Or in Twinkle's case, between the boards of the fence," Mary said as she pointed to the fence where Twinkle already had her head between the top and middle boards.

"My, oh my, the herd on this farm just doubled in a week's time, and here you promised me we would stick with two." Bobby put his arm around Mary. Starlight and Julep would leave, but he couldn't resist teasing Mary about her desire to have more horses.

"You just watch out, Bobby, or I'll ask Twinkle to teach you a lesson or two." Mary walked over to give Twinkle an affection stroke on her neck.

"How soon you forget that I have been a recipient of a few of Miss Twinkle's lessons."

"Ha, yes, you have. And here is a lesson review for you. I'm hungry and what happens when I'm hungry and have nothing prepared for supper?"

"That's easy. We go out for supper or call for a pizza." Bobby grinned like a brilliant student.

Pizza, they all agreed.

Chapter Thirty-Six

Appleridge, Ohio

Kate and Kyiko straightened up the kitchen, and then went outside to do a few more chores. Jennie was at work and they promised to help get ready for the campfire. They also wanted to surprise Jennie with a few ideas of their own, and enlisted Jennie's mom, Ellen, to help.

"Ok, I think that's everything on Jennie's list." Kyiko held out the list for Kate to review.

"Clean and move the tables and chairs, check. Sweep the porch, check. Carry wood from the wood stack to the campfire ring, check. Sweep the barn aisle, check. That's it and I'm tired."

"Me, too, but this is fun." Kyiko had never lived anywhere but in a large city.

"Let's get ourselves cleaned up. Mrs. McKenzie will be here in twenty minutes, and we won't have much time to shop and get back here before Jennie gets home." Kate ran into the house. "I'm in the bathroom first, ha–ha."

"You're rotten. You do know that, I know you do." Kyiko pretended to pout.

"I know, I may be rotten, but I'm quicker than you in the bathroom."

Both girls were still getting ready when Mrs. McKenzie opened the back door. "Hello, I'm here."

Kate finished brushing her hair as she walked to the kitchen. "We're almost ready. Jennie gave us a list of things to do this morning."

"That's Jennie, always busy, always planning. Have you been the victims of the dreaded lists?" Ellen asked.

"Yes, but we usually ignored her lists when we lived together." Kyiko walked into the room.

"So you girls want to go shopping. What are we shopping for?" Ellen couldn't imagine.

Kate looked at Kyiko and shared, "We thought it would be fun to make a little lighted path out to the campfire, and we saw this idea on Pinterest to use canning jars with candles."

Kyiko chimed in, "So we need to go shopping for jars and candles."

Ellen smiled at both. "We'll go shopping at my house first. I have a ton of canning jars in my basement that I doubt will see much use this year. You can have as many as you need. Then, we can go to the little local discount store for candles. Are you thinking the small votive candles?"

"I'm not sure what they're called but they're about this big." Kate demonstrated the size with her fingers. "They're sort of stubby."

"That's a votive candle and you won't need the candles to have a fragrance so you can get the cheap ones." Ellen never spent money unnecessarily.

The three climbed into Ellen's Enclave and drove into Appleridge. I'm starved, so how about my treat at The Café before we shop?"

"That sounds good—we're hungry, too." Kate and Kyiko tag teamed.

The Café was usually busy on Saturdays, but they managed to find a small table near the back of the restaurant. The Café served mostly soups and sandwiches, and all three ordered tomato soup and grilled cheese.

"Well, living with Jennie must have rubbed off on you two since you ordered grilled cheese and tomato soup."

"She used to make it for us on Saturdays, when we were all home doing nothing much but being lazy and watching movies," Kyiko shared.

Kate added, "It was usually in the winter when she didn't have to work at the deli all day. She would work the breakfast crowd and then get home in time to make us lunch. Some days, she brought homemade soup from the deli. Mrs. Samuelson makes a tasty soup."

Kyiko stopped slurping her soup. "This soup is delicious, though."

"Hey, there's Belinda." Kyiko stood up and waved as Belinda walked into The Café. Belinda saw them, and walked over to their table.

"Well, what are you three up to without Jennie in tow?" Belinda thought they were definitely up to something.

"Jennie is working, and I'm helping her friends complete their mission." Ellen confessed.

"Hey, sit down and join us." Kate moved her chair to give Belinda room at their table.

"I would love to, but I'm working. I'm the lowest person on the food chain at Dad's clinic and I'm the lunch messenger. It's my last day working before I leave for Florida. You would think I'd be the one getting special treatment, instead of being the minion." Belinda couldn't resist the poor-little-me act. "I guess I shouldn't complain since Dad's treating the whole staff to lunch."

"I would guess that's your dad's way of making today special." Adrian was a good guy but not real sentimental. Even so, Ellen thought buying lunch was his way of making it a special day. "He may not show it, but he is proud of both his girls."

"I suppose. Hey, it looks like my order is ready. I'll see all of you tonight. It should be fun." Belinda picked up several large bags containing the lunch order, and somehow managed to get them out the door and to her truck.

"I like Belinda. She came over to Jennie's on Thursday morning to meet us and play with the horses, and then she took us to the movie and dinner while Jennie worked at the library," Kate explained to Ellen.

"She's funny, and it's especially funny to hear her and Jennie together." Kyiko grinned. "Almost like Kate and I are sometimes. Right, Kate?"

"Yup, we have fun BFF, especially when we're on a road trip, and we hit the road again tomorrow. Watch out, Pennsylvania, here we come!"

The ladies finished lunch, and walked down a few blocks to the discount store where they found candles, a couple of butane lighters long enough to reach into the jars, and a few other things they needed for their trip on Sunday.

"A few snacks for the road?" asked Ellen as she eyed the red licorice, snack crackers, and candy bars in the basket.

"Just a few," answered Kyiko with a grin. "I think we've worked hard enough down on the farm to afford the calories."

As they left the store to walk back to the car, Kate thanked Ellen. "Thank you so much for lunch and giving us a ride to the store, and thanks for the canning jars."

"You're very welcome." Ellen unlocked the doors. "Sadly, even in little Appleridge it's a good idea to lock your car doors. You just never know."

BACK at the farm, Ellen helped the girls carry the boxes of jars to the back porch, and then returned to her car. "I'll see you tonight."

Kate and Kyiko grabbed a roll of paper towels, and started cleaning the jars. They were only a little dusty so they only needed a quick swipe. Then they went to the barn to get the garden wagon. It wasn't on Jennie's list, but she mentioned that if it was clean, it would work great to carry things back and forth from the house to the campfire.

Kate and Kyiko sprayed the wagon with the hose, and dried it with the used paper towels. Then they loaded it with the boxes of jars and candles stopping every five feet or so to place a jar holding a candle. They had enough to create a little path. It would look great once the candles were lit.

Pleased with their work, they hid the empty boxes in the basement, parked the now-clean wagon near the back door, grabbed a Coke, and sat on the porch waiting for Jennie to come home from work. This farm life was sure busy. They were as tired as if they had danced for hours. Maybe they were finally running out of steam.

Jennie was delighted with everything Kate and Kyiko accomplished while she was at work.

"Wow, I love the luminaries! What a great idea using canning jars." Jennie followed the luminary path to the campfire ring. "Awesome! You already have the chairs and tables set up. You guys rock."

"Thanks Jennie; your mom gave us the jars. What did you call them?" Kyiko was interested.

"They're called luminaries. Usually they're made from small paper bags with sand in the bottom to hold them down, and the same type of candle. But the jar idea is great—and reusable."

"Oh, yeah, our church always sets luminaries out on Christmas Eve at home. I had forgotten that was what they're called. Go figure the writer in our group would use the correct word." Kate always loved seeing the candles lit.

"Well, thank you for making them. And, thank you, thank you, and thank you, for doing all the work. Now I can just enjoy tonight."

The three friends talked as they walked to the house.

"All we need to do this afternoon is feed the horses, and at dusk light the candles, and haul the food out to the campfire." Kate sat down on the porch steps and motioned for Kyiko and Jennie to join her. "But first, let's take a break. I'm tired."

As Kyiko squeezed past Kate to find a comfortable porch chair, Jennie asked, "Are you excited about the dance workshop? It sounds like a great opportunity."

"I am—I've been looking for performance opportunities in Chicago, but I'm not getting any call backs. Hopefully, I'll make a few good contacts at the workshop. I also hope to share some of the video we took this week, because the director of the workshop is merging two of her passions: horses and dance. She's a former equestrian and now an accomplished dancer with her own small dance company.

"I'm excited to do something so unique, but I'm mostly along for the ride, and to support Kyiko. If Kyiko gets asked to stay longer, and I hope you do, Kyiko, I'll fly back to Chicago. I start my dance therapy grad program two weeks from Monday." Kate glanced at Kyiko to confirm her thoughts.

Jennie wanted to encourage her talented friends. "Kyiko, you're a beautiful dancer and talented choreographer, and I think the video we took here at the farm turned out impressive.

I had no idea Jeremy was so talented with media. He created a neat presentation out of all the video and shots we took."

"Thanks for the pep talk, friend. By the way, Jeremy's a good guy, Jennie, but I've never heard you mention him. Is he a new friend?" Kyiko asked.

"I guess he's a reconnected friend. I wasn't very nice to him when we were young and in 4–H together, but he doesn't seem to hold a grudge." She smiled.

"Are you in love with him?" Kate couldn't resist asking.

"I don't know if I'm in love, but I'm very much in LIKE." Jennie emphasized the word like. "Ok, enough talk, we have horses to feed and it's already five-thirty. Then we need to get ourselves cleaned up, light the campfire, light candles, then gather the food and stuff..."

"Ok, ok, wow, what a taskmaster!" Kyiko pretended to complain. "What will you do without us?"

"I'm going to be very lonely." Jennie stopped smiling. "You guys leave tomorrow, Belinda leaves on Monday, Jeremy starts Seminary, and Cassy is picking up a larger load of classes for fall semester. I'm making myself depressed." And she was.

"We've been looking forward to this campfire all week. Don't get all weepy on us now." Kyiko pulled Jennie toward the barn. "Let's spend some time with the ponies. That always makes you smile."

THEY FED, then swept the barn aisle again. Treasure and the ponies eagerly followed Jennie to the pasture gate. The ponies scampered out as soon as it opened. Treasure followed at a leisurely walk.

"Enjoy your early release," Jennie called to the herd, although it was only a little earlier than normal.

The three girls rushed back to the house to change into clean shorts. Since they would smell like smoke by evening's end, they wouldn't wear anything too fancy.

Grayson Corners, South Carolina

Megan climbed down from the ladder and placed her paint-brush in the tray.

"How's that look, Mary?"

"It looks good. Thanks so much for helping me get this done. Now we'll be able to start the design on Monday."

Mary picked up both brushes and walked over to the hose.

"Let's get this mess cleaned up and back to the farm. I know I promised we could take a short ride at the state park this after-noon, but I think I'm too tired." Mary stretched, and then leaned over to start rinsing the brushes. "Go ahead and pour all the left-over paint into the big bucket."

Megan carried the two smaller pails over to the five-gallon bucket, poured in the paint, wiped the top of the bucket, and sealed the lid.

"That's ok, I'm tired, too. I think I'll just groom both Julep and Starlight, and maybe play a little at liberty."

"I'll pull up my chair and watch." Mary put all the tools into a box and carried it to her truck.

"I'll need two showers today, if that's ok." Megan joked but she was also serious. "I need one shower to get all this paint off, and another one after I spend time with my mares."

"Our well is deep so shower away." Then Mary added, "Two showers a day happens a lot around here."

They drove to the farm in silence. They were a lot more tired than they thought. It took the last bit of their energy to carry the painting supplies up to Mary's studio.

Mary retreated to her room for a nap, and Megan decided to do the same. Bobby found them both snoring away when he returned from an emergency. He lit the grill. His stomach voted for hamburgers. Just as he stepped back from throwing the match on the charcoal, his phone whinnied. What a relief! That meant it was a personal call and not another emergency.

"Hello."

"Dr. Gray, I presume." Adrian tried to disguise his voice but wasn't successful.

"Dr. Peterson, to what do I owe the pleasure? Or do I need to help my old vet buddy again?

Bobby couldn't help but give Adrian a little grief.

"No favor this time. I've already exceeded my yearly quota." Adrian continued, "I just want to check on my daughter and her ponies. I hope all three are behaving."

"They certainly are. Mary loves having Megan here. She's putting her to work every afternoon. They ride most mornings. Mary's going to miss that girl."

"Thanks, I can tell Megan feels the same way about Mary. Her stay with you has certainly changed this summer for the better after a rough beginning." Adrian could hear the joy in Megan's voice when they talked.

"We can't take all the credit. Julep, and now Starlight, makes for a happy ending."

"Bobby, we're leaving for Florida on Monday and taking two days for the drive. Belinda can move into her apartment on Wednesday. Unloading the horse trailer shouldn't take long, and Susan and I are going to try to leave on Wednesday, and see how far we get before we hunt down a hotel for the night. Either way, we'll be at your place Thursday."

"That's fine, Adrian. I'll be at the clinic, but I'll tell Mary and Megan to stay home on Thursday and be the welcome committee. Don't you dare load and go. I want to meet Susan. She must be a special lady to put up with you, so you better be here when I get home from the clinic. Hey, plan on spending the night, ok?"

"We'll spend the night, but in a hotel. We sure don't expect you to put us up. Why don't you let Susan and me take you, Mary, and Megan out for dinner that night?"

"It's a plan, but don't be surprised if Mary wants to grill something instead. Nothing fancy, but we could have a more relaxing evening staying here instead of going to a restaurant."

"That's a good plan. I'll stay in touch while we're on the road. Was there any problem with JJ the other day?" Adrian hoped his friend hadn't suffered because of his conversation with JJ.

"No problem at all, except that I had to keep a straight face while JJ pretended everything was his idea. He wanted to make sure I understood he was gifting the mare to Megan, because he's such a generous and caring individual. I stand in a lot of manure while I'm on farm calls, but his manure was waist deep." Bobby laughed.

Adrian was glad to hear Bobby laugh. "He is certainly a work of art—bad art."

Appleridge, Ohio

Jennie used her 4–H skills to light the campfire while Kate and Kyiko lit the luminaries. Then they used the now-very-clean garden wagon to bring out the cooler and supplies.

First to arrive were Sallie and family with Grandpa, followed by Jennie's parents, then a few minutes later, Connie's family, then Belinda and Sam. Where was Jeremy? Jennie tried not to look too eager. She welcomed Cassy and her friend, Sandra, and still no Jeremy. Marcy arrived around 7:30 then Susan and Dr. Peterson arrived after eight and apologized for being late.

Her dad waited with at least five campfire forks.

"Go ahead, Dad, start roasting. I think most of us are hungry." Her dad liked the job of roasting both hotdogs and the marshmallows when it was time for dessert.

Jennie gathered the group and asked her grandpa to pray.

"Good food, good drinks, good God, let's eat. Amen."

"Dad," Ellen scolded.

"Now Ellen, the food is good and so is God." Grandpa wasn't going to be ashamed of his prayer.

With full plates, the group gathered around the small fire to eat, talk, and laugh. They didn't need it for warmth, but with only a couple of lanterns on the tables, the fire was a good source of light.

Jennie noticed Dr. Peterson watching her several times during the evening. It was like he wanted say something, but never did. Instead, he seemed to enjoy the food and conversation, and was much more relaxed than usual.

While everyone seemed content eating and chatting, Jennie snuck away to check her phone. Where was Jeremy?

Her phone displayed both a missed call and a text.

Taking Mom to hospital.

Oh no!

Please, God, be with Mrs. James and with Jeremy. Let them feel your comforting presence. Amen.

Joining her guests at the campfire, she shared the information about Mrs. James. Grandpa asked everyone to join him in prayer. This time the prayer wasn't quite as much fun.

Chapter Thirty-Seven

Appleridge, Ohio

*J*ennie awoke early to feed the horses. No church today. Her friends were leaving for their next adventure, and she wanted to send them off with a hearty breakfast. Both Kyiko and Kate rose early and were already dressed by the time Jennie returned from the barn. Not wanting to climb into bed smelling like a campfire, the shower was busy last night, leaving free time this morning.

"Have you heard anything more from Jeremy?" Kate was concerned.

"No, and if I don't hear from him soon, I'm going to drive to the hospital after you...sorry, I'm not rushing you."

"We know, Jennie. Don't worry." Kyiko didn't want Jennie to feel bad. "Thanks for everything, and I hope Jeremy's mom is home by now."

Kate added, "I bet Jeremy's exhausted but will call as soon as he can."

"Thanks, guys." Jennie was sad to see her friends go, but anxious to check on Jeremy.

Kate and Kyiko loaded their luggage into the rental car while Jennie finished cooking. They repacked the cooler and placed it on the back seat so it was easy to reach mid-trip.

Jennie finished buttering the toast, and took the breakfast casserole out of the oven, glancing up as her friends came through the kitchen door.

Jennie motioned for them to take their seats at the table. "Perfect timing, of course, I wouldn't expect anything less from such accomplished dancers."

Jennie said a quick prayer before they began to eat.

"Your grandpa was sure funny last night with his prayer." Kate reached for a piece of toast.

"My grandfather can be quite a character." Jennie loved him because of his character, both serious and funny.

Kate added, "You have a very nice family and group of friends, Jennie; I'm envious."

"Miss Kate, you forget I met your family in Chicago, and you have a great family." Jennie didn't understand why Kate would be envious.

"I love my family, but we don't joke and kid around. My parents are very serious, and always proper."

"I don't know what to say. I guess my family thinks fun is being proper."

Jennie thought her family had fun because they loved one another and found the joy in life because of their faith. She didn't know how to share that thought without sounding judgmental, or like a bible thumper. What was a bible thumper, anyway? Since both of her friends admired her grandpa, she would share what he said.

"Grandpa believes that we're meant to live joyful lives, because that's God's plan. He recently gave me a little lecture on that very topic. He said if we trust God, we shouldn't worry. If we worry, we'll lose our joy. He also said we should be thankful for everything, and to always try to find something good, even in all the bad things that are sure to happen. That's hard to understand, isn't it?"

Kate didn't say anything, but she was trying to digest that thought, as was Kyiko.

"Did you have a strong faith when you were in Chicago? I know you went to church sometimes, but I've noticed you seem happier now. What made you change?"

"Yeah, I noticed it, too," Kyiko chimed in.

"One day, I asked God for help, and he answered. Then I started to believe my problems were important to God. Tracy, a friend from church, said that if we don't believe our problems are important to God then we don't believe we're important to God, but we are; we truly are loved by him."

Jennie felt bad to think she hadn't shared her faith when she lived with her friends. But then, she was just discovering a relationship with God herself.

"When I finally trusted God, I found a certain sense of freedom. Oh, I'm still learning. Instead of thanking God for all the wonderful things that have happened, I've been worried that everything was going so well—too well. It was like I didn't think I deserved happiness. Grandpa set me straight. He said, of course, bad things will happen, but being a worrier means I'm not trusting God, and worry will suck the joy right out of my life. Well, I don't think he used the word sucked, but you know what I mean. Does that make sense?"

"It's like God is your super hero." Kate added, "I grew up going to church with my parents, but I found it boring most of the time. All I ever heard was, if you sin you'll go down in the earth and live with the devil. Then the list of sins kept growing until I gave up. I'm a good person. Well, at least I try. But I've done quite a few things on the sin list."

"Kate, you're a good person, and you're a wonderful creation and loved by an awesome God. He already knows you can't be

perfect, and, still, you're his precious child. Just ask him to be your super hero, too." Jennie prayed she was using the right words.

"But, Jennie, why didn't I know these things when I went to church and Sunday school all those years?"

"I don't know. It was the same for me, I guess, but it's different now. Now I talk to him like a good friend."

"Jeremy feels that the church as a body has let God down. Church shouldn't be boring. It should be exciting! Jeremy thinks we're all starving for more God, and if we don't fill up on God, we'll fill up on something else."

Kyiko remained silent during the conversation. Christianity was definitely a small minority group in Japan, and she had no exposure to God, other than what Jennie shared.

Jennie noticed that Kyiko was listening carefully.

Please, God, give me the right words.

"Jennie," Kyiko said quietly, "I don't know much about Christianity, but I do see something different in you and your family. You love each other, and are happy, and your family is kind. That's different than most of the world."

Jennie got up and gave her a hug, then reached for Kate to include her.

"This is sort of embarrassing, but I feel like I want to pray for you both. I'm not used to praying out loud, but if you're willing, I'd like to try."

"I'm willing." Kate squeezed Jennie's hand.

"Me, too," Kyiko whispered.

They held hands and Jennie prayed.

"Father, these are my dear friends, and your dear children. Please keep them safe on their trip today, help them to feel your love, and please give them joy, lots of joy. In Your name we pray, Amen."

Jennie saw Kyiko wipe a tear.

Kate stepped back. "Thanks, Jennie, and thanks for helping us out of our little lie. Now we ARE comfortable with horses."

They gave each other several more hugs, and then Kate and Kyiko were in the car, and waving as they left Jennie's farm toward another adventure.

Please, God, be their hero.

It was too late to attend church, so Jennie got busy in the house, cleaning up the breakfast dishes, washing sheets, packing up the air mattresses, and collecting everything else she borrowed for the campfire. Today would be a good day to return those things. She was so busy she didn't hear a car in the drive, but she did hear a soft knock on the back door.

She glanced through the window before opening the door. It was Jeremy. She opened the door quickly, and before she could say anything, Jeremy grabbed her and clung tightly.

"She's gone, Jennie, my mom is gone."

Jennie gasped, "Oh, Jeremy, oh no."

She was now holding him tight. Finally, she took his hand, led him inside, and over to the kitchen table.

"Sit, and when you're ready, tell me what happened."

Jennie went to the sink and returned with a glass of water which Jeremy took gratefully. She sat across the table from Jeremy, but reached for his hands.

"Mom wasn't feeling well yesterday. At first I wasn't concerned, but then she seemed to be disoriented, so I called my sister, and she told me to drive Mom to the hospital. They ran a few tests last night, and scheduled a heart catheterization for Monday. I don't know why, but I felt the need to spend the night

with her, and they brought a cot into the room. Around three this morning, I woke up to all sorts of alarms and nurses running into the room. She was having a major heart attack. They worked and worked, but she was unresponsive. I spent the next few hours watching my mom slip away. I held her hand, told her I loved her, read a few verses from the bible, and then said good-bye. My sister had gone home to be with her family, but she made it back just before we lost our mom."

"Oh, Jeremy, I'm so sorry. I should have checked on you last night."

"No, it was just me and my sister and that was good. Mom went peacefully and I know she's with Jesus. I wouldn't have been so sure a few months ago. This summer, we had a heart-to-heart talk, and I shared my faith with Mom, and she received the peace that surpasses all understanding." Jeremy sighed. "Isn't it sad, my mom went to church her entire life and was such an un-happy person. She never believed she was worthy of anyone's love, so she didn't believe God loved her, and she certainly didn't know how to show love to anyone. Not even her family. She cried a lot that day."

"That's so sad, and so true, for a lot of us. We don't feel like we deserve God's love, and, of course, we don't deserve it, but he loves us anyway. Why don't we believe we're loved?

"Good question. In spite of my mom's hard demeanor, I truly believe Dad loved her and she loved him. I don't think Mom had a very happy childhood. She kept herself behind a wall most of the time. Don't get me wrong, though; our mom took good care of us, but she didn't have much joy in her heart."

Jennie shook her head and gave Jeremy's hands a squeeze, encouraging him to continue.

"She died with joy, but I find it sad that she lived her entire life, except for the last few months, without much comfort from her faith. It explains everything, doesn't it?"

"It does."

"That's why I want to attend Seminary. My prayer is that all the faithful Christians who attend church every Sunday, like my mom, find the true meaning of faith. It's not enough to simply believe in God. We're called to live our lives in a way that the whole world knows we're loved by an amazing God, a Father who will always hold us tight, and surround us with grace when life isn't easy."

Jennie loved hearing Jeremy share his faith in easy-to-understand and passionate words.

"Jeremy, what happens now?"

"Tomorrow, my sister and I will plan our mom's funeral. We think visitation will be Tuesday, and the service on Wednesday. I was supposed to start school this week, but I may delay my start until next semester. I'll call my advisor tomorrow. I don't want to move to Columbus and dump everything on my sister. Mom's estate will need to be settled."

"Jeremy, I'm here. What can I do?" Jennie didn't know what to do next.

"This was the only place I wanted to be when I left the hospital. You're the first person I wanted to see." Jeremy swallowed and added, "That's ok, right?"

"Yes, it's more than ok."

Jeremy was exhausted. "I'm going home to take a shower and get some sleep. I'll call you later, ok?"

Jennie nodded yes.

Alone, Jennie sat on the back porch, thinking about what Jeremy shared. Losing his mom was hard, but knowing his mom

finally believed she was loved gave him peace. He knew he would see his mom again on the day they knelt at the feet of Jesus together.

It was only noon and Jennie felt emotionally drained, but spiritually alive. Her friends had noticed a change. Wow, what a testament to how our actions tell the story! Jennie vowed to be more aware of what she said and did all the time.

Thank you, Father, for giving me the words to share with my friends. Thank you for holding all of them in your loving arms. Father, please be with Sarah and Jeremy. The next few days will be hard and they need you. We need you every moment, God, in good times and in bad. You are the one constant source of love, joy, and strength. Thank you, Amen.

Kate and Kyiko were right when they said she had an awesome family and wonderful friends. She also had a good church family. That's the way it should be for everyone. We should all seek a community of people who love us.

The Red Roan stopped beside Blue Boy and Jennie met Belinda at the back door.

"Hey, Jennie, I figured you stayed home to give Kyiko and Kate a good send-off."

"They left about three hours ago. Jeremy was here, too." Jennie waited to see if Belinda's face revealed the news about Jeremy's mom. When she didn't ask, Jennie shared the story.

"What a shock. How is he?" Belinda motioned for Jennie to go inside the house.

"He's sad, exhausted, in shock, but he has such a strong faith."

"Hey, Jennie, I didn't bring sustenance, because you have a ton of leftovers from the campfire. Can we eat? I'm starved."

"Good idea. I haven't eaten lunch and, yes, I need to do something with all this food." Jennie could always count on Belinda to keep life real.

Together they pulled the leftovers out of the fridge.

"Yum, I love cold cooked hotdogs." Belinda grabbed one and took a bite.

"Hey, we have buns and we can reheat the hotdogs." Jennie wasn't too fond of cold hotdogs.

"Ok, I'll warm the next one." Belinda finished eating the plain cold hotdog she held in her fingers.

"I sure hope you don't eat like that in vet school. You do want to make friends, don't you?" Jennie was only kidding a little.

"I don't think vet students are too picky about table manners, but I'll try to do better, Mom." Belinda finished filling her plate with potato salad, baked beans, and grabbed a bun for her second hotdog.

"Wow, you are starved, my friend, but eat away. I won't have anyone to share this with after you leave."

Jennie wanted to share with Jeremy, but she didn't share that thought with her friend. Instead, she said, "Are you packed and ready for your next adventure in learning?"

"I'm all packed. I filled most of the trailer, believe it or not." Belinda squirted ketchup, then mustard. "Any relish, Jennie?"

"There's some in the fridge. I want some, too, but you're closer."

"Well, so much for offering hospitality to a good friend." With that, Belinda pretended she was going to squirt Jennie with the mustard.

"Don't you dare!" Oops, she knew better than say the word dare to Belinda and prepared to take a hit of mustard in the face. It didn't happen. Belinda put the mustard on the table.

"You're getting soft on me." Jennie was brave enough to tease.

"No, I just don't want your last memory of our summer to-gether to be a mustard face. If I didn't need to leave tomorrow, you would have gotten it right between the eyes."

"Thank you for your compassion, dear friend."

They finished lunch, and Belinda helped Jennie condense the leftovers into smaller containers.

"Will your dad and mom stop to pick up Megan on the trip home?" Jennie was anxious to know how Megan was doing.

"Yeah, she was kicked off the ranch a week or so ago, and went to stay with a local vet my dad knows. Apparently, she told this JJ guy that she wasn't interesting in continuing with an ap-prenticeship, and he told her to pack her bags."

"What a creep, but we thought something was strange." Jen-nie was glad Megan followed her plan of leaving.

"Yeah, it was a bad summer for her. Mom says she's eager to spend her senior year at Appleridge High, and wants to get started on college classes." Belinda stopped and then said, "Don't ask, I don't know."

"Ask what, know what?" She waited, but Belinda didn't an-swer. "Oh, you think I was going to ask what she wants to do with the rest of her life."

"We've been friends a long time and I know you well." Belinda wiped her hands on the dish cloth. "I'm off—laundry calls. Dad says we're leaving bright and early tomorrow."

They hugged. "It's been nice seeing you this summer. I missed you." Jennie was trying not to cry.

"I missed you, too, but I'll be back for the holidays, and it's nice to know you'll be here when I get back."

"Ok, we'll spend Christmas here, but next year, I'm coming down to have a sandy and sunny Christmas. A White Christmas isn't all it's cracked up to be." Jennie was serious.

"Sounds like a good plan." Belinda picked up her purse and Jennie followed her out to the Red Roan.

"Are you driving separate from your parents so you can have your Red Roan at school?" Jennie just realized that the Petersons would need to drive their truck to pull the horse trailer, but Belinda would also need her truck for transportation while living in Florida.

"Dad's pulling the trailer, and I'm following. I couldn't leave the Red Roan girl at home now, could I?"

"No, you and the Red Roan belong together." Jennie couldn't imagine Belinda driving anything but the Red Roan. "But some day, when you're a fancy vet, I bet you'll drive a brand new truck."

"We'll see, girlfriend, we'll see." And with a wave she was off.

It was getting late and time to start the rounds returning all the borrowed items. It didn't look like either Cassy or Marcy would be coming out to the farm today. Jennie made a quick decision to run out to the barn, and give the three equines some hay. Horses need to graze. She liked to keep plenty of hay in front of their faces when they were confined to the paddock.

Jennie heard her phone ping. It was a text from Jeremy.

Feeling better...we'll talk later...will stop by after you get off work tomorrow afternoon.

Jennie worked nine to two tomorrow. *Wow*, she thought, *Jeremy remembers my schedule.* She would need to change her hours to be at the visitation for Jeremy's mom Tuesday evening, and then she would also need to miss work on Wednesday to attend the funeral. Hopefully, she could trade with someone, because

she wouldn't be paid for the hours missed. But if she couldn't trade hours, she would just have to make it work. Some things were more important than money.

Sallie wasn't home when Jennie stopped to deliver the air mattresses. She left them on the back porch with a note. Jennie then drove to her parents' house where she found both Sallie and Connie and her two adorable nephews.

Jennie set the box she carried down on the floor when she saw her nephews.

"Nee!" Both toddlers could say something sort of resembling her name.

"How are my two favorite boys?" Jennie reached to tickle their bellies.

"We're so sorry to hear about Mrs. James." Connie touched Jennie's arm.

"Thanks. Jeremy stopped by the farm, but then went home to get some sleep. He looked beat."

"Will you be able to get off work to attend the funeral?" Ellen asked.

"I'm going to try to trade hours, but if that doesn't work I'll just have to take off without pay. Either way, I'll be there."

"Did Kate and Kyiko get off early?" It was Jennie's mom's way of asking why she wasn't at church.

"Oh, around 10:30, I guess. I made them breakfast. Then Jeremy came over, then Belinda. It's been a busy day."

"Sit down and have a pop. Your dad and the boys are in the garage tinkering with the zero-turn lawnmower. It's not been running right.

Her mom was referring to her brothers-in-law when she said "boys."

"Ok, that sounds good." She could hear the lawnmower engine being started outside. It made a rough sputtering noise. The boys would be out in the garage for a while.

Jennie enjoyed chatting with her sisters and mom while playing with her nephews, but she was tired. It had been a busy week, and an emotional morning. Mom got up to make a quick supper of cold cuts and chips, but Jennie declined the invitation to stay for the meal.

"I'm tired. I think I'll go home, feed horses, and get to bed early tonight."

She walked to the garage to say a quick hello and goodbye to her dad and brothers-in-law. They were totally engrossed in the lawnmower, so they didn't mind when Jennie said she couldn't stay. She walked to her truck thinking, I do have a good family, even if they do find an old lawnmower more interesting than me.

Chapter Thirty-Eight

Appleridge, Ohio

Monday proved to be a busy day for everyone. Jennie worked at the library and made arrangements to get time off work. Belinda and her parents left on the trip to Florida. Jeremy sat in the funeral director's office and made some decisions he didn't want to make. Kate and Kyiko prepared for their first session with the horses at the workshop, wearing their cowgirl boots. Jennie's dad mowed his lawn, her mom sewed, her sisters woke up early to take care of toddlers, and her grandpa met his friends at the Bake & Shake.

It's called life, these everyday things that people do each day. From the most mundane to the most unexpected, they're all important and all should be done with joy, with love, with respect. Jennie was starting to understand this concept. It was a hard thing to explain, but not so hard to live. She thought about her family and friends as she worked. Life was good. In all things, life was very good. And it would really be good if her boss understood her need to have time off work.

When Jennie explained her connection to the family and her desire to attend the visitation and funeral, her boss was very understanding, and suggested a few options so Jennie wouldn't lose paid time. One option was to come in early and work for a few hours before the funeral. It was nice of her to offer, but if the funeral started as early as ten or eleven, she would decline the offer. She didn't want her work to seem more important than being a good friend to Jeremy.

Grayson Corners, South Carolina

Mary and Megan painted the large advertisement for the tack and feed store on the side of the barn in the morning, and remained on the farm to ride in the evening. They would follow this schedule the rest of the week. Megan tried to spend equal time with both her horses, but she soon realized Starlight thrived on attention and Julep didn't object to being left in the pasture to graze with Twinkle while she worked with Starlight.

Megan was anxious to see her parents when they arrived on Thursday. She loved painting and riding with Mary, but the summer was ending and she looked forward to the start of school. Wow, that was a first. It was her senior year and hard to believe only three months earlier she begged to finish her studies online as she traveled with JJ, instead of finishing high school at Appleridge High. Life certainly does change and changes quickly—just when you think you have everything figured out. Megan laughed at the thoughts rolling around in her head. Maybe she learned more than she thought this summer.

Appleridge, Ohio

Jeremy and his sister, Sarah, finished the funeral arrangements, and went to their mom's house to talk. It seemed like only a short time ago they planned their father's funeral. They sure didn't expect to lose their mom so soon. They were now orphans, and even as adults, that is a sad realization.

"I talked to my advisor and he agreed with my idea to start fulltime next semester, but he also advised me to take one or two courses now. If I only scheduled classes for a couple of days, I could commute to Columbus once a week or twice at the most. I'm going to follow that suggestion."

"Oh, I hate that for you."

"It's not the end of the world. It's only a little delay. It will take a while for us to handle Mom's estate. You work and have a family and I don't want to dump everything on you, Sis." Jeremy hugged his sister. "Besides, I don't mind sticking close to Appleridge right now."

"Oh, I get it now. Does a certain girl have anything to do with that thought?" Sarah believed it did.

He nodded. "I just want to take things slow for now with both—getting mom's estate settled and with Jennie."

"I can't complain. I'll gladly hand the estate work over to you. I'll help you sort through Mom's things because that's going to be a huge job. She saved everything."

"Mom wouldn't let us clear out much of Dad's stuff when we lost him. We'll have to go through both of their things, and you're right, they didn't throw much away."

"I have a suggestion." Sarah waited for Jeremy to ask.

"Go ahead. I'm open to any suggestion to make this job easier." And he was.

"First, we both go through the house and garage, and pull out anything we want to keep. We can make a list for the big items. For the small items, we'll just gather them into one place. If we both want the same things, they will go to a different place for us to talk over later."

Jeremy nodded. "All good so far; keep going."

"Ok, while we're looking for things we want to keep, pull out any papers or documents the attorney may or may not need to settle the estate."

"Good."

"Then we need to decide what things we want to give away, and what things we want to sell. Again, large things on a list, small items in a designated area. And, let's throw away any junk as we work. I think there's a lot that can't be sold or given away. She saved the craziest things."

"Mom didn't seem real sentimental, but I bet we'll find all our school drawings somewhere."

"I think you're right, and I'm doing the same thing with Daniel. I hate to throw any of his school papers away."

"I like your plan." He always thought his sister was a good organizer. "Simple and it will work. At least Mom had the foresight to make some arrangements with the funeral home. That was a surprise. She must have done that after Dad passed away."

"I know. I was pleasantly surprised, also." Sarah paused. "That was Mom's last gift to us." She felt herself tearing up. "And here I was doing so well."

"It's ok. We won't worry about tears. Let them fall, that's what I say. I'm sad because we didn't expect this to happen, but I'm celebrating, too. Mom left this earth eagerly anticipating her next life with Jesus."

"It is good, isn't it, Jeremy?" Sarah looked at her phone for the time. "Hey, I need to run and get your nephew. He stayed at a friend's house last night, and I promised to pick him up by three."

Jeremy walked Sarah to the door, and watched as she climbed into her car. Then Jeremy kicked off his shoes and walked to the kitchen for a drink of water. He was packed and ready to leave for a new life in Columbus, but it looked like God had other plans. He would be staying right here, at least for a few more months.

Chapter Thirty-Nine

The funeral for Mrs. James was held on Wednesday morning at ten.

"Jennie, please stand with me as we greet people, and then sit with me. Ok?"

"Are you sure? I'm not family. What will people think?" As soon as Jennie spoke the words, she felt bad. "Jeremy, of course, I'll stand with you and Sarah."

The church was packed. Mrs. James may not have been a warm and well-liked woman for most of her life, but she was active in many organizations and a dedicated member of the church. She served her community well. And the Appleridge community filled the pews of Trinity Methodist in love and support of Jeremy and Sarah during this time of loss.

Jeremy stood up and walked to the front of the church to stand by his mom's casket.

Please, Father, be with Jeremy as he shares what you placed on his heart. I think he is very brave.

"Family and friends, Sarah and I would like to thank you for coming here today. Some of you knew Mom well, some only a little, but if you spent any time with our mom, I'm sure you were a little bit afraid of her, too. You would remember if you crossed Elsie James." There were a few chuckles from the mourners.

"Some would describe Mom as a hard person, and they would be correct. She had a very hard life, before she married our dad. She wore a set of armor for protection, and she used stern words as weapons. But there was a crack in her armor, just wide enough for Sarah and me to see the real person inside. That person was good and she loved us.

"Mom couldn't show her love easily. I guess she didn't know how. She took good care of her family, though. She wanted us to do well in life, and sometimes she pushed a little too much. She probably thought that was how you show love. I don't think she experienced a lot of love when she was young. Dad loved her. Sarah and I loved her. My Mom, Elsie James, didn't love herself— at least not for most of her life, anyway.

"What I want to share today is, recently, my mom found Jesus. Oh, you may think, what? Elsie James was a devout Christian. She went to church every Sunday. Well, that is, unless we were at a horse show."

Again, a few chuckles were heard. Jeremy's warmth put the funeral crowd at ease.

"Yes, Mom was a Christian, she believed in God, but she didn't believe that God believed in her. She didn't believe that God loved her with a passion beyond all understanding. She didn't know that being a believer was so much more than just being good at doing things."

Jeremy walked to the other side of the casket and then continued. He took a moment to look at Jennie, and she nodded to send him quiet encouragement.

"This story has a happy ending. A few months ago, Mom and I had a long conversation. My mom cried a lot that day. We both cried. It was our first honest heart-to-heart conversation, and I had the sacred honor of leading my mom to the faith she was created to enjoy. My mom finally found joy in being a believer. After a lifetime of believing in God, we prayed together, and she turned her fears, and her hard view of life, over to God. When she finally released all that junk, she found peace, she found joy,

and she found herself. She believed she was loved. She kicked the hurt, the fear, the feeling that she wasn't good enough out for good and that left a lot of room for God to fill her up with his love."

Jennie could hear a few quiet *Amens*, and maybe one or two *Praise Gods*.

"My mom found joy, and she will be waiting for me when we meet again at the throne of Jesus. I can't wait to celebrate with her, because we didn't get much time to do that here, but that's ok. Today we celebrate the life of Elsie James, cherished and beloved child of God.

"If anyone here is what I call a dry Christian, don't wait to water those dry bones. Celebrate now. Love now. Fill your life up with God. He's waiting."

Jeremy sat down and Jennie reached for his hand. He was shaking. Jennie gave his hand a little squeeze and smiled and nodded when he looked at her.

Good job, Jeremy James.

Jeremy insisted Jennie ride to the gravesite in one of the black limousines provided by the funeral services. Other than the driver, they were alone in the car, and Jeremy didn't talk during the ride. He held her hand, rubbing the back with his thumb. Jennie didn't read anything more into the gesture, other than he found it comforting.

Sarah and her family rode in the first limousine. There were no other family members in attendance. Other than a few very distant aunts and uncles, Jeremy and Sarah were now alone.

During the ride back to the church, they talked. The worst part was over. All who gathered were invited to the fellowship hall in the basement of the church for a light lunch.

"Belinda called yesterday. She wanted to tell me how sorry she is to hear about Mom, and sorry she couldn't be at the funeral. I told her I understood." Jeremy picked up Jennie's hand again.

"I know she wanted to be here and so did her parents." Jennie looked at Jeremy. "Are you ok?"

"I'm much better now. I'm not a huge fan of funerals." He gave Jennie a strained smile. "But I don't suppose anyone wakes up and thinks, oh boy, I get to go to my mom's funeral today."

"I don't suppose anyone wakes up and thinks, oh boy, I get to go to anyone's funeral today," Jennie added.

"No, I don't suppose." Jeremy was more relaxed. "I also suppose I should get used to funerals and speaking in front of people, given my chosen career path."

"It was good. You have a heartfelt way sharing your faith." Jennie was sincere.

"Thanks for sticking with me, today. I don't know how to say this, exactly, because it's not the best time or place, but I like you by my side." Jeremy looked a little nervous.

"Jeremy, I like being by your side. I think we're on the same page. Just like I told my friends when they asked about our relationship, I said, "We're in like with each other and I would like to stick around to see if it becomes anything more."

"That's perfect. I'm in like with you, too, and I want to stick around to see if it becomes anything more." Jeremy leaned over and gave Jennie a light kiss on the cheek. "I think that's all you get if you are in like. We'll see if it becomes anything more."

"You're on, Jeremy James."

The boy with first two names has stolen my heart. Oh no! If it does become something more I'll be Jennie James, the girl with two

first names. Ok, but maybe we shouldn't name our kids names that begin with J.

Gainesville, Florida

Adrian took a paper towel and ran it over his sweaty face. He hated moving. And he especially hated dragging Belinda's boxes up two flights of apartment steps because the elevator was broken. It must be worn out from all the use during student move-in week.

Susan seemed fine, but she was struggling. In a few hours she would say goodbye to their firstborn. She was thinking, why Florida? Why not Ohio State? Now that was a great school. The University of Florida was a good school, but it was just too far away. Susan didn't like her daughters leaving the nest, not at all. Look what happened when Megan left to spend the summer in South Carolina. Susan said a silent prayer that God would keep her family safe. It was hard giving her daughters wings.

"I think that's it. The trailer is empty." Adrian put the last box on the floor. He looked at his watch. Good, only noon. He planned to stop for the night in Georgia to surprise Susan with a little tour of Savannah. The hotel near the interstate had plenty of parking for the trailer, and they suggested taking a cab into the historic district. That was his plan, anyway.

He asked Belinda, "How about we take you to lunch?"

"That sounds good. Then I guess I'll go to the store so I have something to eat for later."

"Good idea, honey; do you want us to go to the store for you while you unpack?" Susan wasn't ready to say good-bye.

Adrian stood behind Susan and shook his head no. Belinda caught on quickly.

"No, I'm fine. After four years at Ohio State, I've learned to be pretty self--sufficient. But thanks for offering."

Adrian nodded. He was proud of how hard Belinda worked at the clinic this summer. She was going to make a great veterinarian. She was good with both animals and humans. The people part was always a challenge for Adrian.

During lunch, Adrian told Belinda the whole story about Julep, and why Megan left the ranch early to live with the Grays.

"I just knew you were up to something, Dad, because you were much too calm about the whole situation." Belinda gave her dad a stern look. "But I can't believe you didn't tell poor Jennie. You know that's sort of cruel, right?"

"Well, I didn't know how everything was going to play out with JJ. We didn't even tell Megan until she was kicked off the ranch, and I'm sure I'll get an earful about keeping that secret."

"And you're just going to show up at Jennie's with Julep?" Belinda couldn't imagine the surprise.

"I am, and you better not call, e-mail, or text." Adrian tried to look stern.

"Adrian, tell her the rest of the story. Tell her about the second surprise," Susan urged.

Adrian told Belinda about Starlight and how JJ gifted the mare to Megan out of the goodness of his heart.

"That's not exactly how it happened. Your dad held JJ's boots to the fire, but he's allowing JJ to save face."

Susan was proud of Adrian. It must have been hard for him to resist tearing JJ to shreds verbally. And she prayed that he would resist a physical confrontation if ever given the chance. She thought it wouldn't be a good idea for them to hang around Grayson Corners too long when they picked up Megan.

Grayson Corners, South Carolina

Megan put her phone in her back pocket. "Mom and Dad are about an hour away. They're going to stop and get a room for the night and then come on over."

"That will be perfect." Mary put her paint brush down. "We'll have time to get cleaned up and start the grill."

"Dad loves that BBQ place at the interstate exit, and he wanted to know if it was ok to bring over BBQ for everyone. I said I would ask and then text Mom because she's not the one driving." Megan looked at Mary. "We don't have BBQ like that in Ohio."

"That would be good, or I mean great! I like that idea. Tell your mom we already have buns, and I have potato salad, baked beans, and brownies. All they need to get is the BBQ and slaw. I forgot to get slaw when I went to the store for the hamburgers. I'll just put those burgers in the freezer."

Megan sent a text and waited for a reply. Ping, another text came in, this time from Belinda.

julep n starlight happy!!!

Ping. Now she saw a text from her mom.

Got it, can't wait to see you. Love you, Mom. Unlike her sister, their mom always used capitalization and punctuation in her texts.

"Ok, all set, they're bringing BBQ and slaw."

Mary gave a thumb up.

MEGAN JUMPED up and ran down the front porch steps as soon as she saw the familiar truck and trailer turn into the Grays' drive. First she went to the passenger side and opened her mom's door. She could hardly wait for her to climb out of the truck. After giving her mom an enthusiastic greeting, Megan ran to the other side and found her dad for a big hug.

"Come on, come around back and meet Mary. Mom, she's setting up the screened porch so we can eat outside. Dad, Dr. Bobby is in the house." Megan grabbed her mom's hand and took her around to the back porch. "Their house is so cute and cozy."

"Mom, this is Mary. Mary, this is my mom, Susan Peterson." Megan watched her mom walk over and give Mary a hug.

"Thank you so much for taking care of my wayward daughter," she said warmly.

"My pleasure, I loved having her here, and I put her to work." Mary added, "Wait until you see the signs she painted. She's a talented artist."

Adrian and Bobby walked out the back door holding beers. "Your dad wants to see this horse he shamed JJ into giving." Bobby motioned for everyone to follow him out to the barn. The horses lifted their heads to look at the five humans, and then walked to the gate.

"Oh, there's our sweet Julep." Susan sighed. "She looks good, except for that silly haircut. I'd like to take my scissors to who-ever is responsible."

"I'd like to do more than that." Adrian pointed to the chestnut mare. "Is that Starlight? She's nice. How is she doing?"

"She learns quickly but you have to give her time to think." Megan reached over the fence to stroke Starlight's neck. "Thanks for coming over here to see me."

"Mary, that's a nice gelding. An Arabian?" Adrian guessed.

"Yes, he's a good boy." Mary was proud of Windward. "And the pony is Twinkle. We rescued her from a very bad situation, and I wasn't too sure she was going to make it, but now she's

healthy and very bossy." Mary rubbed Twinkle's forehead. "Of course, it helped that my husband is a brilliant vet."

"That he is." Adrian agreed. "And I'm very thankful for the help of that brilliant vet. Bring that vet up to Ohio so we can extend our hospitality, or I'm afraid I'll be indebted for the rest of my life."

"We'll just see what we can do about that. Megan told me about all the beautiful old barns in Ohio. I need to get up there and take pictures. Of course, South Carolina would also have many beautiful old barns if Sherman hadn't marched down here and burned them all to the ground." Mary was originally from the north but loved to defend the south.

"Oh, no, are we in big trouble because Sherman was an Ohio native son?" Adrian pleaded, "Do we still get supper?"

"We won't hold Sherman against you since you have the BBQ." Bobby coveted the BBQ.

The group returned to the porch for cold drinks. It was still early and not quite time for supper.

Mary and Megan entertained her parents with tales of their rides spying on JJ, and some of the barn projects they worked on together.

Susan shared a few things that were happening in Appleridge, and told Megan about Jennie's other boarders, and how she had fixed up the farm with her family's help.

"There's a young girl named Cassy, only a year older than you, Megan. Both she and her horse seem nice. Maybe she'll become a friend and a good riding partner." Susan liked Cassy when they met at the campfire party.

"That would be...," Megan hesitated. She was going to say— great.

"Great!" Both Bobby and Mary said loudly together.

Mary answered Susan's puzzled expression, "We've been teasing Megan about the word great. I think it's her favorite. And now I think it's ours."

"Now I understand. Yes, it's a favorite." Susan smiled at her daughter, happy that she looked so relaxed.

Bobby got up out of his rocking chair. "I'm getting a bit hungry. Can we say hello to that BBQ now?"

"I thought you'd never ask." Adrian looked to Susan and Mary.

They pulled the BBQ and baked beans out of the oven where they were left to keep warm. Mary put all the food on the counter along with paper plates and forks, and they took turns filling their plates and carried them to the porch for a delicious meal and more fun conversation.

"Bobby, I've been meaning to ask, since your last name is Gray, is Grayson Corners named after your family?" Adrian was a history buff.

"The family likes to think so, but actually, a battle of the war was fought by local sons of the Confederate army wearing the gray. They fought hard and won the battle near where two major roads met."

"You mean the Civil War?" Megan joined the conversation, trying to remember her history.

"Well, young lady," Bobby responded. "History is taught a little differently down here in the south. We're taught there was nothing civil about the war. Down here it's what we like to call the War of Northern Aggression."

Susan looked up from her dinner. "Oh, my, I'm so sorry."

"No worries, Susan, I'm from the north, too." Mary didn't want Susan to feel uncomfortable.

"Wow, I'm going to share that in school this year, if I get the chance!" Megan thought sharing a different point of view would definitely start an interesting conversation in history class.

Mary lit the porch lanterns, and they topped off the delicious supper with ice cream and homemade brownies.

Looking at his daughter, Adrian said, "I can see why you don't want to leave. It doesn't get any better than this." He leaned back in his chair and patted his now bulging stomach.

"Thanks so much, Mary. Everything was delicious and so relaxing." Susan leaned forward to hide her stomach.

"You're very welcome," Mary said sincerely. And Bobby added, "Our pleasure."

"Well, Megan, early day tomorrow. Are you going to the hotel with us or staying here one more night?" Adrian got up from his chair and stretched.

"If Mary and Bobby can stand me for one more night, I'd like to stay here. That way I can take care of Julep and Starlight in the morning, and get them ready for the trip."

"Fine with us, and that's a great idea." Mary looked at Bobby and he nodded.

Susan and Adrian thanked their host and hostess again, kissed Megan, and drove back to the hotel with just the truck. At Bobby's suggestion they unhooked the trailer and left it at the farm.

Appleridge, Ohio

"Jennie, its Kyiko."

"Hey, it's good to hear from you. How's the workshop?"

"The director loved the video! She wants to talk to you about a possible collaboration. Can you Skype?"

"Sure, just let me know when." Jennie suggested several possible times to connect. "Do you know if this would be a paying job?" Jennie certainly hoped so. She would love to be involved with the project, but she had to be practical.

"I think so. She's also offering two dancers a contract at the end of the workshop. The dancers are on a salary. They do all sorts of other performance art, not just the horse project. I'm very interested in working with her, and like you, I can't work for free."

"That would be an awesome opportunity for you, Kyiko. A smaller company that thrives on thinking outside the box would be a good fit for a new talented choreographer." Kyiko's talents were just waiting for someone to give them a try.

"That's what I think, too. Hey, Kate's here, and she says to tell you hello." Jennie could hear Kate in the background, singing hello, hello.

"Love you guys, miss you." Jennie hung up without telling them about Jeremy's mom. They were so excited to share their news about the horses and dancing in the workshop, Jennie didn't want to interrupt, or, to use an old expression, rain on their parade.

Jennie smiled when she saw a text from Jeremy.

Can you stop by on your way to work?

Farm work could wait until tomorrow. She sent Jeremy a text.

Ok.

JEREMY ANSWERED the door and guided Jennie into the front room. Sarah was sitting on the floor surrounded by mounds of papers and photos.

"You guys have been busy." She sat down on the floor in a tiny spot not already covered in paper.

"I wanted to show you these photos. Mom kept the photo of you and me leading the grand entry at the horse show. The one they put in the newspaper. And look, she didn't even draw a mustache on your face or anything." Like Jennie, Jeremy liked humor.

Jennie picked up the photo. "I love this, and how did she get this nice copy, anyway?"

"Oh, she called the editor and demanded a copy." Sarah laughed. "You know Mom."

Jennie glanced through the entire stack of 4-H and fair photos. "Did you notice that there are quite a few photos of my grandpa? Did your mom know my grandpa very well?"

"I did, and I also noticed that Mom is always laughing and smiling at him." Jeremy looked over Jennie's shoulder and pointed. "See that one? I don't think that was taken at the fair or a 4-H event, but I can't see anything in the background to give me a clue where it was taken."

"They're a lot younger in that photo. My grandpa is a young man but your mom looks like a teenager." Jennie calculated the years in her head. "This is strange. Do you think Grandpa knew your mom when she was a little girl?" Jennie turned to look at Jeremy's face. "Grandpa shared a few things the other day that gave me the impression he went through some difficult times when he returned home from Korea and my grandma put up with it for a while before setting him straight. Do you think—I don't know what to think, but several of these pictures could have been taken near that time. That would be around 1953 or a little later. How old was your mom in 1954 or 1955?"

Sarah spoke up, "Mom would have been ten years old in 1954. She was always the oldest mom at all our school events. I think that embarrassed her because everyone thought she was our grandmother. She was thirty-nine when I was born."

Jennie looked at Sarah. "Thirty-nine? That would make her forty-three when Jeremy was born, and sort of old to have a baby."

"Jennie, you do know Jeremy and I were adopted, don't you?"

"No, I didn't know. I guess I was aware of her age but I never gave it much thought." Jennie shifted positions on the floor as her leg felt like it was getting numb.

"And to answer your question, I don't know how my mom knew your grandpa, but there was some sort of connection. Maybe there was some sort of gathering for returning servicemen and they met there." Sarah continued to sort pictures.

"It all seems sort of strange. I mean, look at all these photos of Grandpa." Jennie looked through the stack in her hands again. "Should I say anything to Mom or Grandpa?" She looked up, stricken. "Maybe Grandpa had an affair and your mom is his child? Or maybe something else happened that they kept secret all these years?"

Jeremy sighed. "I think your imagination is going full speed right now, and I have to ask, what if your grandpa did have an affair. Would that change anything? Would it change the feelings you have for him today?"

Jennie thought for a moment. "No, I would still love him. He just wouldn't be perfect and in my mind he's perfect."

"No one is perfect, Jennie, no one will ever be perfect. He loves you and you love him. That's what's perfect."

Jeremy reached down for Jennie's hand. "And besides, as crazy as it seems, if my mom was somehow related to your grandpa, I have to say right here and now, I'm very glad I'm

adopted." Jeremy cleared the papers from the sofa so Jennie could get some relief from the floor, and he sat down beside her.

Jennie spent a few more minutes talking to Jeremy and Sarah before leaving for work. She had all sorts of crazy ideas tumbling around in her head. Jennie could always ask her grandpa a few direct questions. He wouldn't lie. But Jeremy was right. She needed to give this some more thought.

Chapter Forty

Grayson Corners, South Carolina

*A*drian and Susan returned to the Grays' farm bright and early on Friday morning. Megan was ready—the horses fed, and her belongings stacked on the back porch. She backed the truck to the trailer and hitched it herself. Adrian taught both of his daughters to hitch and drive a horse trailer. He didn't feel the need to check on Megan's work. She would check the brakes and lights to make sure everything was safe. He would get them on the road and drive as far as the interstate before they switched, and then Megan would do most of the driving. She was an especially careful driver when it involved horses in the trailer.

Both Starlight and Julep walked into the trailer easily—a big plus when traveling with horses. Megan put the security bars into place and lifted the ramp, but waited a few minutes before closing the doors. She wanted to make sure both horses were relaxed and ready for the doors to close.

After goodbyes and hugs, and more goodbyes, the Petersons pulled out of the farm drive and set course for home. It would be interstate travel all of the way until the last hour or so of driving. With this early start, they would be in Appleridge before dark.

Appleridge, Ohio

The pictures of her grandpa with Mrs. James were strange. Jennie couldn't stop thinking about possible scenarios.

If Grandpa knew I was stewing, he would give a lesson on why I shouldn't worry about something in the past that couldn't be changed. I guess I'll just forget it for now. That's easier said than done.

Jeremy admitted he was curious, but he didn't think curiosity was enough of a reason to make anyone uncomfortable, or to force anyone to reveal a story that could be painful. It could be as simple as a young girl looking up to an older man who was a friend of the family. It happened all the time.

She agreed. She was giving more relevance to the pictures than she should. Her imagination often created stories out of things she experienced or thought.

Jennie was thrilled when Jeremy gave her the picture of the two of them leading the parade on their horses. It was a great color photo with Jennie carrying the United States flag and Jeremy carrying the State of Ohio flag. He was riding his nice Quarter Horse gelding, a bay named Bert. Jeremy sold Bert to help pay for college. Boy, did Jennie understand that scenario. She wondered where Bert was now, and decided to ask him the next time they were together.

I need to find a nice frame for this picture.

Somewhere on the Interstate

"Are you getting tired? Want me to drive for a while?" Adrian was in the back seat of the double cab reading a book. His legs were a bit cramped, so he welcomed a turn in the front seat. Susan was in the passenger seat, an easier position for her to fight car sickness.

"I'm more hungry than tired. Do you think we could stop for something to eat? Then you can drive for a while. But Dad, I want to be the one to pull into Jennie's farm, ok?" Megan was getting excited for the big surprise.

Adrian motioned to the next exit. "That looks like a good exit for a stop. We'll grab some fast food and top off the tank."

Megan pulled into a truck stop with a McDonald's. Perfect, Mickey D's and fuel. What could be better?

"I'll fill up and then you can pull around to the other side where it isn't quite as busy. I think the horses will be fine. We'll keep the trailer fans on, and it won't take us long to eat. It'll be just enough time to rest their legs and eat some hay."

Adrian unfolded his legs and stiffly climbed out of the back seat to man the gas pump while Megan opened the trailer side door to check on Starlight and Julep.

"They're traveling well. It looks like they both ate some hay. Julep usually doesn't eat while the trailer is moving." Megan reached in the trailer to stroke her neck. "Starlight must be a good traveling companion."

Megan pulled a bucket out of the trailer dressing room, and filled it half-full of water from a five-gallon container they carried. Neither horse wanted a drink. She would offer water to them again before they got back on the road.

WITH HORSES watered, fed, and rested, and the humans the same, Adrian started the truck and merged back onto the interstate.

"Do you think we should call Jennie's parents and tell them about the big surprise?" Susan asked. "Wouldn't it be fun for them to be there for the big moment? Maybe we could make it a little party." Susan loved celebrations. "I wish we would have thought about it earlier."

"I like that idea! And then they could call Jeremy. I think he's becoming an important person in Jennie's life." Megan leaned forward, and between the two front seats, as far as her seat belt would allow.

"You girls always love a party, but, it's a good idea. I love a good surprise as much as the next person. Give Ellen a call, Susan." They didn't need his permission, but he wanted to be part of the conversation.

Susan left a message on Ellen's cell phone. It was only two in the afternoon and they were still at least three hours away.

It took a half hour for Ellen to return Susan's call. "Hi Susan, I listened to your message. Are you home?"

"No, still on the road, but do I ever have a story to tell." Susan proceeded to tell the story of Julep.

"Oh my goodness, it's unbelievable! And does Megan still want Julep to be with Jennie?"

"She does, and she wants to board another horse at Jennie's. It's a long and very interesting story. We'll fill you all in tonight. Do you think you could arrange a little surprise gathering?"

"I do. Ed and I can be there, maybe my dad. I'm not sure if Sallie and Connie will come with their families, though. My two grandsons were a handful last weekend at the campfire, and I don't think it's an experience either one of the girls wants to repeat. I would guess keeping an eye on toddlers around the horses and barn wouldn't be on the top of their list for a Friday evening." Ellen's mind was reeling. "Jeremy. I'll call Jeremy. I bet he would love to be a part of this surprise."

Susan hung up. "Let the celebration begin."

JENNIE LEFT Blue Boy in the library parking lot and walked a few blocks to her grandpa's apartment building. Maybe he was home checking his busy social calendar and would like a visitor. Well, at least that's what she told herself. No, she didn't have an agenda. She just felt like a little walk on a nice day.

Grandpa was home.

"Come on in, Jennie girl. What brings you to my neck of the woods?" Grandpa certainly had a way with the old phrases. "Sit down. Do you want something to drink? I've got some old-fashioned root beer in bottles."

"No, I'm fine, thanks. I'm not going to stay very long." Jennie sat down on the sofa and left Grandpa's favorite recliner for him.

"I just left work and thought a little stroll around the square before heading home would be nice. I saw you sitting with Mom and Dad at the funeral. Did you go to the grave site? I looked but didn't see you at lunch." Jennie was fishing for comments.

"No, I was meeting a friend from out of town for lunch so I didn't go back to the church. It was a nice service, though. Jeremy gave a good tribute. I don't care much for funerals but since I've known Elsie James for a good long time, I wanted to attend."

Ok, Jennie thought, *I'll go for it.* "How long have you known Mrs. James?"

"I met Elsie when she was a young girl. Her family moved to Appleridge when she was, oh I'd say, about nine or ten and she loved horses. She would ride her bike out to the farm and visit with our horses over the fence. One day I invited her in to meet them up close. Your grandma always made sure to have some sort of treat for her. She was a sad little girl. Her father was a drunk and I don't think she had a good life. Her mom just up and left one day and after that, Elsie stopped coming."

"That's so sad, Grandpa." Jennie hated hearing about abused children.

"It was sad. She was starved for love. As she got older she threw herself at just about any boy who came around. She didn't have a very good reputation—and there isn't any need to share that information with Jeremy." Grandpa gave Jennie a stern look.

"Once she got a little older, your grandma saw her throw herself at me and warned me to be careful. After that, I tried to keep my distance. I didn't want to give anyone the wrong idea, especially Elsie."

"That must have been hard, keeping your distance when she was hurting." Grandpa was a compassionate person and it would have been terrible for him to send her away.

"I was old enough to be her father, and maybe she was looking to me to be a replacement for her own father. He eventually died of the old liver disease right around the time she went to college. He did that much for her."

"Grandpa, how can you say that?" Jennie was surprised.

"Oh, I don't mean that his dying was good, but he did have a small insurance policy and I'm sure it helped with her college expenses. I was surprised when she ended up back in Appleridge after college. She must have had at least a few good memories."

Or maybe she still had a crush on you, Grandpa.

"She married a nice man, and he always treated her well, but she couldn't seem to find happiness."

"Grandpa, Jeremy told me that he and Sarah were adopted. We found some pictures the other night, and he shared a few things while we were trading memories."

"Yes, Elsie wanted children in the worst way and they couldn't have children. When she adopted Sarah and then Jeremy, I think that was the happiest time of her life. She didn't show it much, though. She was bitter. I don't think she could ever forgive her father. That's what I'm talking about when I say don't let the bad things that are sure to happen rob you of all your joy. Elsie let the bad things that happened when she was young steal all her joy, and in a lot of ways ruin her life. She couldn't seem to enjoy the love she felt for her family."

"I understand, Gramps. I see it in the people who come into the library. Some are joyful in spirit even though life hasn't been a breeze. Then there are those who appear to have everything, and they find fault with everything."

"There's one thing you can be certain about, Jennie: a person's attitude doesn't tell the whole story. Just because someone is bitter and hard doesn't mean her life has been any worse than anyone else's. And someone who always has a smile on his face may have a lot more problems than you or I can imagine. I tend to believe people smile because they're thankful for what they have, and aren't worried about what they don't. Life is hard for everyone. I know some have a harder time than others, and Elsie had a real hard time, but she also had a lot of good things in her life." Grandpa paused. "Jeremy's message was good. What a blessing it is to know Elsie found happiness in the end." Jennie saw a smile appear on Grandpa's face. "Thank you, Jesus."

"Amen, Grandpa, Amen." Jennie got up from the sofa. "I've got to get to the grocery store. We've had some good talks lately, haven't we, Grandpa?"

"We have. We certainly have."

Chapter Forty-One

As she walked back to the library to pick up her truck, Jennie scolded herself for jumping to crazy thoughts concerning Mrs. James and Grandpa.

Father, please forgive all my crazy thoughts. Thank you so much for helping Mrs. James find joy before you took her home. Amen.

This was the first Friday evening in a very long time that she didn't have plans. She wasn't sure what Jeremy was doing tonight. Maybe he would like to come out and watch a movie.

I'll make a quick stop at the store for snacks, just in case.

She noticed her mom's car was in a parking spot near the front door. Once inside, she found her mom at the deli counter.

"Hey, Mom, are you looking for something quick for supper?" Her mom was right in the middle of a large sewing project.

"Well hello, sweetie. Yes, it'll be quick sandwiches tonight." Ellen hoped she didn't sound too sneaky and Jennie didn't notice her shopping cart was filled with some interesting party items. She wasn't good at keeping surprises.

"Me, too, I finished all the goodies Mrs. Samuelson sent with Kate and Kyiko and all the left-overs from the campfire. They kept me fed all week." Jennie didn't mention that Jeremy helped her eat most of them.

Ellen picked up her deli packages. "See you later, honey."

Jennie waited for an invitation to join her mom and dad for supper, but it didn't come.

That's strange. What is going on? There I go again, being suspicious.

After Jennie picked up her deli order, she glanced down all the grocery aisles, but didn't see her mom again. Maybe she already paid for her groceries.

Jennie hurried home, put her groceries away, changed her clothes, and called Jeremy. No answer. She left a message inviting him to the farm for a movie and pizza. She splurged and picked the more expensive brand of frozen pizza, just in case he came over. If they didn't eat it tonight, she would save it for another time.

CASSY PULLED into the drive and parked near the barn. Marcy followed right behind. Yeah, a horse girls' night out in the barn. Jennie hadn't seen them since the campfire, and she missed their company.

"Hey, you guys, it's good to see you. You're both working way too hard." That was the truth, or both would be out to see their equines every single day.

"I know. I've been swamped but I missed my Treasure time. She keeps me grounded." Cassy slipped Treasure's lead rope into the tie blocker ring and went to get her grooming bag.

"I missed my munchkins, too. Have they been good ponies?"

"Yes, very good ponies," Jennie answered truthfully.

"I'm not driving tonight. I'm just going to groom them both and then get to bed early. It's been an extremely hard week at the hospital."

"But, I'll be back tomorrow to spend most of the day with Riley and Stuffin."

"I know they miss you. How about you, Cassy, are you coming back tomorrow?"

"I'll be here. I'm going to play with Treasure at liberty tonight and ride her tomorrow." Cassy was getting really good at playing with Treasure at liberty.

"I'll be mowing tomorrow. I'll try to mow all the paths early, so they're in good shape. I may add a few more crossover paths." She had a few new ideas.

As they talked, Marcy heard a text arrive and pulled her cell phone out of her back pocket. She read the text and then quickly pocketed her phone again.

"I just need to get my grooming bag. I'll be right back." Marcy walked to the tack room and answered the text.

At farm with Jennie, Cassy too.

Marcy didn't know why Ellen sent the text. She read it again.

Are you at the farm? Have surprise for Jennie. Is she home?

Then Ellen answered. *Coming—big surprise—don't tell Jennie—you and Cassy stay?*

Ok??? How would she bring Cassy in on the plan?

She didn't know how she was going to share Ellen's message with Cassy, but then she didn't have much to share, except that something was going to happen at the farm and they were invited.

SUSAN SENT Ellen frequent updates as they traveled. The plan was to meet in the parking lot of a country church near the farm and form a caravan so they would all arrive together.

Ellen and Ed picked up Grandpa and arrived first. As they waited, Ellen told her dad the story about Julep. Well, as much as she knew, anyway. Jeremy arrived a few minutes later and Ellen told the story again.

"That's all I know. I'm as anxious as you are to hear the whole story. I can't believe they found Julep alive."

Julep was on the Petersons' horse trailer, but she didn't know how or when she was found.

"I picked up a few things at the store and ran into Jennie. Boy, I should get an academy award for acting. She wanted to talk but I rushed off."

"I'm sure Jennie is wondering why I haven't answered her text. She invited me out for pizza." Jeremy was grinning. "Do you think she'll forgive me for not answering the text?"

"Ha, she won't even remember you once she sees Julep," Grandpa joked.

Jeremy thought there was possibly some truth to that statement, but he hoped not.

"There they are." Ellen pointed to the truck and trailer pulling into the parking lot.

Adrian got out of the driver's seat, stretched, and walked over to the group standing by their cars.

"Megan wants the honor of driving Julep back to Jennie."

"Megan, you look great! I'm not sure what happened, but we can't wait to hear the whole story." Ellen walked over to give both Megan and Susan hugs.

"You simply can't make this stuff up." Adrian walked over to shake both Ed's and Grandpa's hands as he talked. "Well, let's get this party started. We'll lead the parade and you follow." And with that he squeezed his lanky body into the back seat of the truck one more time.

ANOTHER TEXT and Marcy tried to act nonchalant as she read the message.

Please make sure Jennie is at the barn. We're on our way.

Ok, she is in the barn with me and Cassy.

Jennie noticed that Marcy seemed a bit anxious after getting several texts. "Is everything ok?"

"Yes, I'm fine. Ah, Cassy, let's put the horses out in the pasture." She gave Cassy a pleading look that said, "I need to talk to you."

"Ok, but you didn't groom Riley and Stuffin, and Treasure and I haven't played, yet." Cassy untied Treasure.

"I changed my mind. I guess I'm more tired than I thought." She found it hard to look tired when something big was about to happen.

As they walked the ponies to the pasture, Marcy glanced around to make sure Jennie didn't follow, then shoved her phone in Cassy's face to read the texts.

"We need to be with Jennie when her parents arrive. Let's hurry. They should be here any minute."

Jennie was sweeping the barn aisle. Good, thought Marcy. That will keep her busy. Marcy positioned herself near the barn door so she could spot Ed and Ellen. Two cars, plus a truck pulling a horse trailer turned into the drive. What was going on?

"Hey, you have company." Marcy motioned to the cars.

Jennie leaned her broom against the wall and walked to the barn entrance.

"That's the Petersons' trailer, and there's Mom and Dad, and there's Jeremy behind them. What's going on?" Jennie had a strange feeling, but as they parked and got out of the vehicles, she noticed they all had huge smiles.

"What's going on, you guys?" Jennie asked. Then she spotted Megan and thought it was a welcome home party for her.

Megan ran over to Jennie. "You remember our conversation when we talked about you boarding a horse for me?"

"Yes, but I didn't know you had a horse. Did you get a horse?"

"Yes, I have a horse on the trailer. I have two horses on the trailer, and one is for you." Megan was now jumping up and down.

Jennie looked at Megan and then Megan's mom and dad. "You bought me a horse?"

While Megan was talking to Jennie, Dr. Peterson walked around the trailer and opened the back doors.

Jeremy put his arm around Jennie's waist. "Not just any horse, Jennie." He took his arm from Jennie's waist and reached for her hand. "Let's go say hello to a very special horse."

Jennie let Jeremy guide her to the trailer and the whole crowd followed. All she could see were two horses' rumps. One was a bright chestnut and the other a bay. Jennie felt the pain of a memory. The bay rump reminded her of the last time she saw Julep in the very same trailer. It was the day she said goodbye as the trailer pulled away.

Dr. Peterson lowered the ramp and unlatched the security bar on the bay's stall. Megan gave the short black tail of the bay horse a gentle tug telling her it was time to back off the trailer, and Julep backed into Jennie's life.

They all heard Jennie gasp. "Is that Julep?"

Julep heard Jennie's voice and nickered as if she were saying, "I'm home."

Jennie wrapped her arms around Julep's neck and sobbed.

"It's ok, please don't cry." Megan wanted Jennie to be happy.

Jennie wiped her nose with the back of her hand but kept one hand on Julep.

"I can't believe it's Julep." Jennie looked up when she heard another nicker.

"Move over, Jennie. I think someone else wants off the trailer." Megan gave a gentle tug to the chestnut's long tail to tell her to back down the ramp.

As Starlight backed off the trailer, Megan said, "This is Starlight, and boy, do we have a story to tell you!"

Adrian stepped closer to Jennie. "Do you have room for two horses? I'm sure we can work out some sort of mutually agreeable arrangement, and one that doesn't involve taking a horse or two to my place."

Jennie nodded. "Are you giving me Julep?"

"Yes, she wants to spend the rest of her life with you, here at this farm. I want that, too. I've taken on Starlight as a project. Can she stay?"

"Definitely, but only if I get to hear the entire story of how Julep died and is now alive." Jennie was starting to feel like she could breathe normally again. "And what happened to her mane and tail? But first, let's get these horses settled in the pasture for the night."

Jennie led the way, talking to Julep. "Do you remember your home? I can't believe you're here, sweet girl." She ran her hand down Julep's neck, then leaned over and took a big sniff. She remembered that smell."

Riley, Stuffin, and Treasure rushed to the adjoining fence to meet the new arrivals. There were a few squeals and nickers as Riley tried to keep Treasure and Stuffin away from what he considered intruders. It would take a little time but Riley would take charge of all four mares. Not because he was a gelding. He was a born leader.

With arms linked at the elbows, Jennie and Megan returned to the barn, and only Cassy, Marcy, and Jeremy remained.

"Everyone's gone on up to the house. Your mom brought a few things for a little celebration, and your grandpa needed to find a comfortable chair." Jeremy noticed that Jennie looked a little unsettled.

"Hey, let's go to the house and celebrate. I'll walk back out with you later to check on Julep. I promise she won't go anywhere." Jeremy motioned for the group to follow him to the house as Jennie repeated, "I can't believe she's here. I just can't believe it."

Megan ran up to get closer to Jennie. "I can't wait until you hear the whole story. Dad was amazing, but he had help from Dr. Bobby and Mary. Just wait until you hear all about them."

Jennie stopped and looked at Megan. "Thank you so much." She gave her a long hug.

"Hey, you're trembling." Megan stepped back but held Jennie's hands. "It's ok. Everything's ok now."

Jennie only nodded. She couldn't talk. She was so happy, but also so overwhelmed.

The group made their way into the kitchen to fill plates with the snacks, and then gathered on the back porch where Jennie's dad set up a few extra chairs he thought to bring.

Grandpa cleared his throat. "I would like to say the blessing if I may."

Ellen spoke up, "Dad, are you going to behave this time?"

Grandpa nodded.

"Dear Father, we gather here tonight to celebrate something good. Thank you for Julep. Thank you for the safe travels of the Petersons, and the food that Ellen has prepared. Most of all, thank you for all the gifts you have given to Jennie—good friends, a loving family, and a bright future. When life brings challenges, and we know there will be many, please help her to

always be thankful for everything, and to always look to you to find goodness. Amen."

There was a moment of silence, and then Jeremy raised his glass. "Let's toast to Jennie, Julep, new friends and old, to family, and to a good story just waiting to be told."

Jennie looked around at the smiling faces of her friends and family. "And we already know this story has a very happy ending!"

Enjoy a Sneak Peek!

Trusting Truth
Faith, Family, Friends & Horses in Appleridge, Book 2

"Where are you off to this time?" Hank rolled over to follow Elaine, aka Lainie, with his eyes as she moved around the trailer choosing clothes and throwing them into her bag.

"I told you, Hank, I'm teaching a clinic in Appleridge, Ohio this weekend." Lainie Anderson was getting pretty tired of Hank. "I need to get ready to go on the road, so you may want to get up and gather your things."

Lainie wasn't too sure how Hank ended up in her trailer last night, but she was ready to have him gone. The living quarters of her horse trailer were nice but extremely small. Too small for annoying cowboy one-night stands.

What in the world is wrong with me? I love what I'm doing—teaching people about horses. But I'm not happy. Maybe I'm looking for happiness in all the wrong places? Maybe I should start looking for happiness in the right places, but I don't know any right places.

Lainie moved around the small space like a dust devil—her thoughts spinning.

Teaching people about horses used to make me happy. Maybe I've lost my passion for teaching.

Ok, finding her passion would be a good place to start looking for happiness.

Hank got up slowly and stretched. "Sure, Lainie, I've got things to do. I'm heading out on the road, too."

Hank dressed slowly, keeping his eyes on Lainie. It was funny watching Lainie flutter from one side of the small space to the other, like a moth caught in a jar. "Any chance you'll be back in these parts?"

"Probably; I like the idea of having a place to stay in my trailer with my horse nearby."

"Yeah; me, too." Hank looked solemn.

Lainie stopped her flight to look at Hank. He didn't seem mad at being booted out of her trailer. He wasn't a bad guy, and he was pretty good with horses.

"See you around, Lainie. Are you going to be at the big ranch next month for the instructor gathering?"

"I've blocked out that bit of time. I've clinics scheduled for the next three weekends, so I'll be ready for some down time at the ranch."

"Down time? You know we never get down time at the instructor gatherings. It's more like free labor time with the big guy working us to death and then calling it education. Do you ever think about going off and teaching on your own?" With his hand on the door handle, Hank waited for Lainie's answer.

"I'll admit some days I just want to teach what I want to teach without thinking about making enough money to stay in the organization. I'm not seeing all those promised benefits of being a branded instructor."

Hank nodded. "I sure don't get as much of a kick out of following the big guy around—not at all."

Hank leaned over to kiss Lainie lightly on the cheek. He took his cowboy hat from the hook by the door and left the trailer. Lainie watched him walk over to his own trailer before closing her door. He was a good friend. Well, at least that was what she always thought. Last night probably complicated the friend idea.

Lainie sighed. She mentally listed the million errands she needed to run today. First on the list was a trip to the local feed store to stock up on supplies for her Quarter Horse mare, Shadow. Shadow Me, her registered name, was Lainie's pride and joy. They traveled many miles together.

What would I do without my Shadow? The miles are easy with my sweet girl. But what else would make her happy? What did she really want?

Lainie sat down on the bench she used as a step to climb into her bed tucked in the neck of the gooseneck trailer. What did she want? Good question. She wanted to teach without worrying about meeting a quota. She wanted to get off the road, find a little farm, learn from horses, and teach humans.

At first, she loved being part of the branded horsemanship organization called Follow the Leader, and the clout it seemed to carry with the students. Students followed her around like she was a celebrity.

What she didn't love was performing at the shows. Lainie was uncomfortable in the spotlight, and avoided it as much as

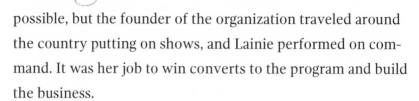

possible, but the founder of the organization traveled around the country putting on shows, and Lainie performed on command. It was her job to win converts to the program and build the business.

Lainie shook her head, remembering how she hero worshipped Brock Rodgers when she first started the Follow the Leader program. It was her dream to study at his ranch and learn from the master himself. Then her dream came true. She won what was labeled a scholarship. The dream quickly turned into her nightmare when the small print required all the so-called scholarship money repaid from future earnings.

She was stuck. The price Brock placed on her education insured her loyalty for many more years. Well, unless she could find a way out of the contract.

Lainie thought about the division in the instructor ranks—some felt the same as Lainie and others still saw Brock as a hero. She had trouble figuring out who was who. Negativity wasn't tolerated, and suggestions of any kind were considered negative. Lainie kept her comments to herself. A simple comment would cause her loyalty to be suspect, and if that happened, well, she wasn't sure what would happen. Some instructors, who were deemed disloyal, were stripped of their instructor status and mysteriously left the program.

I need to find out what happens after they leave. Does Brock have the power to blackball them from the horse world in some way?

She was finding it difficult to hide her true feelings. She felt a little twinge of deceit every time she brought a new student into the Follow the Leader Program. She was spreading a message she no longer believed, and that felt pretty bad. Well maybe that wasn't totally true.

I know the message is good because the horsemanship being taught is really good. It's Brock and the way he does business that makes me feel bad.

And that was the problem. She was the messenger for someone she didn't trust—someone who was selfish, lacked integrity, and didn't always practice what he preached.

Lainie pulled herself off the bench. Appleridge, Ohio was a good day's drive and she wanted to get started early in the morning, and that meant she better get busy today.

Maybe on the drive I can give this whole situation some more thought. I need a plan and a prayer.

Lainie chuckled—now where did that thought come from? A prayer? She wasn't a praying girl, but she did need a plan.

ABOUT THE AUTHOR

Linda would love to be known as a child of God, entertaining author, and savvy horsewoman. She lives on a small farm with her family, two horses, four cats, and one really good dog. The crops grown on the farm are Linda's books and a bit of music. She loves to play the fiddle at church and in jam sessions, and spoils her young grandsons when possible.

Linda loves connecting with readers.
Send Linda a note at linda@fawnsongfarm.com

Follow Jennie and her Appleridge friends at
www.fawnsongfarm.com